EVEN AS WE BREATHE

EVEN AS WE BREATHE

A Novel

ANNETTE SAUNOOKE CLAPSADDLE

**FIRESIDE
INDUSTRIES**

Published by Fireside Industries Books
An imprint of the University Press of Kentucky

Editorial and Sales Offices: The University Press of Kentucky
663 South Limestone Street, Lexington, Kentucky 40508-4008
www.kentuckypress.com

Library of Congress Cataloging-in-Publication Data

Names: Clapsaddle, Annette Saunooke, author.
Title: Even as we breathe : a novel / Annette Saunooke Clapsaddle.
Description: Lexington, Kentucky : Fireside Industries Books, an imprint
    of the University Press of Kentucky, [2020]
Identifiers: LCCN 2020019774 | ISBN 9781950564064 (hardcover ; acid-free
    paper) | ISBN 9781950564071 (pdf) | ISBN 9781950564088 (epub)
Subjects: LCSH: Cherokee Indians—Fiction. | North Carolina—Fiction. |
    GSAFD: Suspense fiction.
Classification: LCC PS3603.L35169 E94 2020 | DDC 813/.6—dc23
LC record available at https://lccn.loc.gov/2020019774
ISBN 978-1-950564-32-3 (pbk. : alk. paper)

This book is printed on acid free paper meeting
the requirements for the American National Standard
for Performance in Paper for Printed Library Materials.

Manufactured in the United States of America.

For Mom and Dad, my original storytellers

The Lovers' Prayer to the Body

O musk & mineral,   salt-slick lips—each
                                    pore's lifted hair a language only felt;

O marrow-mystery,   where bone softens to red
                                      breath & healing's quiet machinery.

We worship skin &   bone but what of meat?
                                      It is muscle's movement we resent:

push & pull & will.   Let us be still.
                                      Let us be still. O let us be still.

—Benjamin Cutler

PROLOGUE

About the place—when I take you there or when you find it on your own, just know that what the old folks say is true. This land is ours because of what is buried in the ground, not what words appear on a paper. But also know this: what is buried in the ground isn't always what you think. It's just the beginning. It's the beginning of the story—the beginning of all of us who call ourselves *Homo sapiens*. Fitting, I guess, that what I found buried, just as I was trying to figure out how to become a man and still be human, was the very thing that threatened to take it all away. Just when I began to see what taking control of my own life might look like, I realized I was not who I thought. And neither was this place.

That summer in 1942 when I met her, really met her—before I found myself in a white man's cage and entangled in the barbed wire that destroyed my father—I left the cage of my home in Cherokee, North Carolina. I left these mountains that both hold and suffocate, and went to work at the pinnacle of luxury and privilege—Asheville's Grove Park Inn and Resort. I guess I had convinced myself that I could become fortunate by proximity—escape Uncle Bud's tirades and my grandmother Lishie's empty kitchen cabinets just by driving a couple of hours up the road. It sounded good to tell folks I was raising money for college; but the truth was, I didn't know what I was doing. I just didn't want to do it *there* anymore. And if I stayed any longer, I would become rooted so deeply I might as well have been buried.

My plan didn't quite work the way I thought it would. When I got to

1

the resort, I mostly stayed outside, cut the trees, mowed the grass, and helped to dig the holes that would sink signs and posts for barbed-wire fences. Music occasionally seeped from the ballroom but was muted by thick, lead-paned windows before one note ever reached the perimeter of the property.

That's where I first found the bone. I was on my hands and knees, pitching rocks and digging holes. It was just as the inn, like its music, was becoming dulled by wartime restrictions and hushed by lead bullets. The prisoners—who were actually diplomats and foreign nationals treated more like guests—weren't really known to me yet. That little girl, God bless her soul, had barely even stepped foot on the property, and I was still as free as I would ever be.

I squatted there by the fence along the boundary of the Grove Park property and grasped the bone by its middle, pointing both ends upward, studying its curvature. A bent bauble for my idle adolescent hands to fidget with in the absence of a ball stick or a soldier's rifle. I can't recall playing with many toys as a child. That's probably why the bone spoke poetry to me as a young man.

It was smooth and porous, its slight c-curve angled in motion, calling to be grasped, used—a weapon, at least in some primitive function of strength—like a subhuman scythe, though innately human. Maybe even the very core of humanity. And now, as I recall the moment out loud, it was an embarrassing indulgence of make-believe for a nineteen-year-old. It's all right to laugh. I don't blame you.

Such an extraordinary object to be inside flesh, it was wholly earthen. Not sterile or cellular. It was natural in a way we pray our body is not.

Momentary. Seasonal. Destined for expiration.

The bone had lost its story. Petrified into a mere alkaline deposit, transient and nameless.

I was immediately spellbound by this calcified opportunity to embrace a remnant of a life's existence in one hand. Dry it. Dust it. Preserve it, and listen. Buried by a story, and I was the only one on this earth privileged to hear it. "Cowney." It seemed to coo my name like the beautiful girls of my daydreams, the ones who never took interest in boys like me. Just as I was yet to know of a certain beautiful girl's power, I was yet to understand the power that bone would wield over my life. I was yet to know how much more I would risk for her, for it.

I am *bits and pieces of the people I meet*, my teacher once told me, though, more accurately, I am of people and places and creatures. And so, because of that summer, and that war and that small, hollow relic, I am bits and pieces of a grand estate, and a half-tamed primate, and a dozen accents, and a missing girl, and a fearful girl, and all the trees and mountains and asphalt in between.

And you—well, I reckon you will be, too, soon enough.

Knowing that she is now gone from this earth, all I am left to do is wonder what remains of her here . . . for me . . . for anyone who knew or didn't know her. What happens to the memories? How long do they survive? I can still see her, dancing. Head thrown back, laughing. If there's one thing old age has taught me, it's that there are many kinds of love. She taught me that sometimes we feel many different kinds with one person. And now it seems possible that love is the only thing that will outlive us all, but only if we continue to tell its story.

I

BONES

That's the thing about ceremony; it must have three things: it must be for the right reason, at the right time, and it must be in the right place.

—Tom Belt, Cherokee Nation

CHAPTER ONE

I don't remember the day my father died. I don't remember Lishie standing at the clothesline when the soldier came to tell her the news. I don't remember the way she nodded her graying head, turned, went back to pinning shirts and skirts, unable to cry for a long while. I don't remember how relieved Lishie was that his body, under the circumstances, would be returned when so many others were not. I don't remember my father's face cradled in the pine casket by one of Lishie's special quilts. I don't remember any of that. Barely four months old at the time, I couldn't have. I've reconstructed images from stories and pictures and stitched them into one of Lishie's quilts.

I do not remember the paleness of the pine box as it was precariously lowered into the deep earthen hole. I do not remember Preacherman sprinkling dry specks of red clay on top, an act that later seemed terribly disrespectful to my six-year-old self when Lishie explained it to me at an aunt's funeral—an act that made me wonder if my father deserved such treatment.

I don't remember Preacherman announcing, "Dust to dust," but he must have.

Sometimes I think that I remember smells, but only when I smell them at new funerals.

Grease.

Lilies.

Tobacco.

Vanilla.

Fresh dirt.

Pine sap.

I remember one taste, though it must have just been repeated so many times after that day that I've convinced myself of it—the bitterest salt I have ever tasted—Lishie's tear when she scooped me up and held me so tightly that my open lips smashed into her cheek.

"You were his," I think I remember her saying. "You are mine," I am certain I remember her saying. Even though all of this is surely impossible.

I don't remember my uncle Bud, or rather his shadow, jutting from the doorway. But there has always been a shadow between him and me, between him and my father; so it must have been there that day.

I don't remember the many different scales of cries from many different throats.

Gunshots surely rang—must have been twenty-one, three from seven men. I seem to remember more.

Lishie wailed.

Bud shouted, garbled and wet.

Too young to even crawl, I could swear I remember running past folded arms and hiding beneath one of Lishie's special quilts until a new sun rose and all I could smell was coffee.

I awoke to find Lishie had curled herself around me, indistinguishable from her homespun patchwork.

That's the impossible memory I've crafted. No amount of time visiting Bud's house changed that.

I wonder if the bones of my father are exposed and clean now. I picture a perfect white skeleton, fully intact, framed within the pine coffin—like the one I saw in anatomy class. So perfectly preserved, the bones could teach. I know it sounds odd to speak of my father like that, but you have to understand, I never knew him in the flesh. I never felt the breath of his lungs. His memory is as much a skeleton as his body.

Yet Lishie was always present. It was as if she radiated—sometimes even radiated right through me. I remember walking in her door after I returned from junior college. I hadn't said a word, and I surely hadn't made up my mind if I was ever going back. She looked up from where she sat in her rocking chair, sighed a heavy sigh, and let her hands fall from her quilting to rest in her lap. "Oh, Cowney," she whispered. That is all she said, but I knew she knew everything. She understood far more than even I did about how I was feeling or how I would come to feel. I knew then and there that I wasn't going back because she knew it first. She wasn't judging me or even pitying me. She just stirred within me until it was all sorted out.

Except for the valley land that began pimpling with improvised storefronts, Cherokee was not the Cherokee of today. Cherokee was mud-chinked log cabins burrowed into mountain hollers, surprising expanses of neat garden rows jutting across rare unwooded land at the end of roughly carved dirt roads—half washed away in the spring and summer and impassable with snow in the winter. But no matter where human life chose to carve its mark on the land, it did not stray far from water—creek, river, stream, or fall—follow one and you would find Cherokee. You would find the smoke from woodstoves. You would find red clay ground into a fine, ginger dust coating the surface of life. And you could not find it directly from any highway. To trust a road is still a road when it looks like a creek is not and has never been for the tourist's heart. Yet it is only that trust that will get you from a road sign to a home. Or, in my case, from Lishie's, where I lived, to Bud's, where I worked.

Bud's cabin was short of breath, strangled by the dust of his daily existence and by the humid draft of his lungs. He was the only man I knew whose sweat seemed to flow simultaneously from the pores of his body and the foulness of his words. I grabbed the besom from beside the front door and walked out to sweep the porch.

"I guess you're glad you're a gimp, for once in your life." My uncle Bud sure had a way with words. "Weren't for that skee-jawed foot of yours, you'd be knee-deep in Nazis." He tossed a tattered, two-day-old newspaper onto a pile, a collection of three months' worth of international posturing and local weather reports, each paper a near carbon copy of the one that lay beneath it.

I shrugged. He wasn't asking a question. He never really asked questions.

"You can thank your momma for that. She was in too big of a hurry to get you out."

He reminded me of this often.

I grunted so the words forming on my tongue couldn't slip through my lips. These were not debates. Not even arguments. Bud was Bud and my only purpose, in his mind, was to be an echo in his presence. If I had cared more about him, I might've tried to offer my opinion once in a while. But I found it no real victory to earn him as an ally, so I echoed. He was a cavern whose hollow center managed to trap errant winds. I drank his vibrations. Still, he was mostly right. Since birth, the bones of my left foot have conspired against my body's natural compass and collectively pointed outward, tempting me to lead my life in circles.

"Better a penguin than a pigeon," my mother was said to have remarked when the midwife laid me in her arms. They both knew then that the foot would never fully correct itself. The midwife had seen too many births and she recounted all similar situations to everyone in attendance. My mother prayed for a "remarkable son." She confessed it to the midwife as if she had signed a legal contract with God. These were stories Lishie told me, not Bud.

Perhaps my foot could have been corrected, but the week following my birth was spent trying to save my mother's life rather than tending to the nonessentials of me. Deep down, I still felt that urgency to protect my mother as Bud placed his irresponsible blame, but I just echoed.

"I reckon 'bout all your cousins are over yonder now. You best believe that means you've got twice the work to do 'round here. Uncle Sam may let you off the hook, but you're going to need more than a twisted flipper to just lay up here all summer. We got a lot of work to tend to 'fore harvest."

"Or before I leave for school."

"Yeah, I'm not holding my breath for that one."

Bud always spoke like I had shied from work, that I had refused to cut and hang tobacco or hoe the tater garden or milk old Bess. My disabled foot translated to disabled resolve in his book. The only work he recognized as *work* was within his gaze. I would spend hours, overtime even, at the inn, but he couldn't attest to my efforts. So it was as if I was on some sort of holiday while he waited at home listing the chores in preparation for my return. He certainly didn't think doing my schoolwork was praiseworthy. This led me to stop altogether when I was with him. Lishie didn't seem to mind me reading or doing arithmetic at the table. I think she might've even liked it. She said my mother used to write poetry—though I've never seen any trace of it.

"I'll tell you one thing. Back in my day, you'd have to have more than just one gimp limb to keep you from shippin' off to fight for your country." Bud punctuated his statement with the ping of the spittoon. He rubbed his knees, acknowledging his gout flare-ups he blamed on old war injuries. Again, no proof of that.

I rolled my eyes but kept my head down so he wouldn't launch into the long version of his tired lecture.

"Hell. If it wasn't for guys like me and your dad, this wouldn't even be *your* country." And again, Bud was only half right. All Indians were finally recognized as US citizens following World War I partially because of the service of so many volunteers like Bud and my father; but I was fairly certain it would have happened without Bud's contribution. The only letter sent home that ever arrived from my father mentioning Bud's service insinuated that Bud spent more time trying not to get kicked out of the infirmary than he did working a post. Lishie used to show me the letter when I got sad. Still, Bud and his brother *had* volunteered, even when they were told that they would not be conscripted. Lishie always said it was because they liked to fight and it didn't matter who or for whom. I think it also had something to do with not having a job. The war was over for all intents and purposes when they arrived in Europe.

Outside Bud's cabin, the black-capped chickadee whistled a lonesome song, the notes piercing and unrequited. The indigo bunting darted between tree limbs like the woodland sprite I had once seen in a book Lishie brought home from the Goat Man peddler.

Lishie had asked a cousin in Charleston to write her when the Goat Man made his way through their city so that she might time his arrival in Cherokee. Even though exhibiting amazingly accurate travel estimations, Lishie made futile journeys to town three times before he arrived and she was able to trade a month's worth of savings from her humble mending services for the volume. The copy was well worn and two pages were completely missing, but what remained seemed magical and questionable in the context of Lishie's conservative religious practices. This was a woman who damn near burned *Ulysses* when she found it (and read nearly a quarter of it overnight) among the books I overconfidently resolved to complete before the age of twenty after my teacher, Miss Marjorie, assured me I was bright enough to do so. Joyce being "the Devil's whisperer," according to

Lishie, I barely glimpsed the final pages before the book was confiscated. Perhaps the bunting-esque spirits of a fairy tale were somehow godlier than man's quest for godliness.

The indigo bunting reminded me that the merging of the forest's stillness and its interruption marked by fierce velocity was what made the woods the wilderness. Hovering just outside Hawthorne's darkness, though less romantic than Sherwood Forest, it was a wood not yet known in literature or picture shows. Now, I know what you must be thinking. That all sounds starry-eyed, maybe even romantic. But that's why you need the stories of this place. No outsiders seemed to know what I knew, what we knew about these woods. Few outsiders knew the contradictions of poison oak and healing salves growing side by side, or the way in which grapevines have nothing to do with eating and so much to do with flying. And that . . . well, that was fine by me then. But you will need to know.

I was also one of the few who recognized old man Tsa Tsi's capuchin monkey, Edgar, simply by the way the tree branches bent overhead. Tsa Tsi, or George (his English name), was one of those fixture characters many of us have known in our childhood. He was a man who never seemed to age nor would ever die. As a child, I was perpetually nervous in his presence, fearful he could see deep to the root of my motivations and ambitions and judge them ceaselessly without saying a word. One sideways glance from the old man and I was transformed. I never actually saw him move from one place to the other, now that I think about it. I can't recall when or how I met him or when I decided we should go on conversing like lifelong friends. Of course, there were lots of folks like that back then. Formal introductions weren't needed. Just like I never introduced myself to the stream below my house or my great-aunts that I saw maybe once or twice in my lifetime. Some things, some people just seem to always have existed within our own sphere of being, indefinable by common terms of friendship or familial relationship. Just people, peopling our world. And of course, I still laugh to think that such an apathetic man cared for a ridiculous monkey named Edgar. But as a child, it all made perfect sense.

Edgar's leap caused the limbs of the trees to dip much lower than a squirrel's jump, though he was also far less clumsy than the local woodland flyers. He made very little noise. Tsa Tsi insisted it was because he was deaf. I wasn't so sure about that because I couldn't figure how a monkey could survive the panthers if he couldn't hear them sneaking up on him. I've never heard that monkeys have a strong sense of smell. I'm pretty certain Edgar was quiet because Edgar had to be quiet. To survive. I know a little something about that.

Often, standing on the porch, even though I could not see his tiny black, brown, and white body, I could see his path zigzagging back to Tsa Tsi's place over the hill. Pines bending. Oak leaves dancing. Maples swaying as if a strong gust of wind had managed to coil its way within the confines of the forest. His movement was in such congruence with the treetops I couldn't help but feel he was naturally meant to be there.

I guess it's safe to say that the old man was the only one around who kept a monkey as a pet and the only monkey owner in the whole wide world who thought it perfectly natural to let said pet roam at will. Edgar caused more than one hunter to go into near cardiac arrest a time or two. But more folks in the area by then knew to be on the watch for him and would relay sightings to Tsa Tsi so he wouldn't worry. Not that he was prone to worrying.

A few years back, while I was up at his place helping to split wood, the old man, sitting on a stump rolling cigarette after cigarette, told me how he came to acquire Edgar. It seems that the carnival was making its way through Cherokee one summer. Early '30s, late '20s . . . something like that. The carnival wasn't stopping here for a show because no one in Cherokee had any money anyway, but sometimes it would set up camp for performers to rest before moving on to another town for a week of shows. Edgar was a trained tightrope walker, wore a top hat and tiny red vest. Unfortunately, he also had a problematic tendency to lift ladies' skirts and nip at children who tried to pet him. The carnival manager kept him in a minuscule metal cage for those reasons. "Weren't fit for a possum." Tsa Tsi shook his head, thinking back.

Tsa Tsi told me that one day while the carnies were in camp, he went down to see if they might be interested in buying some wild greens or deer jerky. "They paid a fair price for fresh goods." He told me that the place looked pretty deserted, so he eased his way into one of the larger circus-style tents *for a look-see*. When he saw Edgar the first time, the monkey was clenching the bars of his cage and shaking the entire structure so hard that the bottom kept lifting from the ground. As Edgar saw Tsa Tsi enter the tent and approach his cage, Edgar just stopped, and as Tsa Tsi says (though who's to know what's really true), "he began to grin like a fool" at Tsa Tsi and calmed right down.

It all seems like a crazy story to me (and probably you) now, but the old man did tell me something that I took to heart. We were sitting outside the trading post on a split-log bench. I sipped an RC Cola, desperate to cool off from the walk down the mountain and he, as he always did, seemed to have been sitting there his whole life. I took a long drink as Tsa Tsi picked up the story at its midpoint.

"And right then I knew what I had to do. See, Pap used to tell me about sneaking down to the stockade and taking food to his older brother and his family right before they moved 'em west during the Removal. He used to tell me that the government had made an animal of his brother and that he knew he could never get caught or he'd become one too. So he hid out in the mountains and later stayed with a family who'd been traded a small piece of land 'cause freedom was worth more than life."

And that's why old man Tsa Tsi never left the Qualla Boundary either and how he came to end up with a capuchin monkey named Edgar, who I'm guessing he just up and stole—because Tsa Tsi wasn't much for negotiations with white folk.

I asked him once why he'd named him Edgar. He told me that he'd named him after Edgar Allan Poe. I don't know what I think about that. Wouldn't have suspected Tsa Tsi to have even read Poe; but then again, Tsa Tsi didn't seem to fit into molds so easily.

Now, as for Edgar, he was even more adventurous than Tsa Tsi and loved to explore and that's why he nearly sent quite a few people to an early grave. Edgar had been seen as far away as Tennessee and Georgia. He always made his way back to Tsa Tsi, though. He might be gone a whole month, but he'd come ambling into Tsa Tsi's cabin, hungry as hell, no worse for the wear. So I think Tsa Tsi saw no point in keeping him tied or locked up, and the rest of us got to enjoy having our very own capuchin monkey hanging out in our woods. We didn't even have to go to a zoo for a taste of the exotic.

Ever since I could remember, I wanted to escape Cherokee, and that feeling of suffocation just kept growing with my body. But just as I was about to finally get out, at least for a summer, I felt as if I was rushing carelessly out of the woods, saw briars pricking my bare forearms and legs, leaving trickles of blood to mix with the sweat of haste. I started thinking of all the things I would miss, like ripe berries left on the bush. Lishie's hand over her mouth when she got tickled. The way a cool mist rises from the Oconaluftee as if sighing at the rising sun. The chattering of the indigo buntings. And a place where a monkey could scamper across oak and maple limbs like a tightrope performer. If I thought too much about the sweetness of my place in the world, I might never be able to leave it.

CHAPTER TWO

Bud had one more job to scrounge up before I left for the summer to work at the Grove Park Inn in Asheville, and though he would never admit it, he needed me. Bud and a few of his cronies had managed to covertly fell several trees following a major storm but were unable to convince the remaining railroad bosses to haul the load to the lumberyard. The river, with its infinite ability to expand and contract due to cloudbursts or man's manipulation, offered the only solution. They would burden the beasts that had been retired to farming life and drag the load to the Tuckasegee River. They'd dam it, anticipating the expected summer rains, and wait for the push.

The Smokies had long been a logging economy, ending only with the inception of the Great Smoky Mountains National Park. I had mixed feelings on such and probably harbor more distaste for the industry in my later days; but back then, logging was just another way to survive. Bud made what semblance of a living he could out of those woods.

As the logging companies dried up, he siphoned every last opportunity they leaked on their way out of town, as if it were maple sap. The timber companies used to build great splash dams to push their haul down the rivers into the timber yards. Railroads couldn't do all the work. The rivers and animals, as they always have, bore the burden of man's desire to do things faster and cheaper.

I was seated on a stump at the lumberyard removing my shoes at the edge of an ever-rising pool, watching the rounded, slick logs race down the river toward me. Waiting. My job was to be a river hog. "Gas money," Bud reminded me. "'Bout time you can get off the teat."

"Yeah, just try and relax." Thomas, a man I barely knew, nudged me. "Ain't no big deal."

Little did I know I'd hear those words again in only a matter of weeks. *Just try and relax.* It took me a while to understand why suspicion would feel so much like drowning. I know now it was those words that connected the sensations for me. It was those words that would outlast the men who spoke them. But I'm getting ahead of myself.

The log runners (those skilled, balanced men who spun endlessly on the glassy logs, prodding them into alignment) had left with the last whistle. I knew with my foot useless as it was, and well, to be honest, my body useless as a whole, I could never maneuver the way they had. I could swim, though. I could swim for hours. Surely I could push the few dozen poles into their stalls from the pool's rim and, if need be, wade among them. I needed the money. Not just to put away, but to make sure I had the necessities when I got to Asheville. Places like that'll make you pay for your uniform before you even clock in. That's how you became more of an indentured servant than free-will staff, and I couldn't let that happen.

Bud gave no direction on how to accomplish the objective. He told me where to wait, where the logs should rest, and to keep my mouth shut about the splash pool to anyone else.

The logs rushed down the river in a collective heap, fast and bulging from the waters like dark storm clouds mounting. I immediately felt my pulse quicken, and I turned, momentarily considering leaving this impending mess to Bud alone. How could I corral such a force of nature? It was obvious I would never be able to swim between the poles as I had imagined. I would need to, at the very least, mount them on all fours to float among them.

I've tried many times to recall what happened next, but much of it will forever be blackened from my memory. Here is what I know.

I was wet—head to toe, submerged in the frigid spring waters. I felt slick bark on my fingertips and managed to pull my torso atop one undulating log until I became nauseated from the pressure against my gut. I found some sort of strength, some sort of urgency, that pulled me into a straddle position, and then I made the mistake of trying to stand. This lasted no discernible time because the balance of my memory is veiled by water and darkness and desperation. I've had a similar sensation when I drive beneath a bridge in a rainstorm. There is a brief void of silence, and then everything rushes in again. In this case, the void was when my head dipped below the water, suffocating my senses.

Logs were coming faster, and the pool was rimmed three, sometimes five, deep. To reach the bank I would have had to scramble over multiple rows of the hewed trees. I ducked beneath the surface as each new wave came, fearful that the next time I tried to emerge there would be no space for my body or that the space would be swallowed, crushing me. I couldn't see a thing beneath the surface. The water reddened with clay and frayed bark. I was blind. Calling for help was a waste of time. The skeleton crew of men were stationed elsewhere. My survival was my own.

I forcefully pushed my legs downward, propelling my torso above the surface as far as I could, like a trout gasping in silted waters. I inhaled deep and sank just as quickly as I had risen.

And then I swam.

I swam as hard and as straight forward as I could manage, knowing that coming up for air was no longer an option. Logs loomed overhead, blanketing the surface and blocking the sunlight. I swam until my lungs no longer held and I expelled a burst of bubbles, what I felt was surely my last contribution to this earth. I waited for my body to rise and rest beneath the barrier of wood, having nothing left in me to breach it.

And just as my body began to rise, my fingertips sank into soft mud. I had reached an edge. I could stand.

I clawed my way up the receding bank until my face rested on grass, and air once again filled my lungs. I tried to blink my eyes open, but they were stung by the splinter remnants and fresh light. I am unsure how long I lay there, but it was Bud's voice I heard first, followed shortly by other men's. They were laughing; he was not. "Get up!" he roared, rolling me over with his boot and pointing the way to his truck. I never saw a dollar from that day and we didn't speak again until I returned to his cabin one last time before leaving for Asheville. This was all I needed to assure me that if I stayed, if I became Bud's dispensable errand boy, I would die young—if not physically, most assuredly spiritually. My father had not died for his country merely to have his son die for someone else's pocket change.

CHAPTER THREE

"Cowney! Be sure 'n' kindle the fire 'fore you head out tonight. Blackberry winter's settin' in," Bud rumbled, shaking me from daydream. Blackberry winter was an impossibility that time of the year. Bud loved to refer to the little winters—sarvis, dogwood, blackberry, locust, and so on—as much as possible, I think because he believed it made him sound wise.

Bud stoked a fire every night, seven nights a week, 365 nights a year. It did not matter whether it was blackberry winter or the Fourth of July. Bud was cold-blooded in that regard, probably in a few other regards as well. He'd mumble something about tradition when questioned by his buddies—saying a fire always had to burn in a *real man's* home.

I swept the accumulated pile of wood shavings from under Bud's rocking chair off the far side of the porch, selected a few twigs from the yard that had yet to be scavenged by Bud for his nightly inferno, and took the top three or four additions of old newspapers from the pile just inside the cabin. The twigs fit neatly into the fireplace like vertebrae, and I began to crumple the paper into tight balls of tinder. But something in the second layer gave me pause.

A bold headline warned of rumored brutalities occurring in Poland. I scanned the article enough to imagine a child caught up in the conflict, a child in a cage, or a child watching his parents being hauled away. My imagination folded into the stories I had been told about when my people had been removed from this land. I could see my own ancestors in pens or hiding in caves, while their neighbors and fellow clan members were marched out, prodded along by soldiers' rifles. I pictured a child alone, scared, and probably no longer alive when the paper was printed. This was war's game piece—a skeleton covered in the indistinguishable color of newspaper gray as if his skin was made of the broadsheet itself. Even back then, I remember feeling that if I stirred, or turned the page, the image, the picture would come to know the merging of stillness and velocity that I had known standing on the porch looking out into the forest. But this merging was much deadlier. The paper preserved the truth's existence, and, as I held it in my hands, I believed crumpling the page or tossing it aside would erase it forever.

"I didn't ask you to read the funny pages, boy. Get on with it," Bud thundered.

I folded the paper, setting it aside until I could tuck it into my back pocket on the way out the door.

The fire was stoked to a moderate roar in no time. "You be sure and take the rest of those pintos with you to your Lishie tonight. I get awful tired of hearing her complain I don't feed you enough while you're here," my uncle gargled.

"Yes, sir. You remember that I'm leaving in the morning for Asheville, right?"

"Ehh, shit. That tomorrow? Just make sure you get everything done here you need to before you take off again." Bud stood from his ladder-back rocking chair and walked over to the table. "I been reading about this place you say you're working at."

"Reading about it? Where?"

"Hell, son. I ain't illiterate. The goddamn newspaper that every other folk in the country reads."

I wanted to know more, but knew it was best to try to ignore him when he appeared to be keen on a topic.

"The Grove Park Inn. That's the place, sure nuff?"

"Yes, sir." I hurriedly spooned the remaining beans from the cast-iron pot into a small blue bowl to take with me.

"Paper says they've got Krauts holed up there already. Gonna move in Japs soon, too. Best watch your step or they're liable to lock you up with 'em. You probably look more like a foreigner than a soldier."

"I'll be careful, but I think they keep everyone pretty well separated. I'll be doing outside work anyway. Doubt they let them outside much."

"Ain't no resort with sightseers now. Says they're diplomats and foreign nationals. Shit, that means they're high-class prisoners. 'Fore the summer's over, you'll be serving them tea and rubbing their Nazi-lovin' feet."

"I think they pay other people for that," I offered, grabbing the folded newspaper I had set aside, tucking it in my pants, and hurrying out the front door. "Night!" I called back.

Lishie was waiting at the kitchen table when I came in. "I thought you would've beat me home." She smiled.

"I brought you home some beans."

"Sgi, sweetheart. There's a pan of cornbread on the stove if you're hungry."

"No, thanks, I still need to start packing for the week."

"Well, okay. If you're sure. I'll make you some sandwiches to take with you. I put your momma's old suitcase on your bed, too. You should use it. The lining still smells like her." Lishie was tearing up, whether over Momma or me I couldn't tell. Sometimes I think Lishie may have missed her daughter-in-law more than her own son. I would not have been surprised by either motivation for the tears. Lishie had two emotions: sternness and complete, utter compassion. There was no moderation.

I wouldn't know if the suitcase smelled like my mother or not. I wish I knew. I only even knew what she looked like based on what features folks said I had of hers, what some of her cousins looked like, and one faded black-and-white photograph, taken by one of the ever-present ethnographers or anthropologists or archeologists passing through, of her holding me, my hair still wet and face still swollen from birth.

"You spoil me, Lishie. You know I won't starve between here and Asheville."

"Well, you need to be ready to work when you get there. Show them you're good help."

"Yes, ma'am." I kissed the top of her silver head. "I'll make you proud."

"You always do."

I walked to the back room Lishie had divided with a flannel sheet curtain on my tenth birthday so I could have my "privacy." Though I'd built a doorframe and hung a door two years later, we left the curtain out of sentimentality. I took the newspaper from my back pocket and laid it on my pillow. I could hear Lishie slide her chair away from the table, change into her nightgown on the other side of the curtain, and pad into the living room as I folded my clothes into my mother's woven sweetgrass suitcase. This was Lishie's nightly routine. I knew she was opening her Bible to read in her rocking chair until she fell asleep. I pulled the quilt, one of many Lishie has stitched over the years, from the foot of my bed and took it in to her.

"Thank you, dear."

"Thought you might get cold. Bud said it's blackberry winter."

She looked up from the scripture and smiled. "Shhhiii . . ." She shook her head and we both laughed softly.

Returning to my packing, I was unsure of what I would need but knew that I would return in a few days to get anything left behind. I didn't have a heck of a lot of choices of what to take anyway. I closed the suitcase just before 9:00, went to my dresser, and pulled the folded yellow sheet of paper from the drawer with the Preacherman's handwriting scribbled across it.

> Essie Stamper
> Pick up 5 a.m. on Monday, May 18th
> Soco Road—2nd left past trading post

I folded the paper again and put it in the pocket of the shirt I planned to wear the day we left. Something about the girl's name written on the paper made me want to keep it close. I sat the suitcase by my door and tidied the room as best I could. Hearing Lishie begin her soft snoring, I padded out to the living room again and helped her to her bedroom.

"You mind if I read a little bit before bed?" I asked as I pulled the top quilt over her. Lishie was a sound sleeper, so she never really minded my reading at night by the lantern.

"Of course not, darlin'. I'm sure you're a little anxious. Just make sure you don't stay up too late. I don't want you noddin' off on the road tomorrow. It's a long trip."

"Yes, ma'am." I changed into my nightclothes, dug out the newspaper article, and slid into my bed. The bedframe creaked its nightly distress signal. Out of courtesy, I kept the oil lamp turned so low I could barely make out the words on the paper.

I wasn't sure this was the same article where Bud had gotten his information, but it did tell of the foreign diplomats, foreign nationals, and US citizens who had been moved to "remote locations" in the United States to be held under surveillance. It was odd to think of these mountains as prime surveillance real estate. The newspaper identified Indian reservations out west as sites to hold Japanese Americans. I shook my head. You see, not much has changed. Axis in the country's finest resorts. American citizens scratching around on land only fit for America's forgotten stepchildren. I wondered how close I'd get to the prisoners. *Should I be afraid? Are they afraid?*

Our local paper had taken to picking up trailers from other publications across the country. Apparently, San Francisco had woes I'd never understand.

> The women might have something to say about this, however, as the departure of the Japanese has sent them into a spin which looks, Mr. Roosevelt, like a cost-of-living spiral. Anyhow, they're going round and round in a battle to get household help, never before equaled in intensity. It looks like total war on the distaff side.

According to the article, the real tragedy of Japanese internment was not a loss of freedom or a pseudo-criminalization of innocent human beings on the grounds of name, language, color, or great-grandmother's country of origin. It was that white women of upper-class San Francisco might not have someone to fold their skivvies. They may have to sweep their own floors. And, most horrifically, they had turned to stealing servants from their nearest and dearest friends.

> The bidding for household help hasn't been equaled since Simon Legree went out of business. Fine friendships are falling apart like a tired cemetery bouquet, as women lure price[les]s human jewels from women.

Oh, these poor women. Certainly the death of former servants is nothing compared to broken pinky promises and the end to afternoon gossip sessions. It was sickening! *Did no one else see it?* Now some might think that I was just sympathizing with my distant Bering Strait–linked relatives (a suspect theory). I sympathized, sure. But I sympathized as a human being, one whose ancestors knew what it was like to be forced onto a reservation.

Empathy is fossilized in our bones.

I thought about Tsa Tsi's great-uncle and if I would sneak food to an internment camp if the government chose Cherokee, North Carolina, as its next prison site. Would they just throw me in with the rest of the "others" who fit into the wrong box? No one would miss me if I didn't show up to work. For once in their lives, those Japanese Americans must have wished they were just Japanese in America, like the diplomats and nationals that I'd be serving at the inn. Being American had somehow made being Japanese harder. Citizenship by choice complicated an identity assumed at birth.

Funny how things get twisted when people are in a hurry. I guess Bud was right sometimes.

He was right, too, that there is value in work. Even if that work only serves those who aren't aware of your existence. Would the next few months ahead of me help me understand the San Francisco situation far better than I really wanted? I laughed a little thinking that I might be considered some woman's "human jewel." Hopefully all of my orders would be coming from the inn's remaining skeleton staff manager. He, of course, was the one who had placed the ad and responded to my letter of interest. No matter where I was, the US military would expect me to fall into their tight, neat lines. And that'd be okay for the summer. The truth is I didn't know what to expect, and no amount of reading newspapers was really helping with that. I could be thankful the unknown was just over the mountain and not in some foreign country, like where all my cousins had been sent. Lishie would say that I should give thanks for whatever little morsel I could find.

I closed my eyes. *Whatever morsel.* I had a paying job. Maybe even one that would pay enough for the first semester of college if I decided to actually go. I had a good excuse not to spend all summer at Bud's feet, listening to his quarrelsome ranting in the muggy heat. I wouldn't waste my life never seeing what life could be like away from Cherokee. And probably most importantly, I had the girl, Essie, to look forward to. A couple of hours alone with a beautiful girl would certainly be more than a morsel's worth.

CHAPTER FOUR

The rattling gearshift seemed to rise between us, expanding into a border separating our two worlds. She smelled of lavender and honeysuckle, a scent that defied all boundaries and invaded my awareness. So I revved the engine, forgetting what my uncle had taught me: "Clutch is clutch, dammit!"

Despite my nervousness around her, we had practically grown up together, caught in the slow churn of the Qualla Boundary, tiny Cherokee, North Carolina, hours away from Asheville, the nearest city anyone could call such. We were products of "the reservation," pronounced low and quickly by us—*rezervashun*. Broken into at least five whispered syllables when spoken by visitors or neighbors across the mountain—*thuh-rez-her-vay-shuuun*.

We were "cousins of cousins' cousins, or something like that," Lishie often recalled. A classification less about tree branches and more about confined timeless existence.

Of course, I instinctively knew who she was. I was fairly certain I knew who she would become. Watching her was like watching a summer storm's lightning charge, the flash that illuminates the sky. She was the bolt that strikes fast across the horizon, downward toward its target, an unsuspecting lone tree whose roots are no longer its security, but rather become the very circuit for which the charge swells. The energy's force overcomes everything idle and ordinary. And you know it from the moment the air vibrates with warning thunder. Her future, everything

25

that would come after her nineteen-year-old reality, was too powerful for most of us to follow.

I knew this the first day I saw her, over a decade prior to our trip. She was a child of maybe seven or eight playing in the cool shallows of the Oconaluftee River, downstream from where I fished for speckled trout and dug ruddy crayfish from beneath mossy rocks. Her goldenrod skirt was hiked up to just above her scarred knees, and dark strands of hair fell ragged along the slopes of her downward-peering face. She, too, was searching for fish, but not to snare as I had set out to do. While I was dedicated to their capture, she was more concerned with studying the free movement of the fish that maneuvered past her stick-thin legs. Out of a patient stillness, she darted after a quick-moving knotty head, marveling at its agile speed, then snatched it from the water, only to release it immediately. Within minutes by the river, I had slipped on the filmy rocks and busted my ass. I was soaked. Though she took far fewer precautions, she never fell. She never even seemed to come unbalanced.

However, judging from the way she introduced herself on the sagging porch of her father's cabin all these years later, she remembered nothing of me. And judging from the past fifteen minutes of this car ride from Cherokee to Asheville, she did not care to.

The sum of her words amounted to "Hello. Pleased to meet you. I'm Essie Stamper. Thank you very kindly for the ride."

I'd done my best to conceal my excitement when the request came from Preacherman to help Essie arrive safely at her summer job at the Grove Park Inn. I wanted credit for a burden borne, and to earn that I had to at least appear as if I were actually burdened. I figured it could help to pardon me from a few Sunday or Wednesday nights' church services. Despite my resolve, it was still difficult to shoo away the grin as I loaded her suitcases into the car's trunk. I felt something intimate about preparing for a trip together, even if others had arranged most of the preparation.

Preacherman told me that Essie was just working at the inn for the summer to earn money for college. "One smart cookie," he offered one day after church. "If you keep your mouth shut and ears open, you might just learn a thing or two."

I hoped that Preacherman did not provide Essie with an overview of my own background, which would include a failed attempt at Oak Ridge

Junior College (an institution I'd only been accepted into as recognition of my father's World War I service and been able to afford with federal relief aid dollars), and the last year of my nineteen-year-old existence working odd jobs in Cherokee. I coveted this opportunity to introduce myself on my own terms, to present the Cowney detached from family binds or awkward tales of my fumbling youth. Though I was unsure if she had any impression of me at all, I wanted desperately to craft one for her. I wanted us to be immediate confidants, as if we shared years of inside jokes, had nicknames for each other, could speak without vocalizing words. I wanted to assume that Lishie's recollection of being distant cousins was merely the ramblings of an aging grandmother insistent that the whole damn reservation was related. I wanted to speak to her like I am speaking to you now. I wanted her to have never heard anyone else's opinion of me save, perhaps, my mother's and Jesus Christ's.

Some apparent nervousness pinched the tint from her lips. We were well into our two-hour drive and she hadn't uttered more than her initial introduction. She clutched her black purse on her lap and left her ankles uncrossed, though seemingly fused together.

The silence pressed deep into my chest. I waited for a change in her demeanor as if I was checking the ripening of a Cherokee purple, unsure of the perfect time to pry it from the vine when it peaks—before it spoils.

Oh well, I rationalized. *No better way than to just jump in.*

I leaned over and gave her a sideways glance. "There's rumors about this place, you know." I shrugged. "Heard it's built on graves."

The car's vibration unnerved my voice.

She feigned interest. "Oh. Whose?"

At least maybe she wanted to pass the time as much as I did. Optimism grew. "I don't know. People's, I guess."

"No. Which people? Indian? White? Your great-aunt Sally?" Essie sighed as if exhausted with her own questions.

"Cherokee," I gushed. Grateful I had an answer. "That's what they say."

"*They* do, huh?" From the corner of my eye I saw her slip out a smile too glassy for me to grasp.

"Yeah. Lots of people. Heard it's built on graves."

The smile disappeared as quickly as it had come. "Of course it is. White folks with money tend to find moving dead Indians easy."

"Ah, they're not all bad," I offered, thinking she might like to hear me acting diplomatic.

"That's true. But they sure don't like to be reminded of us."

I felt a warm, wet embarrassment wash over me because of how confidently she spoke when I was always grasping just to stay in the conversation. I had pissed away my opportunity. Preacherman was right. Anyone could tell by the way she cut her dark, Greta Garbo eyes toward me that Essie was smart or mean or both. I knew I had better figure out which one as quickly as possible or the rest of the ride would be miserable. More troublesome, there would be no second ride, and I could not imagine an existence without at least the possibility of seeing how fully Essie's long, perfectly curved body would fill out the baby blue maid's uniform at the inn. These daydreams did not help my execution of words.

"Anyway. Makes sense given some of the rumors about that place at night."

"Oh, you have friends there?"

"No. People just tell you things when you say you are going to a place like that." The truth was, if I didn't have friends in Cherokee, which I didn't, then I sure as hell didn't have any in Asheville.

"What kind of things do they say?"

At least she was listening.

Essie stared out the window at the blurred crimsons, gingers, auburns, and verdant greens of the budding trees, a Monet masterpiece appearing through the Model T's passenger window.

"You've heard the stories, right?"

She still did not turn. "What stories?"

"Of those people staying at the inn. Of why they're there and why the owners can't keep no help longer than a few weeks." *This would get her.*

Essie turned her face toward me, but did not commit her body to the same engagement. "Any," she responded. It wasn't a question and she noted my confusion. "Any. They can't keep *any* help." Her tone was sharp.

"Yeah, that's what I said. Anyway, you've heard rumors of those death camps? These are the types of people who run those places. Higher-ups. You think they just left all that behind when they got captured? It's like a blood thirst." My hands gripped the steering wheel as if I was driving a tank myself.

"So you're telling me they're some sort of German vampires?" She had a way of twisting my words to make me sound fool-ignorant.

I loosened my grip. "Never mind." I looked into my rearview mirror so she'd know I was too busy to be chided.

"No . . . I'm sorry, Cowney."

She remembered my name.

"Go on. Tell me what you think. I need to get as much background as I can if I am going to work there."

I was beginning to see that this was typical for Essie. That she was somehow cold without wanting to be, just needing to be. My early impressions of her could have been wrong. Maybe all those years ago she wasn't scowling down at the river but shielding the summer sun from her eyes so that she could better locate the fish. Walking into town alone, speaking to no one, was not chosen isolation. Maybe she was concentrating on the shopping list streaming through her head or, like me, she feared straying too far from explicit instructions, leading to an inevitable whipping, maybe even beating. For me it was the difference in who sent me—Lishie or my uncle Bud. For Essie, maybe there was no option.

Regardless of how I justified her coolness, I wanted to believe that I had something to do with her warming. I wanted to believe that years ago I had distracted the fish in the river so that they all swam her way. I wanted to believe that my shying away from the beautiful girl in the trading post allowed her to complete her purchase with accuracy. I was her space to breathe, her freedom to warm in the margin I left for sunlight.

"Well, there's been children come in to work with their folks, but you never see them leave. Staff can't report it 'cause they're not supposed to have kids around anyway." I took my eyes from the road so as to better gauge her reaction.

"Oh, Cowney. Do you really believe someone would just keep their mouth shut when they've lost their own child just so they don't lose their job?" She rolled her eyes like she'd been practicing the motion her whole life.

Of course I did not believe much of what I found myself telling her, but it seemed to keep her attention and that was motivation enough to continue. "All I know is there ain't a helluva lot of jobs floatin' around and maybe they're afraid for their own lives. Who knows why people do what they do."

"So why are you going to work in a place like that?"

"Correction. I work *for* a place like that. I won't set foot inside unless I have to. And even then, I sure as hell won't go up to the guest floors. Excuse my language."

"So I guess I'm just a fool, huh?" Her lips pursed again.

"Oh, gee. No. That's not what I meant. Ahh. I just wanted to tell you about the place. I didn't mean to scare you. We all have to work some-where. It's probably nothing. Plus, they have all kinds of security at the place. US Army detail scattered like ants on a hill."

"Are they really prisoners?"

"The guests? Yeah, but not like soldier prisoners. That's why they call them guests, by the way. Best to remember that. Have to call 'em guests. The way it's been explained to me in the letter I got last week, they're foreign diplomats and foreign nationals. Not American, but not Hitler's frontline henchmen either. Been in the United States for some time, but had to be moved during the war."

"Diplomats? I thought you said they were bloodthirsty vampires run-ning death camps."

"Oh, here we go again. You said that. Not me. Just tryin' to hold a con-versation." I checked my side mirror needlessly. The steep, green banks hugged the car as we bumped along what were little more than plowed dirt paths. A sweet honeysuckle scent seeped in through the cracked windows, fighting its way past the swirling dust. I mentally marked the point in case Lishie needed vines for new baskets. There were only a few wooden guardrails periodically placed, and I worried that I'd take a curve too liberally and we would careen off the bank and roll down into a ravine—possibly never to be seen again. "The manager will tell you all you need to know anyway," I conceded.

"I'm sorry, Cowney. Sometimes I poke fun when I'm on edge." Essie settled deeper into her seat and pulled a small, golden mirror from her handbag. She drew an errant strand of dark, chestnut hair from her left cheek and tucked it behind her ear. With her other hand, she steadied the compact in front of her and admired the reflection of the procedure. If she had been like most girls I knew, her next move would be to produce a shiny tube of deep red lipstick and slowly apply it as I wiped away the beads of sweat forming on my own upper lip. Unfortunately, at least in this moment, Essie was not like most other girls. She tucked the mirror back into her black bag and balanced her chin in the palm of her hand, resting her right elbow on the passenger side door.

And still the perspiration came. It edged its way up my spine, forcing me to pull my chest forward into the steering wheel so that fresh air could dry the back of my damp shirt. The sweat then ringed my collar and finally framed my hairline. I rubbed my face as if I was still sleepy from the early-morning departure, but the foggy embarrassment was too much to absorb. Until now, I assumed that I looked at Essie like I looked at every female of a certain age. There was little distinction in my immature lust, not that I had the right to be discerning. She did nothing to evoke a deep longing. She sat prudishly, reserved and so utterly unaware of her femininity that it was as if I was compelled to seek it out on my own. Though I was slightly older, I felt ingenuous in her presence.

From the margins of my peripheral vision, she appeared almost wistful. The car's right two tires grumbled across the rocky shoulder of the road, and I eased the steering wheel straight so as not to worry her. I was sure the awkwardness of my lame foot anywhere near the gas pedal had already done enough of that, and I didn't need her questioning my equilibrium on top of everything else.

"It's okay. I talk too much. Everybody tells me that."

"No. I mean, it's a long ride, right? Tell me more. I like a mystery." Essie smiled, crossing her arms and leaning back.

Fresh air in the car gently circulated and for the first time during the whole ride, I began to really see Essie for who she might want to be: a respected lady rather than a respectable lady. Maybe she would be a detective, a mystery writer, or a scientist. Maybe we would both become scientists, discover cures to childhood diseases and deformities together in our shared laboratory. The possibilities coursed through my thoughts, but I forced myself to confine them there. I gave her that moment. Shut my big mouth and just nodded.

Within half an hour, Essie was drifting in and out of sleep, jerking her head upright periodically and fumbling to make a pillow of her clenched hands. There was a sweet innocence in her uncontrolled movements. It was a vulnerability that made me feel that at least her unconscious self had some level of trust in me, that maybe she wasn't worried that my gimp foot would cause us to wreck or that my unsophisticated ways would lead us down the wrong road.

The only two people who had ever trusted me to drive them before were Lishie and my uncle Bud, and Bud had to be pretty damn desperate or incapacitated to allow someone else to drive him anywhere. He would huff like a deflating balloon because I was driving too fast or sigh, with a slow leak, because I was driving too cautiously. We shared the car between the three of us, so with me working in Asheville, Bud would have to get used to walking while I was away or get his broken-down pickup fixed after three years sitting idle in the yard. But Essie's trust, that was something far better than Lishie or Bud could provide, and even though she didn't say another word to me on the drive for quite some time, I still relished knowing she might be dreaming next to me.

When Essie and I arrived in Asheville proper not long after, she yawned, arched her back, and smiled again. The sidewalks on either side of us seemed to move like conveyor belts as sharply dressed men fell into office buildings and tightly dressed women pulled small children behind them, careful not to drop purses or their early-morning purchases. An almost rhythmic opus of car horns signaled lackadaisical street-crossers and distracted drivers. A haze of dust and cigarette smoke billowed from passing cars. The starched pallor of city *dappers* (as my uncle liked to call them) was threatened with each turn of the steering wheel or application of the squeaking brake pads. Emerging sunlight sparkled off copper guttering and art deco tile designs framing doorways. I wished desperately that I could tune a car radio to mellow jazz. One of the first items on my list after a few paychecks was to buy a radio. I wouldn't be able to buy one just for the car, but maybe I could take it with me on long rides if I stockpiled enough batteries. In truth, I didn't know a whole heck of a lot about jazz, but there was no denying that one true fact—Asheville was a jazz city. It breathed blue notes.

By the turn of the second signal light, I was swerving consistently to avoid an errant stray dog or misguided fruit cart. The tempo had taken a strong upturn. Essie, now fully awake, gripped her purse with one hand and the edge of the seat with her other, signaling her distaste for my navigational talents. "We're not in that big of a hurry, are we? I think we

32

could have bypassed some of this. That way you wouldn't be in such a rush."

I had little time to consider her comforts, not entirely sure of my route, though I had navigated the streets before. In truth, this was not the most direct route to the resort, but I thought the excitement of downtown might conjure a smile from Essie. She seemed more "city" than any other girl I knew back home. I gambled on her inborn metropolitan inclination.

My foot ached from the constant stop-and-go pressure on the brake and clutch. I needed to stretch my legs. My toes started to go numb. I was quickly regretting my decision to prolong the ride. The slow traffic allowed me the opportunity to fully sense a distinct nervousness about Essie as well. She lifted her chin as she looked out the windows, as if to imply to the passersby that I was most certainly her driver and that was all. She brushed the skirt of her dress flat and patted the sides of her head, sticking her up-do into permanent alignment. None of this was for my benefit. Her breathing became deep and rhythmic, in the way that nearly forced me to mimic it myself. She was calming herself. I never would have thought a girl like that got nervous.

By the third traffic light, as we now eased into the heart of Asheville's downtown, Essie sighed again; but this time it was different. The tall buildings folded around us, concrete sisters of the Smoky Mountains edging the horizon. Essie squared her shoulders. A peaceful energy surrounded her. It was almost as if she had finally aligned herself with the morning sunrise, a calm after an invisible storm. The golden glow cocooned her body.

Given the week I had in Cherokee under Bud's surveillance before Essie and I made our trip to Asheville, though I know now I was wrong, I would have thought it was sheer luck or divinity that placed me in the driver's seat. *Try and relax*, I told myself. Perhaps it was the discussion about the inn's rumors or what it might be built upon, but the road ahead felt uneasy in more ways than one—as if the wheels of the car were rolling over secrets.

CHAPTER FIVE

I eased the Model T up the private driveway, feeling as much a newcomer as Essie probably did. Essie's fidgeting in the passenger's seat seemed to feed my own unrest as we wound our way up the driveway to the inn. Iron gates and alabaster homes lined the path, each in competition with the Grove Park's opulence. As we edged the top of the hill, newly erected barbed-wire fencing, completely at odds with the serenity of the property, unsettled me. The only barbed wire I had seen at home was used to keep cattle and horses corralled. I had ripped more than one pair of good jeans on those fences.

Aside from the temporary military structures dotting its grounds, the Grove Park Inn looked as if it had been forcefully extracted from the rocky earth by some red-gloved god. The base of the main structure mimicked the stone-formed mountain landscape. Succeeding generations of stonemasons must have labored to jigsaw the fragments together. It splayed across the hillside, dipping down and rising with the ridgeline. With its bright red terracotta tile cottage sag, the roofline was anything but natural. Nothing camouflaged this edifice among the blue-gray mountains; it set the Smokies ablaze. Even though I knew the buildings were older than me, I reminded myself that they were not older than the land on which they amassed. I felt as if I was arriving at some sort of sacred site. Not sacred to my people, but to the people of Asheville—or, more accurately, to the wealthy whites of Asheville. I approached with a sense of reverence and fear of the inn's inherent power. I was a caretaker of a phenomenon. I wondered if Essie would feel the same impulse to say a prayer. *Dear Father, dear Lord, dear God!*

To the south, the grandiose Biltmore House pierced the horizon. To the west, Thomas Wolfe lay in rest at Riverside Cemetery, home again at last. To the east, Black Mountain College's artist community woke the dead. To the north, Governor Vance's old homeplace held fast to the landscape of stagnant time. There seemed to be many secrets in this town, far more than I considered the Boundary to have. But, of course, Asheville townies likely felt quite the same about Cherokee. So, during our time in Asheville, we would pass one another with both curiosity and secret-keeper confidence in our eyes.

"We have to check in at the gate first," I explained to Essie, pretending that I knew what I was doing. She nodded. I slowed the car to stop at the makeshift gatehouse, a small white box of a structure much more recent than the rest of the property, and cranked the window down. "We're here to work. I'm Cowney Sequoyah and this is Essie Stamper."

The M.P. scanned his clipboard. "Yes. You're right here. I was wondering how you pronounced your name. See-coy-ya. Good to know. Just a moment." He walked behind my vehicle and wrote down my license plate number. "Take this pass and put it inside your windshield so it can be seen from the outside." He seemed nice enough, even smiled as he waved us through the gate.

That was the last smile I saw for the remainder of the day.

Two other M.P.s waved us into a parking lot situated just above the resort's main hall. I slid the sheet of paper onto the dashboard. Essie looked at me, silently, but still communicating, *Well, here we go.*

"Not too shabby, is it?"

"I've never seen anything like this," she confirmed.

"Yeah, me neither. But I don't think most folks have. Probably even a lot of people from Asheville have never been here."

"Wonder why they thought to put prisoners here?" Essie asked as she opened her car door. I had intended to open it for her, but my left foot was knotted into a tight cramp from working the clutch, and I could only manage to get myself halfway out the door by the time she was stepping out.

"Guests," I reminded her. "You mean to say guests."

"Yes. Of course." She nodded, straightening her back and lifting her chin.

I moved to the back of the car and opened the trunk, setting all three suitcases on the ground. "Not sure. I guess they figure they'll keep them pacified in a resort and, well, we are in the middle of nowhere."

"And I thought *Cherokee* was the middle of nowhere."

"Apparently they save reservations for *real* prisoners. Let's go. We can check in with the manager together."

Essie nodded and picked up her bags with no indication that she was accustomed to anyone else ever carrying them for her. I was relieved, certain I couldn't have carried so many down the hill without tumbling into the front lobby.

"Alright. Keep up, will you!" She was almost cheerful as she started down the slope ahead of me.

That is, until we reached the large oak doors. She stood motionless in front of them, inhaling and exhaling slowly.

"You okay?" I asked, catching up to her.

"Yes. It's just . . . Well, what you said about the children . . ."

"Oh, no! No, no, no. Just ignore me. Heck, everybody else does. It's fine. Come on. You'll see."

I moved in front of her and pushed the right door open. I imagined how just a matter of months ago there would have been someone who looked a lot like me to open the door for us. And then there would be someone else who would sweep in and take our suitcases. They would have assumed we were on our honeymoon, perhaps. And though we weren't exactly on some sort of upper-crust holiday together, my chest swelled to think that I was about to lead Essie anywhere. In truth, I can't say for certain that I had ever led *anyone* anywhere.

I stepped back against the open door so Essie could walk through without shifting her bags. I watched as she cautiously surveyed the enormous lobby.

Stone-bolstered walls fortified the space, an impenetrable holding cell for the *haves* and the *pretend-they-haves*. I felt as if I was exploring a cavern, finding the only entrance through a tiny door compared to the enormity of open space inside. We were tumbling down Lewis Carroll's rabbit hole.

"I wonder where we go," she whispered.

"This way," I motioned with my elbow, hands still holding my bag. "The main office is over here."

She continued to follow me over to a small glassed-in office. A uniformed guard stood out front, but no weapon was visible.

"Can I help you?"

"We're here to work," I said.

"Well, I figured you weren't checking in for holiday." His eyes drooped in line with his tone.

Essie leaned forward past me. "I'm Essie Stamper and this is Cowney Sequoyah."

She remembered my name again.

"We just got here and need some direction. So please excuse us. We need to find the person in charge." Essie's cool demeanor fully returned. I think she may have scared me more than the guard.

"Letcha off the rez, did they? In there." He pointed.

As we continued through the door, I leaned over to her. "How'd you know he wasn't in charge?"

"His rank."

"How'd you know his rank?"

"My brother's in the army. My brother orders flunkies like him around."

I felt strongly that she was about to order flunkies like me around, too.

"Wait there." A thin man in a tan linen suit sat at the desk in front of us. He held the black phone receiver to his ear and pointed us both to a couch with his other hand. As he talked into the device, he kept his eyes on us.

The glassed room gave us a view to the sheer massiveness of the inn's lobby. Great pillars formed an exoskeleton of dark wood, flecked with stone joints. Scaffolding lined the colossal windows, most likely to replace original ornate draperies with canvas tarps and to reach the delicate chandeliers so that they could be wrapped in protective sheets during the army's tenure. In their desperate attempt to shield the resort from the economic laceration of the Depression by contracting with the US government, the inn's owners would still go to great lengths to protect their architectural treasure from the scars of the war. I wondered just how much light, natural and otherwise, had been stripped from the palatial space when the military arrived. It was now hard to imagine the light ever being here.

"Alright, what may I do for you?" the thin man asked briskly.

"Yes, sir." I wanted to speak first, before Essie had a chance. "I'm Cowney Sequoyah and this is Essie Stamper. We're new employees."

"Sure. Sure. Well, come on. I will show you where you're staying and introduce you to the shift managers. They'll take it from there. Show you where to eat. Go over the rules. All that." He opened a file in his hands. "You're Indians from over in Cherokee. That right?"

"Yes, sir."

"Hmm. We'll make sure you get a proper orientation then. Things are probably quite different."

"Yes, sir. Thank you."

"It's late to start the day. Keep in mind you won't be getting a full day's pay today, starting so late and all."

"Yes, sir," I answered and then immediately regretted it as I could feel Essie's stare beating down on me.

"But we have been traveling for hours!" she interrupted.

The manager stopped shuffling papers and looked at Essie inquisitively. And then, as if it all made sense, he nodded vigorously. "Oh, yes, I see what you're saying. Of course. The shift managers will give you your uniforms, so don't worry about those wrinkled clothes. You can wash and iron them out later."

"Excuse m—" Essie began to push.

I placed my hand around Essie's elbow to calm her. She jerked her arm away, but let the comment drop nonetheless.

"They're prisoners, you know, but it's our job to run this place just like they're any other guests," he continued. "Leave the politics to the military, I say. It's much easier for everyone that way." He returned to his papers, readjusting his wire-rimmed reading glasses. "Any other questions before we head off?"

"Yes," Essie answered. "The soldiers. Are we to treat *them* as guests as well?"

"Of course. You are to accommodate their needs, but . . . word of warning, miss." The thin man rose from behind the desk and walked around to the front, taking a seat on its edge. He removed his glasses and stared hard at Essie. "Don't let them get too used to your *accommodations.*

They do have a tendency to take advantage of the services here. And other things." He paused as he turned to face me. "Well, let's just say this crew should count themselves lucky that they're spending the war at a resort. Most boys their age are out serving our country in foreign lands."

I rose, picked up my suitcase, and exaggerated my limp as we walked toward the door. Essie followed closely behind. Have you ever felt like everyone was staring at you, like every single pair of eyes in a twenty-mile radius was on you, but when you glanced to check your suspicion, you realized absolutely no one was looking? That's how walking through the Grove Park Inn's lobby felt—probably still feels. It was as if my bones were crumbling under the weight of an imperceptible gaze.

After brief tours of our respective dormitories (spartan, dank, and life-less), the thin man led us back to the main entrance of the inn. Waiting, arms folded, were a short, stout woman in an ill-fitting navy suit and a large burly man in khaki coveralls. Jet black wires sprouted from her pale chin. Her lips naturally curved downward in direct opposition to her eyebrows, which seemed frozen in constant disbelief or surprise. She held a clipboard in front of her rounded stomach and only glanced up from it when the thin man spoke. The burly man, in contrast, eyed us both from the moment we came into sight. He also withheld any hint of a smile, but his eyes rested on us in such a way to convince me that he was never surprised. Not ever.

"This is Miss Ulana Parks and Mr. Iliam Jenkins."

"Call me Lee," the burly man interrupted, thrusting out his hand to shake mine. I was relieved that Lee seemed welcoming, humble even. I worried that Essie was not likely to be greeted with the same kindness by her new shift manager. Ulana Parks's demeanor was distinctly unwelcoming.

"Pleased to meet you, Lee. Thanks for taking me on."

"Your good work will be thanks enough. Let's go ahead and I'll show you around and introduce you to the rest of the crew."

Essie nodded to me with reassurance that she was perfectly fine on her own and then turned to Ulana Parks with surprising readiness. As Lee and I walked off, I could hear only pieces of their introductions.

"Pleased to meet . . . Miss Parks . . ."

"Mrs. . . . . Are we clear?"

I looked back to read Essie's face and watched as the confidence I had seen earlier fell away. I tried to share a smile with her, but her eyes were locked on Mrs. Parks. She didn't appear scared or intimidated, exactly. It was as if she was newly poised, her core countenance bared. We were both starting a new life, one that demanded we forfeit certainty for opportunity. We had a chance to do everything new and fresh and start our lives away from the suffocating safety of the familiar. I saw in her what I hoped was in me—the courage to step into one's true self, whoever that might be.

CHAPTER SIX

I didn't see Essie again for the rest of the day. I worried I probably wouldn't see her again for most of the summer since my work would be outside and we likely would rarely see the sun touch any of the women's faces except for the diplomats' wives and daughters lounging on the back patio as they sipped lemonade.

Lee was by no means chatty, but hints of Scots-Irish heritage twisted anything he told me into the most incredible story of Grove Park survival.

"And over yonder's the tool shed." My head spun to follow each point of his finger, causing me to become both dizzy and disoriented.

"Supper's served in the mess hall at eighteen hundred hours for military and at 8 p.m. for staff," Lee continued. "Guests eat in the dining room at 7 p.m. Go ahead and change into your coveralls. There's a couple pairs on your bunk. We'll start bustin' up some wood when you get dressed. Guests fancy a fire after dinner." Even with his drawn-out speech, the information flew at me with ungraspable speed.

My coveralls were made for a man twice my size. I rolled up the pants cuffs so as not to wear holes in the hems. Even the Sunday trousers Lishie sewed by hand for me frayed on the left cuff from the unavoidable drag of my foot. Somehow I had to make two pairs of coveralls last all summer, weeks and weeks of outdoor labor. I wouldn't be able to afford mending, much less another pair, if it came to it. Lee warned me not to leave the grounds with any Grove Park property, which I assumed included uniforms for Lishie to mend during a weekend visit home.

41

I could tell from the number of disheveled beds that at least five other civilian men would be working on the property. All the beds were made, but some were military-grade smooth. I knew I could never achieve that, and from the look of the dorms, I was not alone. I imagined at least a couple men would be working inside maintenance, a few more in the kitchen and, judging by the muddy boot tracks, it looked like Lee and I'd have some company outside.

Though the dorm couldn't have housed workers for more than a couple of months, it smelled of acidic metal and earthen sweat as if decades of men had laid their heads on the matted down pillows and tossed beneath the rough, woolen blankets, metal bedrails, and dangling pendant light fixtures sweating right along with them.

It was relatively clean, though. I was glad of that. At least I wouldn't have to pick up after Bud or worry about supper for him. I just had to worry about myself and that was plenty for now.

"Cowney? Son, you coming?" Lee called to me through an open window. "Don't have time for a housewarming party."

"Yes, sir. Sorry. I'm coming. Just . . . are we staying in here with the soldiers?"

"Yep. This whole thing is temporary—rushed, really. Ain't got time for formalities."

Back outside, I found that another man had joined Lee. He too was large, with broad shoulders and thighs as thick as my torso. He smelled of minted tobacco, which was also evidenced in his few remaining teeth.

"This here's Solomon," Lee nodded at the foul-faced man.

"Glad to meet you. I'm Cowney." I extended my hand, to the apparent displeasure of Solomon.

"Mmm hmm," he replied.

Lee snorted. "Sol's a man of few words." He glanced in his direction. "He warms eventually . . . not sure you'll want him too, though."

I nodded, unsure whether to smile and please Lee, or smile and further annoy Sol.

"Come on, boys. Already getting a late start. Let's kick this pig."

Sol and I followed Lee to the edge of the property. I quickly found that Sol consumed more than his share of the talking space. The warming had begun.

"Where you from?" Sol asked after about five minutes into our work.

"Cherokee." And then I waited.

He hefted the ax onto his shoulder and eyed me. "Wagon-burner, huh?"

"No," I said, and turned away. "Cherokee."

The ax fell. "Thought all y'all supposed to be out west now. Or dead."

I spoke over my shoulder, refusing to face him again. "Some are. My people survived the Removal. Hid out for the most part until they could make a deal—"

"You know I really don't give a shit, right? Don't need a history lesson," Sol interrupted. "You're a young fella. Why you not overseas? You get shot or something? Noticed the limp."

Lee was right. I now wished Sol had never found his comfort level.

"No. I mean, yes. I mean, it's because of the leg, but I wasn't injured. Born this way."

Sol looked at me as if I was lying, as if in a moment of pure teenage dumbassness, I had injured myself.

As odd as it may sound, I was grateful. Usually, I received pity. "Poor fella" comments and sad headshakes that included infuriating tongue clicking. *Tsk. Tsk. Tsk.* In some ways, I wish it had been my fault. I wish I had been on some reckless adventure or attempted a grand feat of heroism. Pity just made me more protective of my mother because, in essence, if I were the object of pity, she must consequentially become the cause of my unjust fate. At least that was what the tongue clicking seemed to translate to in the dialect of the sanctimonious.

"Don't worry. I can still pull my own weight," I offered, immediately regretting it.

"Apparently Uncle Sam doesn't agree," Sol shot back, seemingly refocusing on his work. Odd how people were so concerned about me risking my life for a country that wouldn't even let me vote.

"Load 'er up, boys!" Lee interrupted, motioning to the empty wheelbarrow. "Ought to be able to get it all out in three trips if we stack it right."

Sol systematically laid the logs beside the first wheelbarrow. In an effort to further prove myself, I doubled my effort, causing the wheelbarrow to rock at times and Lee to shake his head. "I'll get it," I announced as the last log was placed. "I'll take it where it needs to go."

"Alright," Lee said. "Take it on around to the rear entrance of the lobby. Only got one cart, so you'll have to empty it a couple of times. Otherwise you'll break the handles. Sol and me's goin' to grab a sandwich."

I hadn't realized that I was volunteering to shoulder the whole morning's work, but that was Lee's first lesson of the summer for me. Humility has its place.

They lumbered away in silence as I stood there balancing twice my body weight on a rapidly deflating wheel. A small group of soldiers, looking like human erector sets, marched by me. They were silent except for the rhythmic crunch of their boots on the earth beneath.

I couldn't help but wonder why neither an upscale resort such as this nor the US Army couldn't afford a couple more wheelbarrows. By the final load, I began to wonder why the hell the guards weren't doing this work, saving taxpayers a nickel. Better yet, weren't these "guests" technically prisoners camped out in resort rooms? Why not have them work for their room and board?

And then I reminded myself that all this was a good thing. Thank God, I at least had a paying job and was out from under Bud's hand. I dumped the last load on the rock patio veranda outside the rear of the lobby and entered the building through the massive glass doors that stayed open most of the day and on into the early evening to help cool the halls. Guests were milling about, all paying no mind to me. They really seemed to pay each other little mind as well.

Immediately, I realized I had made my second mistake of the day.

"You again!" A voice bellowed from the corner. It was the same soldier who had met Essie and me at the door earlier that day. I kept my head down and walked as quickly as possible toward the front entrance. The guest room halls flanked both sides like a protective ribcage of the massive lobby, the heart of the inn. Its rhythmic echo matched the pounding of my own cardiac pulse.

"Hey, you! I'm talking to you," he continued, his voice getting closer. I had no other choice but to stop.

"Yes, sir. On my way out."

"Why are you coming through here?"

"Just delivered some wood out back and thought—"

"That's your problem. You tried to think. Your kind haven't had much practice with that."

"Private, can I help you with something?" I blurted before I could stop myself. And, in fact, I wasn't certain he was a private. I hoped Essie had been right in her estimation of his rank. Her identification had somehow emboldened me, as if I myself were some sort of officer. I'm not sure I could have reacted the same way if I had not been assured that his superiors weren't within hollering distance.

He stopped walking immediately. His eyes cut to both sides, as if scanning the room to see if anyone else had heard me. "Just get on your way."

Once out of sight of the main porch, I picked up speed and headed directly to the dining hall across the lawn, eager to join my fellow workers, even if they had already abandoned me once; being among coveralls seemed far more comforting than uniforms. My adrenaline carried me there, but left me utterly depleted by the time I arrived.

I was out of breath, and sweat beaded my forehead and matted my hair to the temples. The blue-gray of my coveralls (only Lee donned the khaki variety, another distinction of rank, I surmised) turned a deep blue-black down my chest and under my arms as if I were bleeding out. I must have looked like a disoriented jaybird smacking against an overly clean window. I had no idea where to go next and my stomach growled loudly, reminding me that I'd better figure it out soon. The intense smell of burning coffee and cigarette smoke further stunned my senses.

"There ye are," Lee called to me as I stepped through the doorway. "Almost missed lunch."

Sol looked over his shoulder without turning his body toward me. He shot a smart-ass grin at me and turned back to his meal.

Asshole.

"Grab it and growl, Sequoyah," Lee called.

"Yes, sir," I agreed, finally locating a buffet-style cart in the back of the room.

"Hurry up," Lee continued. He and Sol stuffed the remainders of their sandwiches in their mouths and laughed, spewing bits of moist bread across the table. Sol, seated to my left, slid his empty plate toward me, motioning toward the kitchen. I clearly was not done cleaning up after him, and the day was not just about to get better. Sol's laugh was a little too hearty for that.

Sol stood, palms on the table, and leaned over so that his mayonnaise-dripping lips rested inches from my ear. Lee stared at him, but instead of speaking, stood and took his own plate into the kitchen. He had left me with Sol hovering like a roadside buzzard. "You can take my plate now, son." He breathed hot, wet spittle into my ear.

Here's what I wanted to say, what I should have said: *I have an idea, son: shove that plate up your ass!*

But of course I didn't. I closed my eyes just briefly enough to see Sol's face melt into that of Bud's. How similar their bone structures were; how easily one could transform into the other. I had nineteen years devoted to the practice of echoing; I could do it at least one more day so I wouldn't lose my job. I tried to stand, but Sol ground his elbow into my shoulder until my knees buckled. The force was so great that I could not fully turn my neck to search his eyes for further instructions.

"Let's get one thing straight, boy. If the old man wants a new pet to play fetch with, that's his business, but I don't plan to share my scraps with any more mongrels than I have to. Do us both a favor and get on home 'fore your momma's teats dry up."

"I'm not taking nothin' from you." I shook my head.

"Takin' my air every time you open that trap of yourn."

"Just here to work."

"We can handle it. All you do is cause 'em to water down the milk."

Sol eased back, alleviating the pressure just enough for me to collect my leg strength. I picked up the plates, almost head-butting Sol in the process.

"And hurry your ass up," Sol called after me. "We need to break you in right." Sol laughed. He laughed as if the whole exchange had been a joke all along, though the bruise congealing just beneath my skin confirmed otherwise. I looked to Lee as he returned to the table. I can't be certain, but I think he looked slightly remorseful either for what Sol *had* said or what Sol *would* say.

Years later I would read about Dr. Jekyll and Mr. Hyde. I think these two may have been the prototypes for that character, both just too damn big to keep holed up in one measly body. When I returned to the table, I braced myself for what *strange case* the two were about to lay before me.

CHAPTER SEVEN

Several hours later, I found myself negotiating the hidden rules of the staff dining hall again. The wilting bodies warmed the room almost past the point of tolerable. The sun held strong, the evening breeze had yet to blow the dust and dank from the hall's wooden floors. I was unsure if it was allowable for me to join Essie at her table, though she sat alone, though other tables of men had little space, though no one attempted to make eye contact with me when I walked in for supper. Of course, that included Essie as well. *Was dinner more formal than lunch?* There were not *Colored* or *Whites Only* signs I had heard tale of being in the city, but perhaps there were unspoken rules. Likely there were unspoken rules.

I went straight to the serving line, filling a tall glass of sweet tea from a pitcher, guzzling until the glass was empty, and refilling it again before I moved on to the food. It was heartening to see—and better yet smell— the richness of the food being served for dinner. While lunch had been cold and sparse, the spread before me was rich with grease, butter, and sugar. I think those are the three real Cherokee Sisters. Corn, beans, and squash would be nothing without them.

Golden-fried chicken overflowed from porcelain blue serving dishes. I could smell the rich tang of buttermilk batter. Mounds of white whipped potatoes, skins and all, were carved by melted butter rivers and piled high in a huge metal bowl. I scooped an oversized serving, barely balancing the glob on the spoon. Then I topped them off with a heap of bright green winter peas. I added candied carrots and sweet corn on the cob and completed my plate with a yeast roll.

I'd be eating better than any American I knew. The country was experiencing noteworthy rationing of the rich ingredients I readily found on my dinner plate. While fresh vegetables were nothing new, most families in the area having productive gardens and at least a few farm animals, I had to wonder if ordinary citizens were conserving so that stateside soldiers and their prisoners did not go without.

I sensed that Essie had noticed my arrival, even if she was careful to offer no physical evidence of it. She hadn't hurried out the door, so I took that as a sign that she wouldn't mind too terribly if I joined her at her seat. As uncomfortable as Sol had made me earlier, I was glad that I had more news to tell her than just the trite and boring recollection of a day's work. I sat my plate on the table and slid down the bench, planting myself directly in front of her.

"Hiya! How was your first day?" I forced a smile.

The ridge of her brow pinched, but her eyes did not move from her plate. "Sure. You can sit here."

"Thanks, don't mind if I do."

"My day was fine. And yours?" Essie focused on the potato sculpture she was making with her fork.

"Pretty good. You know. Pretty much what you'd expect. Did hear some interesting stories, though."

"Oh, did you?" It was obvious that she didn't believe me. She looked tired. Or annoyed. Probably both.

"Yeah, guy stuff. You know." I crunched down on the juicy chicken, grasping for a napkin to catch the grease before it dripped from my chin. "You jusff stay mmnnsfide?"

"What? For Pete's sake! Chew your food."

I blushed through my tea glass. "Sorry." I dabbed my mouth with the napkin. "You stay inside all day?"

"Yes, looks like I might get out to the porches some, but I'll be mostly cleaning guest rooms."

"Oh. Are they . . . I mean, do you have to . . ."

"Don't worry. They're never in there, far as I can tell. We have to make sure the sign is not on the door before we go in, and we have to knock, too."

"Oh, good." I reached for the saltshaker.

"How about you? You see the guests at all?"

"No. Not really. Don't have time to. We were outside all day pretty much. 'Cept for cutting through the lobby once . . . which I will *never* do again." Essie looked up. "That private was still there. He's a real *jerk*."

"Oh, yeah. You need one of these. Then you can go another way." Essie pulled a small iron key from the pocket of her white smock. "It's a skeleton key. It's supposed to unlock any room I need to get in. One of the other girls said it probably unlocks some of the doors I don't need to open, too." She smiled, twisting the key between her fingers.

"Let me see that." I reached out across the table.

"No way. Do you know what trouble I'd get in? The shift manager says I can't tell anyone I have it. Military doesn't know we have them. They say it's bad for security purposes, but the girls say our job would take three times as long if we didn't have 'em." Essie looked down at the key in her palm as if she held tangible power. She wrapped her delicate fingers around it and secured it back in her pocket. She smiled at me, tasting a small bite of potato from her fork. "I think I've already found a room they don't even know about."

I swallowed hard and almost covered my chest in potatoes as I leaned toward her. "Really? How you know?" What I wanted to ask was why she thought she should tell me if she wasn't supposed to tell *anyone*. Instead I assured myself that my imagined answer was far more satisfying than the truth. I also couldn't help but wonder how she even had time to find another room on her own. I could barely keep in step with Lee's to-do list.

"There's just too much for all of us girls to do. No way we can even work in pairs."

"I think that'd be safer."

"Oh, stop worrying. Anyway, I went up to the fourth floor and noticed my list had left off a room around the corner at the end. I think it must be one of those odd-shaped rooms." She moved her fork through her potatoes as if she was drawing a map. Unsuccessfully, I tried to follow the gravy-laden path. "You know, when a building isn't exactly rectangular, you're going to end up with some odd rooms. I almost missed it at first. It doesn't even have a room number on it."

"Did you ask the shift manager about it?"

"Why would I do that?"

I had no idea why *she'd* do that. I would. I'd ask everybody of authority I could find, most likely. But that was me, and I was pretty sure that that was most certainly not Essie. However, since the moment we got in the car together earlier in the day, I had been wrong about her.

"Essie. It's day one. Don't do anything to get yourself fired already."

"You mean, don't do anything to get *you* fired."

"That's how it goes in places like this. Heck. I drove you here. Of course they'd send me down the road just as quick as you. Especially in places so tight on security and all. And look at us. It's not like we're like the rest of the help. Just be glad most of these guards are still trying to figure out what an Indian is. We so much as drink from the wrong fountain in front of some of these folks and that's the end of this job."

"Don't worry. I'm not going to push my luck." She rose from the table and walked to the coffee urn. I pretended not to watch as she poured herself a cup of steaming joe, stirring in cream and a teaspoon of sugar. She returned and slid into her seat. "Still." Essie took a sip. "What would it hurt if we just opened the door? It's in a corner that I am sure no one looks."

"We?"

"Well, if you don't want to go . . ."

"It's not that. I surely wouldn't let you go alone. But still, it would be twice as bad if they caught us both and the guys were saying . . ." Essie leaned in, smiling. I tried not to get pulled into those brown eyes. They threatened, like bottomless pools, to pull me under. "Ahh. It's nothin'. I just mean, let's just say the guys talk about some of those rooms. You might be surprised who you'd find behind locked doors, that's all."

"Cowney. Is this another ghost story?"

I laughed and then stopped myself. "No. No ghosts or vampires. Let's just say it seems like everyone around here likes his privacy and it can be hard to come by. You girls may not be the only one with a key like that." I blushed at my own insinuation. When Lee and Sol told me about the other men and their *conquests* of sorts, it all seemed so—I don't know—hopeful, I guess. That the workers could find more than just work here. But with Essie sitting squarely across from me, her eyes now so focused and serious, it all seemed stupid. Just more bullshit to complicate the rules of this place. *Was I really going to tell Essie that she had one more thing to be afraid of?*

"Well, I'll be. I didn't get *that* part of the tour today." Essie raised her eyebrows, further reddening my cheeks.

"Don't say anything. You know how fellas talk. Probably not even true."

"Just so you don't get the wrong impression, Cowney Sequoyah. I want to see what's in the room. You are welcome to join me. But let's be clear. You and I going into that room is not what your *fellas* are talking about. I am not that type of girl. I've seen some of these chambermaids and . . ."

I held up my palms in front of her. "I gotcha. Trust me. That's the farthest thing from my mind." Of course it wasn't. Hadn't been since Lee told me about secret rendezvous earlier in the day. But I was darn clear on where Essie stood and that anything between us, other than friendship, was more than a long shot.

"When were you thinking about going?" I asked.

"Tomorrow night."

"What!"

"Yeah, why not?"

"You know, most people come from a ways to work at a place like this, they tend to be homesick. Spend the first week crying into their pillow. Too afraid to even talk to folks."

"Oh, I'm sorry. Was that on your agenda?" She cocked her head. "Like I said, you don't have to go."

"I'm just saying this seems a little quick. Don't you want to check things out a little more?"

"Thought that was what we were going to do."

I shook my head and was disappointed when she started stacking her dishes and cutlery.

"I guess I better enjoy not doing the dishes tonight." She rose to take them to the kitchen.

"What do you mean?" I questioned her. "You've got all summer."

Essie let out a harsh laugh, one that made me feel like a rookie sitting on the sideline of some ill-defined game. "Well, all summer for you. They told us girls this morning that we will take turns with all the staff upkeep duties. Cooking. Cleaning the dorms. Luckily there are enough of us that we get a week off here and there." Essie smiled slyly. "So, are you coming with me tomorrow?"

"I don't get it. Why are you so intent on going into some mildewed old room?"

"I'm looking for something."

"What?"

"Anything. Anything someone doesn't want me to see."

I collected my dishes and followed her to the kitchen. She placed her dishes in the stack beside the large sink. A clumsy matron jerked mine from my hands. Essie swung open the kitchen door and I trailed her back through the open hall.

Before opening the door to exit she turned to face me. "We shouldn't leave together. It looks inappropriate." Essie scanned the dining hall. "Meet me at the cellar door on the west end of the lobby at 6 tomorrow evening. Most of the guests will be out of the hallways. If you're not there, I'll just assume you aren't coming."

I shook my head and walked back into the hall, feebly searching for a reason to justify my lingering.

The whole next day was a slow grind. I was tired. And hungry. And thirsty. Sol's constant complaints about my work hit my better sense of reason at just the wrong angle. He was a crow, I quickly recognized. Cackling crows chase—no, terrorize—the hawks over the fields. There are almost always two or three crows circling the poor, though obviously stronger, hawk. That was Sol, a crow. I was too out of place for him. Didn't look like him and that ensured harassment in his book. He was constantly looking for the other crows, expecting them to be there, but they weren't. It was just me. I knew they weren't because every time I stepped into a building or turned a corner, I would make sure I knew exactly where every guest, every uniform, every worker placed themselves. I would know how many steps stood between each human being and myself and which ones noticed my existence. I would note every beautiful woman and each serious-faced man clutching her. I would notice their almost carefree children stumbling after them. I would notice who noticed whom. Which men looked at which women. Which adult looked at which child and how they looked at him or her. The whispered rumors of the missing children still tortured my thoughts, so I made sure to notice. And while I'd never consider my will or strength that of a hawk, I could surely scare off an annoying crow flying solo.

Ten minutes before Essie's meeting time, I lay motionless on my tiny brass-framed bed, staring at the planked ceiling. I wondered about Essie. How could a girl be both a master fisherman and grammar prude? How could she speak so boldly to men in uniform and seek out secrets in new forbidden places? How did she arrive with such assurance on her very first day when I was still too cautious to even enter the main building willingly? I thought about the children I saw on the property and how they, too, played freely as if they weren't caged between swaths of barbed wire and military khaki—about a little girl with a purple ribbon in her hair who smiled at me each time I passed, acknowledging our shared space.

I was bored and anxious and could not imagine Essie wandering the halls of the inn alone. *Surely she has no idea what she is about to do.* At that thought, I bolted up and slipped out the door before anyone could notice.

"You came," she whispered as I crouched down beside her at the cellar door just outside the entrance to the lobby.

"I couldn't let you go by yourself, now, could I?"

"We'll see how brave you are when we get inside. Don't rush it," she coached. "Remember what they say; good things come to those who wait." Her smile inspired every imaginable obedience in me except the deference to wait. I watched as she inhaled and walked through the doors.

How someone from such a very different place could feel such a right to go where and when she pleased, I did not know. I still really don't know to this day where Essie's wellspring of certainty came from; but wherever that place is, it must have transferred from her fingertips to me, because I did exactly as she instructed, took my own deep breath, and walked into the inn like I had every right to be there.

I tried not to run as I chased after Essie, up the staircase and into her hidden corner of this mysterious estate. Unsure if she was leading us into a wonderland-style dream or a nightmare, I followed with every ounce of courage I could muster. I tried to slow my pace, to assure her that I was only there for her protection, but my mile-wide eyes and breathlessness surely gave me away.

The steps trembled beneath me as the shrill wail of a siren swept down the narrow passageway. I'd never heard such an alarm. I slid down the wall and sat on a step, certain that I would soon be met by a host of guards. My head dropped onto my knees.

"Come on!" Essie bounded back down the stairs and tugged at my arm. "What are you doing?"

"Don't you hear that? They must know—"

"Of course they don't. It's probably just some drill. Listen. Do you hear anyone coming?"

"No. But what if there's a fire or something?"

"Get up now." Essie shot me a warning and bounded, two steps at a time, up the stairwell. I had no other choice. I stood and ran after Essie as quickly as my body would allow.

We slipped behind the hall's final corner in unison. Doubting I could have found my way alone, I was positive that I could now not leave without her navigation.

Before us was a door. Just a door, no different from any other in the hall. Essie was right. There were no longer brass numbers like on the other doors, just faded wood outlining 447. Essie held up the key. I turned and craned my neck around the corner to confirm no one else was in the hall.

"Oh, come on. No one is coming." She elbowed me in the shoulder. "I just hope it fits." Essie inserted the key, paused, inhaling, and turned her wrist. I silently prayed against the sound of a click, but to no avail. The lock gave as if it had been awaiting the key's arrival for decades, centuries, surely since the beginning of time. "Okay, ready?" she threaded her arm through mine.

I pulled the Rayovac flashlight, given to me by Lee, from my hip pocket and clicked it on.

"The bulbs must be blown," Essie surmised, as she fidgeted with the closest wall sconce. I scanned the room slowly with my flashlight, terrified of what might be illuminated. "At least it looks like we're alone. Stay here. I think there are more bulbs in the supply closet." Essie bolted from the room before I could protest. The room was cold, even drafty, which further concerned me as it meant something was open to the night air. The floor was the same wooden planked floor as the inn's lobby, though my feet stumbled across some sort of rug as I scooted inside. I scanned the ceiling, fearful of squirrels' nests or perched bats. The light reflected from a large chandelier, twinkling back like a visual wind chime of moon's glow. It brought a strange magic to the room, both hopeful enchantment and mysterious wonder. I wanted to be there, to see more. Not prepared for a solo exploration, I also wanted Essie to return immediately.

"Got one!" Essie announced, far too loudly, as she entered the room again. She leaned in the door, removed the old bulb, and screwed in a new one. The light flickered on, seemingly as eager as I was to bring light to the space. "Let there be light!" Essie threw her arms out wide. I crouched a bit, still wary of varmint settlements yet to be exposed.

The room glowed. We stepped onto an oriental rug, dulled and worn thin. I expected a typical guest room, but there was no sign of a bedroom suite. Instead, a threadbare velvet chaise anchored one corner, and two leather couches, divided by a small, scratched cherry coffee table, faced each other in conversation. In front of them was a still-sooty stone fireplace with wooden mantel framing it from above. On the mantel, a golden clock, time frozen at 12:27. There was a tall brass lamp stand in another corner of the room, no bulb or shade attached. Half-filled bookshelves flanked the fireplace, indicating that this might have been a small library at one time.

"Perfectly cozy," Essie remarked.

"Perfectly eerie, maybe."

"It's just a room. Just an empty space. Nothing scary about nothingness. It's the 'something' you ought to be afraid of."

"I didn't say that I was afraid, Essie."

She paused for a moment. It was the first time I had addressed her using her name. She took it in like I had spoken it in some foreign language.

"Well, anyway. I think it is a fine place."

"Now that you've seen behind the curtain, are you ready to go? I can still hear the alarm."

"Oh, Cowney. What's the rush? It's early. You know good and well that if we go back now, we'll both just lay around listening to someone snore. And if that alarm is anything to worry about, we'll hear people on the floor soon enough."

I sat down on the couch and wove my fingers together behind my head. "Okay, but much longer here and you are going to be listening to *me* snore."

"Surely there's something interesting here." Essie ran her hands carefully along the bookshelves and began pulling open the doors of the cabinets below them. Dust rose and dispelled into the darkness. "Here we go!" Essie held a tin box above her head. "I think we're in luck!" She blew the dust from its raised lid design and placed the box on the coffee table.

"A box? Great. Should make for hours of entertainment."

"Not the box. It's what's in the box."

I picked up the metal container. Small pieces of some kind slid about inside. I desperately hoped that I hadn't already broken the one thing that Essie was convinced would keep us together, alone, in this room.

"Open it," she urged.

I obeyed and pried off the lid, almost spilling out the set of small alabaster tablets inside.

"I hope they're all there." Essie peered over, digging her slight fingers into the box.

"What are they?"

Essie let her hand fall to her side and looked at me, surprised. "Dominos." Each syllable slowing as she reached it. "You've never played?"

"Played? It's a game?"

"For heaven's sake, Cowney. You've never even heard of dominos?"

"Guess not." I felt ridiculous.

"My folks used to play all the time. Every Saturday night after supper." Essie beamed. Her memories of family were pleasant and it made me smile to know that.

"I don't guess we had anything like that."

"You didn't play games growing up?"

"Not with adults. I mean, my family sounds like it is a little different than yours. My mom . . ."

"Cowney. I know your folks. You know that, right?"

"I mean, everybody knows everybody in Cherokee, but sometimes . . ." I lied, unsure of which line of Stampers she came from.

"You're right," she corrected herself. "I'm sorry. I don't presume to know all about you. Just, well, you don't need to explain. I know about your mother."

I wondered if that meant that she also knew about Bud and Lishie and everything else in between. *Did she know anything about my dad? Did she know more than even I knew about his life and death?* "No, to answer your question. No games that I played at home. Played plenty with kids, but not like this."

"Well that is the most exciting thing I've heard all day. You, Cowney Sequoyah, will learn something brand-new tonight. And it's fun!"

"Well, I guess I'm your captive. I'd rather stay here than try to sneak back out, anyway." I picked out one of the tiles from the box and turned it over between my fingers. "You hear about my dad then, too?" I searched her face.

"Yes. I mean, he died a war hero, right?"

"I don't know. He died away from here, but a hero? Maybe. Maybe not."

"Most people think so. Why don't you?"

"Ahh. No real reason. Sometimes stories don't line up and I never feel like people are telling me the whole truth, you know? Maybe you're right. Maybe he was a hero."

"That why you wanted to come here? Be like him?"

"I ain't nothing like him. I'm here because I can't serve my country." Saying it aloud made me nauseous.

"I guess we all do what we can with what we got."

"Yeah. Guess so."

We played that night for hours. Probably hours. Neither of us had a watch, but when we landed back at our respective quarters later, even the nosier inhabitants were so far into their dreams that they could not wake to interrogate us. The siren too had faded, leaving no evidence as to its meaning. I told Essie more about Lishie and Bud, still careful not to incite sympathy or disdain. She told me little of her family, speaking mostly of her girlfriends, a tight-knit group of five who were growing apart as they got older. I told her more of what I had learned from Lee and Sol, still careful to censor the language a bit. I told her just which girls were lonely, which were most definitely not, and which guests to stay far, far away from. I pulled the napkin-wrapped chicken leg I had smuggled from dinner out of my pocket and picked it clean until there was nothing more left than delicate bone as she shook her head at my uncouth manners.

But mostly, we talked about what was ahead of us. At least, what we hoped was ahead of us. Miss Essie Stamper was not the girl I thought she was when she climbed into the Model T, and I was desperately trying not to be the Cowney Sequoyah she had taken a ride from. By the end of the evening, she was just Essie, and that was more than enough.

CHAPTER EIGHT

There were few days at the inn that I wasn't in a hurry to leave work, scarf down dinner, and escape to the room with Essie. But on the day I found the bone, everything and everyone else around me—all the soldiers and guests and Sol and Lee—just seemed to fade from existence.

Noting my growing frustration with Sol's bullshit, Lee sent me mid-morning to the perimeter of the property to dig new holes for warning signs—*No Trespassing—Federal Property*—ominous threats with an ambiguous intended audience. The morning rain had slowed to a mist, but my boots still sank into the ground as I trudged across the property. While I was glad to be shed of Sol for a couple of hours, the heavy stick of outside felt anything but freeing. Nonetheless, I began my work, all the while daydreaming about the fresh cool waters of the Oconaluftee. As I knelt to remove rocks that slowed my shovel strikes, my coveralls absorbed the wetness of the ground. I worked quickly and mindlessly.

So much so, I almost tossed it away.

Covered as it was in soft dirt, I only recognized its solidity at first. But as my fingers curled around it, I recognized it for what it was—a bone.

It most likely had been carried there by a wandering scavenger—one of the many hungry animals that translate a being to a body, to a carcass, to a bone, to an artifact now for my amusement. I marveled at the thing, holding it above my head so as to find some bit of sunlight to illuminate it. Small and solid, cleaned by tooth and claw, stained by mountain earth.

I had certainly seen my fair share of animal bones, either happening upon them in the woods or excavating them from a fresh hunt. Something felt different about this one. I couldn't quite place it. Maybe it was because it was in Asheville, an environment I assumed was devoid of elemental remnants such as discarded bones, castoff feathers, and rock faces that scowl like relatives. There was brick and concrete and glass and steel in Asheville, for certain—anything else seemed misplaced. The bone, in such a tangible state, reminded me of home and what I loved about home—the simplicity of knowing what each day held and the certainty that people said what they meant and meant what they said. There were no flashy distractions, but there was strength, there was resolve, and they were foundational. I knew exactly where I stood and when to stand there. I had wanted so badly to fit into the *shine* of Asheville, but it never seemed to fit me. Back home, being Cherokee meant I fell into a role. Unfortunately, it also meant I had only a few options: I could farm. I could work for a white man. I could leave. I learned that pretty quickly in school. They instructed us in the trades, but they were trades to stay, to exist, to fit into a slot already carved out for me. Sure, it was safe in a lot of ways. I didn't worry that I would starve; my family and church and neighbors saw to it that no one would starve. But oh, the hunger! I always felt half empty, like I was missing out on some grand feast just over the mountains. I was tethered in all the good ways and in all the bad.

I pulled a red bandana from my back pocket, wrapped it around the bone, and tucked the parcel into my pocket. With the rain starting to pick up again, I haphazardly planted a *Federally Restricted Area* sign, filled in the dirt around it, and hurried back to the barracks. Before changing clothes, I tucked the bone inside my suitcase so that I wouldn't forget to take it home when I returned to Cherokee for the weekend. I needed more time with it. I knew I had junior college textbooks at home that might just help. Maybe I would finally be able to put them to use.

CHAPTER NINE

Asheville Citizen-Times
Local Hero's Whereabouts Unknown
Reports this week indicate that Lt. "Peanut" C   o   l
of   Nor   C   lina   Camp   after surviving
miles   Death March.
served with   returned safely and recounted the
harrowing acts of his brother in battle. Likely, a combination
starv   , disease, and   ible t   led

A name, folded and smudged. Misspelled. I probably didn't even know him. Wasn't related. Maybe the family was even from Oklahoma. But it was a Cherokee name. No doubt about it. Even incomplete there was no question. My eyes jumbled the letters of his name, struggling to spell out my own. I knew it was an impossible feat, but that did not sway the compulsion.

I pried apart the folds of soggy newspaper, carefully salvaging what remained of the brief report. No telling how long it had been there. The date was completely faded, and the guys had been using the paper to wipe their muddy feet since the rain started. It felt like it had been raining almost a full two weeks straight now. Maybe more. It started the night Essie and I had entered room 447, baptizing us as we made our way back to our dorms. I can't remember more than a few hours' break from it. And oddly enough, according to folks back home, there had been nothing but a dry heat all summer. It was odd that we could be only a couple of counties over and yet it felt like two totally different worlds. I found myself eager to escape the weather of one place only to quickly crave it again shortly after leaving.

I laid the broadsheet across the cage of the floor fan nearest my bunk, turning the dial to its lowest setting. As the blades churned, the words dried and separated from each other, forming legible sentences, solidifying into their story.

We didn't get much news at the inn. Not that the newspaper didn't come a whole day earlier than back home. People just didn't talk about it like they did in Cherokee. Someone would read a line or paragraph over lunch, but it was usually just greeted with a "Mmmm" or a "No kiddin'?" No one offered another version or an opinion. Maybe they were afraid of what the guards would say. And the guards never told us what they thought. At home, everyone had their own version, their own theory, their own take on *the rest of the story.*

Back home, Lishie was like my own personal Ernie Pyle: "Paper says it's going to snow this week. We'll see about that. Blueberries are budding. Probably just the stores overstocked winter coats."

I pulled my suitcase from beneath my bunk and unfolded the bandana around the bone. I needed to touch something tangible, and ever since finding the bone at the edge of the property, it had served that purpose. It was real when so much of the inn felt staged. I wanted to share it with Essie so she, too, would feel grounded. Or maybe I shared it for other reasons— for the mystery of it. Either way, just like Essie had given us the room, which was becoming our own sanctuary, I wanted to offer something no one else knew about. I had waited until I could clean it and consult my books at home, but now, having returned to the inn, I was eager to share it.

So the Monday following its discovery, as we arrived in 447 soaked and chilled, I barely let her enter the room before blurting out, "I found a bone. A human bone . . . Probably a little kid's or something." I shrugged. "It's pretty small."

"Oh. Which one?" She feigned interest.

"I don't know. A dead one, I guess."

"No. Which bone? Leg? Jaw? Pinky toe?" Essie sighed.

"A rib," I gushed. "Curved just like one."

"Maybe it's Adam's." From the corner of my eye I saw her flash a tiny smile.

"Adam who?"

The smile disappeared as quickly as it had come. "Never mind."

I felt a warm, wet embarrassment wash over me. I had pissed away my opportunity. "Oh! Ha . . . right." *Jesus, I'm an idiot.* Biblical references were not exactly my nineteen-year-old self's forte.

"Anyway. I found it when I was digging fence posts."

"Are there more?" She asked, seeming already bored without even knowing my answer.

"Didn't see any others. Figure some bear or bird or coon ran off with this one."

"Then how can you be so sure it's human?"

"I have an anatomy book at home. The one thing I kept from junior college. Right measurements and all. Plus, it's not brittle and thin like any animal I know this size."

"How close was it to the inn?"

"Oh, it was out a bit. Still on property, a goodly five hundred feet inside the woods line."

"And it was just laying there? All by itself? No other bones?"

"Yep. That's why I figure some animal carried it there."

"Where is it now? Did you keep it?" I could feel her eyes on me. Perhaps secretly searching my person for the bone.

I wasn't sure how to answer this. It might sound creepy if I told her the truth. That I'd wrapped it in the red bandana taken from my back pocket, carried it home, washed and dried it, then slid it in the bottom of my bureau drawer so no one else would find it and claim it as their own. When I returned to the inn, I brought it with me. "Yes. I mean—I know where it is."

"If you think it is human, why don't you tell the police? Did you move it?"

I was quickly approaching taboo. Moving human bones, even one that was obviously far removed from its whole, was questionable, at the very least. If Essie thought I had disturbed an actual grave, she might never speak to me again. I was pretty sure my Darwinian obsession with scientific inquiry was not compatible with what was most likely a Baptist upbringing or a traditional Cherokee value system. Neither permitted room for my curiosities.

"Well, I wasn't sure when I saw it. Like I said, I have this book and until I looked in there, I thought it was just some animal bone I could make a knife handle from. Then after looking it up, I figured I had taken it out of its rightful jurisdiction. I mean, who do I call? Asheville City Police Department? That would go over really well. *Hi, sir. Yes, my name is Cowney Sequoyah from Cherokee and I'm here with some dead person's rib that I think belongs to you.*"

Essie snickered. "I can see your point." She paused for a moment and then gave me a curious look. "Hey, what if it's Cherokee? I mean, our people used to hang out around here, right? There are all those stories about burial grounds."

"Could be, I suppose. Shit. Then I *really* can't tell the police I found it. White people are the only ones allowed to dig up our bones and move them." I laughed.

"Yeah, and put them in the ground in the first place." Essie shook her head and sighed.

"Well, I figure it's on me to make sure it gets buried properly. I'm just not sure where that should be, though."

At dinner, I asked Essie if she wanted to read the newspaper, the one I had dried in the barracks. She didn't. She barely even lifted her eyes while shaking her head. So I packed the paper away in my weekend bag and let it marinate among the dirty socks and soggy work boots.

I couldn't figure why Essie wouldn't want to read it. I knew she was a reader. I'd seen her read plenty. She read books from room 447 and almost always had a magazine with her during her breaks. Lately, she studied a single page of stationery over and over. Probably from someone back home ensuring that her summer paycheck made its way back to Cherokee. I guess she was homesick enough to read even that multiple times.

I especially liked to watch Essie read. She fell into pages like they were deep lagoons. She bit her nails when she read. Yes, I know this shouldn't have been particularly attractive, but it was a rare moment when Essie forgot proper womanly etiquette. It was honest and natural and completely unacceptable to everyone but me. As much as she pressed her uniform or pinned her hair or reapplied her lipstick, she was just a curious young girl when she read, and that made it alright for me to be just a curious young boy for once.

Maybe Essie didn't want to read the newspaper because she was afraid.

Lots of people were afraid of the news. Still, I was glad I had something to take home. Once the paper was completely dry, I folded it like a store-bought gift for the journey to Cherokee, and that's how I presented it to Lishie as soon as I unpacked during the next weekend visit back home.

CHAPTER TEN

I handed the crisp clipping to my grand-
mother, along with her reading glasses. I knew she would mimic reading
it on her own, but I would need to fill in the gaps, tell her the content.
Her eyes failed her more and more every day. Her English-reading skills
were fading even quicker.

"Mmm. I see," she mused.

"Do you know him?" I asked her.

"Can't make out the name."

"No, it's faded, but thought you might have heard about someone who
was over there. Looks like the last name might start with a 'C.' Catolster.
Cornsilk. Calhoun. Something like that."

"Sounds familiar, but can't place 'im. You know we got plenty of boys
over there, but some of 'em come straight out of boarding schools out
west and up north. Readymade soldiers. Hadn't seen 'em 'round here in
so long I forget they's grown."

"Says he survived a *death march*, but died in a prison camp. Starva-
tion. Disease. Something like that." *A death march. Aren't we all just death
march survivors?*

"For heaven's sake." Lishie twisted a pale blue dishrag in her hand. "I
thank the Lord every day that you . . ." she trailed off.

I hated when she said things like that.

"Does it say who his folks are?"

"No. Mostly about all the torture he likely went through. I think
most of it's speculation. Says another soldier was with him for part of it,

65

but he escaped from the prison camp so he didn't know all the details." I turned the page. "They included this picture, too. Don't think it's him. Just a stock photo they have of another prisoner. Nothing but a sack of bones." I shook my head.

"They really shouldn't put things like that in the paper. Just awful," Lishie complained.

"But it's real. I mean, don't you think people need to see what's really going on?"

"I just think about your daddy and uncle. Oh, how I worried myself sick with 'em gone. Your father was about the same age as you are now and so sensitive to each way the wind blew; and Bud, he was a great deal more patient, but wasn't that much older than your dad. There's got to be a lot of mothers and fathers out there looking at these pictures and seeing their young'uns faces on those bodies."

"Yeah, but weren't you proud? With them war heroes and all. Didn't you want people to know how brave they were?"

"Well, I didn't know that at the time. In all honesty, I was just surprised your dad made it off. He signed up in one of his fits of restlessness, thought he might change his mind again. Those other things come later. Too late, really. When nothing else matters, especially not some rusty metal and a folded flag." Lishie stood and walked over to the kitchen to pour coffee from the kettle. "I guess I should count my stars that at least Bud made it back."

"Yeah," I agreed unconvincingly. I guess I should have been more thankful, too. I mean Lishie couldn't have raised me alone. Bud had served a purpose. Still, he would have made an easy trade for my father.

"Lishie. Tell me the story again."

"Oh, son. Dontcha get tired of it?"

I laughed. "You know it's different every time."

Lishie smiled. "Okay. Okay." She wrapped the dishrag around her coffee cup and nestled herself into her rocking chair by the fireplace. "Let's see if I can remember . . ."

Lishie had the letters, but she only pulled those out anymore when she was alone in her room. She much preferred to recite from memory, building the story each time she told it.

"He still seemed like such a boy to me. Even in his uniform. They both did, though Bud has always had that hard edge to him. That's what being the oldest does to you. Your dad, though, he just grinned from ear to ear when we dropped him off at the station. They'd gotten into the war late, really. By the time they finished training, it was practically over. I was grateful for it, to tell the truth. Otherwise, I guess you wouldn't be here." Lishie closed her eyes. "Yes, he was so pleased to finally ship out. I hadn't seen him that happy in a long time."

"How long until you heard from him?"

"Way too long. A good month and a half, I believe. But once the first letter came, they seemed pretty steady every week. Sometimes I got two in one week. I was still getting letters after we buried him. Now I tell you, that's mighty hard to take. Hearing your son's voice about how well he's doing when you already know he ain't coming home."

I wanted to ask her why I had only been allowed to see one of his letters, the letter she read to me about Bud being lazy; but I didn't want to upset her or delay her story.

Lishie stopped and walked over to the stove. She busied herself by making another pot of coffee. "You want a cup?"

"Yes, ma'am," I agreed. I needed to hold something warm in my hands.

"So most of the letters just talked about what things looked like over there. It was like he was on some kind of European holiday—just like the rich folk take. He told me about the other men and where they were from. He'd make fun of Bud." Lishie smiled.

"I guess Bud wrote similar things."

"No. Bud never wrote." Lishie dropped her smile. "He just sent word by your dad that he was okay. I was just thankful that they were stationed together; otherwise I guess I would've never heard from Bud."

"He didn't even write after dad was killed?"

"Well, in all fairness, he probably didn't have time. The army was at least good about that. They knew you didn't have a mother and her folks had long been gone. Bud was now the man of the house for us all. The war ended soon after, anyway. They sent him back not long after we received your dad's body. Made it back in time for the sittin'-up."

I had never heard Lishie refer to my father's "body" before.

She lit the stove and circled back. "So they sent a courier to tell us what happened." She stopped and turned to me. "You've heard this a hundred times. You sure you want to hear it again?"

67

I nodded.

"Well, now the army and Bud have a little different story, so what I take as truth is really just me piecing the two together, that and just knowing your dad and what I think he'd do."

"Can't imagine anyone knows better than you."

Lishie continued, "Early one morning the men woke up to the sound of a gunshot. That's what the army says. I think the rest of the story is that those boys stayed up too late playing cards and maybe even drinking whiskey and the night watchmen fell asleep, so the enemy had no problem sneaking up on 'em without firing a shot."

"That does make more sense."

"So our boys start runnin' around, grabbin' their weapons, waking everybody up; but nobody can find your dad. Course, nobody is takin' a head count either. They're just tryin' to stay alive. Bud starts yellin' 'round for him, even goes lookin' for him, but he's not in his bunk."

"Did Bud tell you that part?"

Lishie didn't answer.

"Finally, he hears your dad's voice, but he can't make out what he is saying. Shoutin', really. He's yellin' something, but Bud doesn't know what. So Bud follows the shouts and finds your dad standin' on the other side of the barbed wire. And for the life of him, Bud can't figure out how he got there or why he crossed the line. And then he sees the body of another American soldier hung in the wire and your dad's runnin' to him, shielding him from the incomin' fire."

I know the answer, but I ask anyway. "Why was the soldier in the wire?"

"Best they could figure, he was a sleepwalker. He did it a lot, they said. Of course, never got himself into trouble like this, but he must have just walked right into the wire and barbs woke him up. By the time he was trying to free himself, the enemy had started comin' at him. He fired a blind shot. That's what the men heard. That's what woke them up. Your dad must've run out to see where the shot came from and realized his buddy was in trouble."

It was late in the war. While I knew Lishie envisioned uniformed German enemies, it is far more likely that men across the fence line were remnants of a resistance. No longer formal soldiers recognized by any responsible government. Still, I remember the first time I heard that part. I had never felt prouder.

"They ever figure out how Dad got through the wire to the enemy side so fast? I mean, without getting caught in the wire himself?"

"No. But it doesn't surprise me. That's just how he was. Your grandpa used to swear that that boy would go in a cave and come out a waterfall clear on the other side of the mountain."

I shook my head. I didn't need my father to be any more magical than he had already been built to be. I needed him to exist in the world I lived in, flaws and all.

"He stood in front of that man and shot at the enemy until he was out of bullets. Then he took the other soldier's gun and shot until he emptied all of his bullets, too. Army said that for sure. Said they checked the guns."

Lishie pulled another coffee mug from the shelf and stared at the kettle.

"Who'd you say found him?"

"Bud got to him first. Lots of men saw him later, but there was too much gunfire. They had to wait until the enemy retreated."

"And it was too late by then," I finished her story. I knew she wouldn't be able to. Up until that point it was like someone else's story, a film she projected.

"Milk?" she asked, holding up my cup. "Good for the bones."

"No thanks. Black's fine."

"I like mine with a little sugar." She grinned. "Need all the sweetness I can get." I was glad I had smuggled some from the inn back for her.

Later that night, I lay in bed and played out the story again. Details from my father's story mingled with those of the soldier's in the newspaper, to the point that I was afraid I could no longer separate them. It's not that surprising, when I think about it. I knew just about as much about my father as I did the man in the paper. Lishie told me many stories over the years, but I only believed what I saw in print or what more than one person had said about him. I guess I was hoping one of the men's stories would fill in the missing pieces for the other, but neither, no matter how much I wanted, could answer the one question that still lingered amid the faded newsprint and Lishie's well-worn memory. Neither could answer the question churning over and over in my head ever since I was old enough to hear my father's story from Lishie for the first time—old enough to hold a question deep inside when it didn't fit the narrative on which it was precariously perched. *How does a sleepwalker carry a loaded gun through the barbs without waking?*

CHAPTER ELEVEN

A muted haze of morning sun leaked through the cabin slats into my bedroom. I was pulled from indiscernible dreams so abruptly it took me a moment to determine whether I was at home or the inn. Once I got oriented, my next concern was the oil lamp beside my bed.

Something was burning.

I inhaled deeply to confirm this fear and flung the quilt forward.

Something *was* burning.

It was not the oil lamp. My body relaxed momentarily, reasoning that perhaps Lishie had gotten an early start preparing breakfast. I slid out of bed and fumbled into my clothes. Before I made it to the kitchen, Lishie met me in the doorway.

"You smell that smoke?"

"Yeah, what you cooking?"

"Not me this time, boy. Get your boots on and take a look, will you?"

"Yes'm." Lishie's weather reports had been true. Cherokee was bone dry—had been bone dry practically the whole summer. It was as if Asheville's torrential rains had sucked all the moisture from the west. It was unusual for places of such close proximity to suffer in such distinctly contrary ways, but this was an unusual summer, after all. Just as I escaped one extreme, I found myself planted in another.

The sky was grayish pink by the time my feet hit the front porch. A dense grayness limited my view to about twenty feet in any direction. It was impossible to determine the course of the smoke. Winds initiated a dreadful game of hide-and-seek. The smoke billowed toward our house like smoldering tumbleweed. Stepping back, I stood poised to run as best I could, or call out to Lishie at the very least. I opened my mouth, sucking in filmy air and expelling it back in a fit of coughing that left me bent, clutching my knees. When I straightened again, Preacherman's truck breached the opaque barrier and skidded sideways right at me, stopping a mere two feet from the front step.

Lishie opened the cabin door and pushed the screen so forcefully forward it knocked me out of my infantile pose and straight onto my ass. She had fastened a red bandana over her nose and mouth. The thin cloth rose and fell with her exaggerated breath.

"Shut tight the windows and carry water to the washtub, son." She stepped over me and squinted into the yard. "There's Preacherman. When you finish the other, get on back out here and help him with the clearing. I'll get yuns some breakfast to stay you in just a bit."

Preacherman eased out the driver's side coughing and rubbing his eyes. "Your uncle here?"

"No, sir. We just got up. Haven't seen him." I wanted to tell him a likely truth. That Bud was laid up drunk or sleeping off a drunk. That he'd be here as soon as most of the work was already done.

"You seen a fire line yet?"

Was he serious? "No, sir. Just got up. How close you think it is?"

"Hard to tell. Won't know until the sun's fully up. I haven't seen a line myself. Just the smoke. And it's been so dry."

I nodded.

"You go help your Lishie. I'll get started out here and see if I can figure out the direction."

"Yes, sir. Be right back."

Preacherman and I worked until the sun turned the smoke a grayish mauve and then dissipated into a blue summer sky. By noon, I began to wonder if it had all been a shared dream—how quickly the smoke cleared seemed almost unexplainable. I would have kept questioning this reality had Bud not lurched through the doorway just as Lishie, Preacherman, and I were sitting down to lunch.

"It Sunday already?" he hawed, reaching for a plate from the stack beside the sink.

"Preacherman's been helping us in case the fire saw fit to make its way over here," Lishie said.

"That so? Little skittish, ain't you?"

"Have you seen the fire line, Bud?" Preacherman asked.

"Nah. Heard it's down Painttown, though. Shouldn't be nothin' for us to worry with."

I must have breathed a heavy release.

"Going to check it out after lunch, though." Bud turned toward me. "Ride along if you want." By "ride along," of course, Bud meant I would drive. At least that way I'd know I'd get the car back in time to drive to Asheville on Sunday.

An hour later I was driving Bud down the mountain across town and within five hundred feet of the fire line. The long, curved red glow painted its way horizontally across the bank, designing an almost magical barrier between charred earth and dull, brown roughage. We were not in the heart of the blaze. Though the air was smoky, the heat was tolerable.

"What are we doing here?" I asked Bud.

Bud reached into the back seat and pulled his shotgun from the floorboard.

"Has that been in the car the whole time?"

"Since this morning."

I exhaled deeply. Had the gun been in the car while parked at the inn and found, I certainly would have been fired, arrested, court-martialed— hell, whatever they do when a brown boy is within inches of a deadly weapon and white people. Especially if the weapon is tucked out of direct line of sight.

"What are you doing?"

"Huntin'."

"What?" I opened my car door as Bud had his and stood beside him as he stared up the side of the bank that hadn't yet burned. "Are you going up there?" A charge of birds—cardinals, hawks, and several others I couldn't distinguish in their haste—clouded the sky.

"Hell, no. What kind of fool do you think I am? There's a goddamn forest fire up there."

"Yeah, but—"

"Shit, Cowney. You're right dull, ain't you? I don't have to go in. That

73

fire is about to send every living creature, 'cept those with wings or scales, running off that bank. When they come this way, I just point, aim, and shoot. Easiest day of hunting I've had all year."

"That's not quite fair, is it?" Before he could respond, two whitetail, a doe and fawn, sprinted through the smoke and down the bank. Bud steadied the gun against his shoulder. Two blasts echoed and the mother fell. He shot again, but the fawn was already running back into the smoke.

"Fair? Fair's where you get cotton candy." Bud shrugged and leaned back against the car, staring toward the ridgeline. "It's sportin' enough. Natural. I can't help it if Mother Nature saw fit to set a fire."

I walked over to the mother deer; her round black eyes stared into me as I watched her chest rise and fall quickly, and then cease altogether. The thirsty earth drank in her blood before it could pool at my feet.

Of course Bud and I both knew these fires weren't usually the handiwork of Mother Nature. There had been no storms, so it wasn't like lightning struck a tree and then all hell broke loose. No, these summer fires, especially the drought fires, were set by locals. Sometimes by men from fire stations in nearby towns who were bored and wanted some action. Sometimes by disgruntled hunters who hated the National Park Service and wanted to watch them squirm a bit. Sometimes by campers too careless to extinguish their campfires completely.

"You best move, 'less you wanna be next," Bud hollered.

"They're running for their lives. They're trapped. That just doesn't seem right."

"We'll see if you complain after a supper of deer steak or bear stew."

"I'll be back in Asheville by the time you get one cleaned and cooked anyway. How you going to get it home? You can't put that in the car. You need a truck."

"Yeah, yeah. I know. Just stop in town and tell Joe I'm here. He's supposed to come pick me up."

Joe hung out between the bus station and the trading post and traded rides in his pickup for groceries or stamps or a new pair of shoes. Really, whatever he wanted that day. Likely Bud would be sharing any meat he procured with Joe for a ride back to his house.

"Those prisoners they got over there. They's some Japs there, right? You ever talk to 'em?"

"There are some, but I don't talk to the guests."

"Guests? Shit, son." Bud shook his head without looking at me. "As long as you're over there, you might work up a deal for me."

"A deal?"

"Yeah. See, I had a buddy I was stationed with. He married a Japanese girl. He had this whole business he had worked up for when he got back. Turns out Orientals pay a pretty penny for bear gallbladder. Bladders supposed to be some sort of Oriental medicine. He said if he ever found a way to export it, he'd be able to make a year's pay just off one huntin' season. You believe that?"

"No. Not really. Seems far-fetched to me."

Bud stepped back and leaned against the car hood. "Yeah, probably right. But it's worth a try, I figure. I'll do the heavy lifting here. All I need is for you to ask around at work. See if there's an interest. Try to get a price. Next time you're home, I can send the bladder with you. Maybe a few of 'em if this fire keeps up."

"Bud, that doesn't sound like a good idea. I just can't be trading with prisoners. I am pretty sure that's against the rules. Plus, I don't know if any of 'em even have any money now."

"Oh, hell. They got money. They got money somewhere. Even the nationals, or they wouldn't be holed up there."

I shook my head and walked to the driver's side. Bud stood and looked back at me. "You gonna take my car all summer, least you can do is ask a few questions."

"Sure," I lied, or at least I hoped I was lying. "I'll see what I can find out."

Lishie was quilting when I arrived home and had already laid out my packed suitcase on my bed. I knew that by this time the following day the suitcase would be filled with freshly washed and dried clothes without me having to lift one finger. I thanked her and slid the suitcase onto the floor so I could lay down a bit and rest my eyes. The smoke was still thick in my nostrils and my entire body felt dry and rough beneath the quilt I pulled over me. *Gallbladders? Was he serious? More importantly, was he right? I could take a cut. Make enough to not have to go back to Bud's ever again. Make enough to see that Lishie was taken care of. Make enough to even impress Essie.* But I couldn't shake the gaze of the doe—left to wonder if her fawn had returned to the fire.

I must have drifted off sometime, my head still filled with questions, because the next time I checked the clock it was almost 3 in the afternoon. It was too hot to sleep any longer. I flipped my pillow over, hoping the opposite side was cooler, trying desperately to think of anything other than the humidity. There are some nights, some days, you just pray it will rain. Not because the crops need it or the wells are dangerously low. Sometimes you just need the clouds to burst and release the pressure building around you. The smoke, its constant swarm and release with changing winds, smothered the skyline, suffocating me in the process.

I wanted it to feel like it did back at the inn, with the rain pouring nearly every day.

2

STAINS

Who has fully realized that history is not contained in thick books but lives in our very blood?

—Carl Jung

CHAPTER TWELVE

After a couple of weeks, it grew soggy and weighty in contradictory ways, but during the first couple of days of downpour, Essie and I found dry sanctuary in 447. The weather gave me the excuse to retreat to the room as soon as possible after my work had ended, with the near certainty that Essie would be there as well. The heat had finally dissipated, and the second day of rain must have caused Lee to feel drowsy because he sent us off for the evening early.

Lee grabbed my shoulder, stopping me on my way out of the storage shed and pulled a camera from the shelf above the workbench. "Son, hold up a second."

"Yes, sir." I stopped, eyeing the camera.

"Do me a favor, will ye?" He handed me the camera. "I've been tinkering with this thing. Think I've just about got 'er fixed. Take 'er for a spin. Let me know how she does."

I was too afraid to hold the expensive equipment, let alone use it.

He pulled a canister of film from the shelf. "Here, let me show ye how to load it." Lee triggered the latch and told me where and how to place the film. Then he held it up to his eye and pretended to take a picture. "You've never had a camera?" he asked, handing it back to me.

"No, sir."

"Well, this will be a good one to practice on. Just promise you'll show me the pictures when you get finished."

"Yes, sir. But how will I know when I'm done?"

Lee smiled. "Yer done when the film runs out. Just like a book when the pages run out."

I nodded and thanked Lee. "I'll be careful."

I took the camera with me and raced to room 447, stopping only once to snap a test picture of some of the children stringing plucked red clover into green and purple crowns—the girl with the purple ribbon from earlier stopping to share her smile again. I couldn't wait to show Essie. If I was lucky, she would want to go with me to take pictures around the property.

As I approached 447, I noticed that Essie must have arrived ahead of me. She, too, must have been in a hurry because the door was slightly ajar. It would not have been noticeable to a passerby, but as I reached for the handle, I realized that I did not need to turn it. This discovery and my excitement about the camera emboldened me to attempt to scare Essie if I could sneak in while her back was turned. I eased the door open and peeked in. I blinked into the soft pink light, sparkling with dust particles.

At first I could not see Essie, but as I opened the door further, I saw her in ethereal motion. She stood high on her tiptoes, holding her arms above her head. Essie stared longingly at her outstretched fingertips as if they were grasping for the most delicate, most precious object one could ever hope to hold. But there was nothing there. She let her head drop back, her hair wrapping the curves of her shoulders. She closed her eyes and spun her body around, leading with her hip. I pulled the camera to my eye and pushed the button as Lee had instructed. A flash burst into the space, unsettling 447, stopping Essie, and nearly causing me to drop the camera.

"Cowpie! I'm gonna . . ." Essie lunged toward me, fist clenched, and holding back an embarrassed smile as tightly as she could. She had coined the nickname on our third visit to the room when I had scolded her for leaving behind a plate of cookie crumbs, calling her "Messy Essie." That name didn't stick. Cowpie did.

I pulled the camera behind my back with one arm and shielded my face with the other. "What?" I couldn't contain my laughter. "Just documenting the Grove Park's very own prima ballerina."

She reddened with embarrassment, ashamed anyone had seen her dancing so seriously and so alone. My smile faded. I had never seen anything so beautiful, and I knew I was not deserving of that joy in the least.

"You're not that bad." I worked up a compliment when our breathing had settled and we sat on the couch together.

"Of course I'm terrible. You don't need to lie to make me feel better."

"No, really. I mean, I can't say I'm an expert, but—"

"Me either. I've never even had a class. But gosh, I just love to watch ballet. I mean, when I can."

"Where do you watch it? Do you go to shows . . . or whatever they're called?"

"I've been. Once in Asheville when a company came to town. The best day of my life, I think. But mostly, I go watch movies with dancing in them. Rarely ballet, but dancing all the same."

I had never seen a movie with any dancing, and truthfully, had no desire to do so . . . that is, unless I was taking Essie.

"One of my favorites is *Dance, Girl, Dance*. Ever seen it?" she asked.

"Can't say I have."

"Well, you're missing out. I had to sneak off to see that one at a play-house in Georgia when we were visiting family. Lucille Ball is just a riot! And gorgeous. Oh, and then there's *Broadway Melody*. Just wonderful. But, you know, it's New York. If you're a real dancer, there's no other place to be than New York City. Both of those movies take place in New York."

"You ever think about moving somewhere like New York City?" I asked.

"All the time." She fell onto one of the leather couches and stared at the ceiling. "Just imagine how much there is to see."

I sat across from her. "Plenty to see here, too."

"Yes, but it's different. It's cultured."

"Cultured?"

"Yes." She sat up and looked directly at me, hands grasping her knees. "Think about all the music and artists, and oh, just think about the dancing!"

"We have those things."

"Sure, but not like New York. Not culture from all over the world. Everything you could ever want to see, hear, or do in one city."

I wanted to tell Essie that New York City was sounding a lot like room 447. She was all I wanted to see, and 447 made that possible. Her voice was all I wanted to hear, no matter what she was saying, and 447 was her microphone. And to kiss her, well, that was all I wanted to do, and I wanted to do it in 447. We were slowly creating the most beautiful culture I had ever known. It grew richer by the day and, as new as it was, it felt ancient, ageless. 447 held our own language, our own art, our own system of existence.

"So, you think you'll find yourself a Yankee to marry." I smiled, hoping she would call the thought absurd.

"Oh, I don't know. I may never marry."

"Why would you say that?"

"Well, I can't see myself settling down back in Cherokee, and from what I've seen of other men, well, I can't imagine myself living with one of them forever."

"What other men?"

"The guys here. Your buddies, probably. They're just uncouth."

"*Uncouth?*" I shot Essie a look letting her know just how ridiculous it was for her to use such a word. She was certainly more sophisticated than me, but not so much so that words such as *uncouth* should be on the tip of her tongue.

"You know what I mean."

"No. Tell me what you mean," I pried.

"They flirt with the women here incessantly. Doesn't matter which one of us it is. Next time you're in the dining hall or walking around on the property in the evening, notice how none of us girls ever turns her back to the men here."

"Why's that? I mean, it's safe. Heck, over half the men here are sworn to serve citizens like us." Sarcasm peppered my words.

"I can't count the number of times I had the back of my skirt flipped up or was catcalled in my first week here. Men that have never even said a word to me."

"I'm sorry, Essie. But it's not all of us. I haven't done that."

"Of course not, Cowpie. But you're different, you know. Women don't need to worry about guys like you."

My heart fell, and I was ashamed that it did. I should have taken her words as a compliment, but I knew that they were placing me squarely in the category of men who would never travel to New York City—who would never carry Essie Stamper over some foreign threshold.

"It's just how I was raised."

"Exactly. I think you're exactly right. You can almost tell which family folks come from just by the way they act in public."

I wasn't so sure that was accurate. I mean, that meant that Bud and I acted the same in public. "Tell me about your family."

"Oh, you don't want to hear about them."

"Sure I do."

"Well, there's Mom, Dad, and my brother Charlie, who's in the service."

"What about your parents? What does your dad do?"

"I'm surprised you don't already know all my business. Everyone else in Cherokee sure does."

"You're the one who said I wasn't like the other guys."

Essie shook her head. "He's away on business a lot. Salesman."

"And your mom? She stays home?"

"Yes, she stays home and tells me how much I need to marry someone unlike my father."

"What does she mean by that?"

"She thinks I need to find someone well-off who isn't always gone. Or at least if he's gone, that he leaves me with enough money to keep me entertained."

I hesitated, but had to ask, "Isn't your mother from Cherokee?"

"Yes, of course. Why?"

"I don't know. Just doesn't sound like something you hear from Cherokee mothers too often."

"What would your mother . . . Oh. I'm sorry, Cowney." Essie blushed and covered her mouth with her hand.

"It's fine. I guess that's why I ask so many questions—because I don't know what a mother would say."

"But you have your grandmother, right?" Essie recovered.

"Yes, she's been like a mother, I guess. Not that she cares too much about who I'm going to marry. I think she is too worried about who my uncle Bud is going to marry."

"So she doesn't pick out your girlfriends?"

My face grew hot. "I've never really had one."

"Well, Cowpie. We need to fix that! I will find you—"

"So you're turning into your mother now?"

"I sure hope not! She'd be grilling every girl that grinned at you." Essie shook her head. "My mother is different. She went off to Carlisle and, as Dad says, never got it out of her system. What she doesn't realize is that in the end, we'll all just be buried together. She won't get to choose her eternal neighbor based on social status."

"You think she's right? About finding someone away from Cherokee?"

"Maybe. I don't know. I just want to fall in love with Prince Charming. Too much to ask for, you think?"

I smiled and shook my head. "Nothing is too much to ask for the prima ballerina."

"Well, one thing's for sure. You aren't going to get any good pictures with your new fancy camera and I'm not going to find my prince if we are cooped up in this room all summer. What do you say we go on an adventure when the rain quits?"

"Sure. What do you have in mind?"

"Let's go canoeing!"

"Canoeing? Where'd that come from?"

"I don't know. It just looks so peaceful."

"You've never been?"

"Well, not really. A couple of girls from school tried one time. A couple of the boys had been burning out a log to make a canoe like they used to. We were the best swimmers, so we offered to try to it out. Barely got past wading waters." Essie shook her head. "Disaster. All their hard work sank to the bottom of the Tuckasegee in just a few minutes. It was fun while it lasted, though. You ever canoed?"

I was immediately taken back to the splash dam. The walls of 447 felt like the logs pressing down on me as the rain poured outside. Essie's description of the canoe seemed so similar. "No." I laughed, shaking off the memory. "I guess we aren't very good Indians, are we?"

Essie laughed with me. "No, Sacajawea and Pocahontas would be so ashamed."

"And I wanted so badly to be on a postcard."

"Sorry, Cowpie. It's not in the cards." Her smile grew. "Literally!"

"Sure does sound like you could use some fresh air for those jokes. So where are we going to get a canoe?"

"Some of the girls mentioned that some of the soldiers have access to a couple. Just have to make the right friends."

"Sounds good to me. I don't really know any of the soldiers, but as long as I get a few hours shed of that damn Sol, I welcome it."

"What's his story?"

"You know how it is. You get out of Cherokee and people like to remind you how damn dark your skin is."

"What a fool." Essie shook her head.

"Yeah. Ah, forget him. About this trip—and just where are we going canoeing?"

"Supposed to be a place where the Swannanoa and French Broad meet. People back home call it a-na-to-ki-as-di-yi."

"The place where they race? So this won't be as leisurely as you described."

"A little competition gets the blood pumping, don't you think?"

"Okay, I'm in. Assuming this rain ever stops." I was thankful that the opportunity to compete, especially against the soldiers, would not require me to be on my feet. I might just have a fighting chance.

"Should be the perfect place, from what they say back home. Cherokees used to race there all the time."

"Can you imagine what it would be like if Cherokees still lived here? Lived in Asheville—all over this region?" I mused.

"We do. You and I are living right here."

"You know what I mean."

"Is this about the bone again? You really are fascinated with that thing, aren't you?"

"I guess it's the mystery. Once you see it, you'll understand. It's not gory or anything."

"Maybe. It's not the bone itself so much as it is thinking about it belonging to someone. I can't help but feel sad about it."

"Think about it this way. You said your mother would want to choose who she was buried with. Mingle bones with the upper crust and all. Maybe this person was just trying to do that at the Grove Park."

"Cowney Sequoyah! You speak of the dead so easily. And that's my mother you're talking about!"

"Ahh, Essie. I'm just kiddin' around."

"If it's all the same to you, let's talk about something else."

"Fair enough. Here." I handed the camera to Essie. "Give it a try."

Essie took the camera and instructed me to pose by the fireplace. I smiled wide and confident, pleased that Essie had focused her cultured eye on me for the moment.

I left the camera high on a shelf in 447, certain that the best pictures would be made in that room.

CHAPTER THIRTEEN

Despite the fires, the next Sunday I went to church with Lishie. Essie stayed in Asheville, and I had had my fill of imposing buildings already that summer at the Grove Park, so I pretended to sleep in; but Lishie knew this game all too well. She began by banging around in the kitchen and then by humming "The Old Rugged Cross" until the kettle whistled and she broke into a full-on belting of "Amazing Grace" in Cherokee.

> U ne la nv i u we tsi
> I ga go yv he i
> Hna quo tso sv wi yu lo se
> I ga gu yv ho nv.

I never could resist that song. I knew both the English version and the Cherokee version better than I knew any other song, well, except for "Boogie Woogie Bugle Boy," and that was Essie's fault. She sang it incessantly.

"How sweet the sound—"

I crawled out of bed, following the smell of bacon grease, and shuffled into the kitchen. Lishie smiled without turning from the stove. "Well, sunale, sleepyhead. Thought I might have to wake you for dinner."

"Mornin'." I kissed the top of her gray head and inhaled the comfort of lye soap and sweet corn. "If you're cookin', you know I'm awake to eat."

"Everyone should have a full stomach on the Sabbath."

"And go to church?" No sense in waiting on her to ask.

"Well, if a body's able, I reckon one should."

"Go on and get dressed. I'll finish this." I took the fork from her hand.

She wiped her palms on her housecoat and smiled. "Oh, good. I have a new dress I've been wanting to show off."

"Now Lishie, Preacherman's married."

"Oh, Cowney. Stop that foolishness." She was blushing. "Besides, you know I just want to show Myrtle how much better of a seamstress I am than that good-for-nothin' daughter-in-law she's always crowing about."

Lishie had a way of making boasting sound humble.

The smoke still lingered in the air, graying the sky, though it felt somewhat lighter than the evening before. As we crawled into the Model T, I couldn't help but think about how much I would have preferred it to be Essie sitting shotgun. Nothing against Lishie. For every moment of reserved silence Essie offered on our ride to Asheville, Lishie offered stories tenfold. In truth, I often enjoyed the stories that allowed me to sit silent, stare off through the windshield onto the road ahead, regardless of who was telling them. On this particular ride, Lishie was not disappointing.

" . . . and then that old man plumb near blew a hole straight through his overalls," she chuckled.

"That's funny," I offered on command. After a lifetime, I knew exactly where her punch lines fell, when to laugh, when to shake my head, when and how to respond to ebb and flow.

"Uh-oh." Lishie frowned. "What's on your mind this morning, boy?"

"What? Oh. Nothing. Just tired."

"Mmmm. Maybe. Maybe not." She jammed her left elbow deep into my rib cage, the worst of all bad Lishie habits.

"Ow! Lishie! You gotta stop that! That hurts. I don't care who you are."

"Toughen up, tsu-ts!"

She called me son just like she did Bud, probably just like she had my father. She dug in once again.

My right hand flinched, trying to deflect her swift jabs. The car swerved, sending us both upward until the roof forced us back into our seats. I overcompensated and nearly landed us in a drainage ditch on the right-hand side of the logging road we followed. I bore down hard on the brake, swinging us forward and then back again. We sat still, both panting, eyes wide in wait.

In front of us, eyes wide in wait as well, stood a black bear on two legs, as tall as our vehicle and just as black.

She screamed at us.

She opened her mouth and shook her head like a wife whose husband has tracked in mud for the tenth time. Annoyed. She did not roar nor growl. She screamed a deep, tonal screech. Neither Lishie nor I said a word. We just stared forward as the bear dropped back to all fours and was immediately joined by two small, equally annoyed cubs. The family took one last look at us and scurried into the laurel.

We arrived at the white cinderblock church just in time for the morning announcements. The parish was stuffed with small, elderly women in floral patterned dresses, hems barely greeting knee-high stockings, like in-laws at a family reunion leaving a slight gap in their embrace of one another. The women's graying heads were tucked neatly beneath red, blue, or purple bandanas. Men waited on the steps, taking the final drag from hand-rolled cigarettes and waving to children racing through the dusty churchyard to end their game of tag and join the others inside.

Lishie loathed lateness so she did not wait for me to help her from the vehicle before climbing out of the passenger side and scurrying as fast as she could toward the church steps. I took my time joining her inside. If I waited long enough, one of the men would offer a final drag of his half-smoked cigarette in lieu of tossing it wastefully away. Mothers were still settling into the pews, rocking infants, and the choir was warming up with weekly gossip. Lishie walked in ahead of me, nodding to the other ladies and clutching her Bible beneath her arm. She slid into our pew and I followed. Same spot every Sunday. Third pew from the altar. Right side. Middle of the bench so that others could join on either side, though they never did.

The choir stood in unison, the signal to mothers to hush their children, men to find the most inconspicuous resting position, and older women like Lishie to assume a pious pose. Preacherman Davis moved from the back of the church where he had been greeting parishioners and joined the choir in song.

"How great thou art," the chorus concluded.

"Good morning," Preacherman greeted us.

"Good morning."

"Sunale."

"Mornin'."

"Mmm."

"Yes, sir. Yes, sir."

The responses, varied and disparate, joined in piecemeal harmony. "We gather once again in the name of Jesus Christ, our Lord and Savior, who shed his blood so that we might be saved."

"Amen!"

Lishie nodded beside me. She would not uncross her ankles nor unfold her hands from her lap throughout the entire service. While younger folk might raise their palms in the air in praise, she sat composed and reserved. The gentle rocking of her head and cadence of Preacherman's sermon did little to keep me alert.

I tried to focus on the meaning of the words, " . . . and set me in the middle of the valley; it was full of bones—and I saw a great many bones on the floor—bones that were very dry. He asked me: can these bones live?"

I thought back to the bone I had found and resolved to make sure it was still wrapped safely in my room when I returned. Had my sharing its story, true or fabricated, brought that bone to life?

Preacherman continued in his own words, "And then, brothers and sisters, Ezekiel witnessed the Lord breathing the four winds into the bones, bringing life back into them."

What kind of man must have Ezekiel been for God to perform such a miracle before his eyes? There were a great many bones that deserved life, a great many graves needing to be unearthed. Both then and now.

" . . . and stood on their feet, a vast army . . ."

Soldiers resurrected. Would God call up the skeleton of my father to rejoin the American army during this new war? And if he didn't, were we to believe that this war was not worth such a miracle or simply that my father's life was not?

The single ceiling fan did nothing to stave off even the earliest of morning heat in the tiny building and did much to provide a sleep-inducing soundtrack. My eyes grew heavy, stung by the lingering smoke, my body warmed until I could only remain upright by cupping my forehead in my hand and resting my elbow on the windowsill.

There's a kind of terrifying quality to this type of sleep. Fire and brimstone, condemnations of Hell and glorious songs of angels weave their way through the unconscious conscience. Reality, fear, and hope served to jolt my body upright at the most inappropriate moments, yet I felt paralyzed, unable to produce any voluntary movement, even to pull myself awake. I can't say that I was dreaming, nor can I say that I was crafting wakeful thought. Images coursed through my mind, seemingly at their own will and pace.

Essie's laugh

Lishie's song

447

My father's name

My father's name

The newspaper

The bear's scream

Bud's muffled cursing

Laughter

Dry bones

Song

God's voice

Tendons and flesh

In our father's name—

Amen!

Lishie pinched the fat of my arm.

"Ow!" I flinched.

"Wake up, boy. The Devil doesn't sleep on Sunday morning and nor should you."

"Yes, ma'am." I rubbed my arm and reached for my hat. "We staying for dinner or you wanting to go home?"

"I'm going to stay. Myrtle's boy can bring me back after. You go on. Bud's got some chores for you before you head back to the city. There's beans on the stove if you get hungry."

"Thought we weren't to work on the Sabbath." I smiled.

"Devil works on Sunday morning and so does Bud." Lishie smiled back and patted my rapidly bruising arm. I dug the keys from my pocket and handed them to her. Because what Lishie didn't have to say was that Myrtle's boy didn't have a car of his own, nor did any member of their family, and so he would be driving ours. This was how she could disguise her favor as his. They lived as close as anyone to us and so the four would avoid the long walk from church by giving Lishie a lift.

I never minded Lishie's convoluted charities, nor commended her for them. She could go to great lengths to ensure that no one publicly recognized her for kindness, fearful that it might insinuate weakness, gentleness, or naiveté. She couldn't afford such labels. None of us could.

Preacherman grasped my hand tightly as I shook his on my way out. I was eager to be on my way, but he nearly jerked me backward with his grip. He leaned in, questioning, "How's Miss Essie Stamper?"

"Getting along quite fair. Don't see her much since they keep us busy," I lied.

"Good to hear. You two take care of each other, being so far from home and all."

"Yes, sir. We surely will."

As the congregation unbundled picnic packs, I began the walk across the ridge, a quicker route than following the logging road. The forest provided cool shade beneath the summer sun. I was in no hurry to reach Bud and his list of demands, so I took the opportunity to listen for bird songs, attempting to identify the singers before seeing the first feather. I peered into the small pool of one of the many mountain streams, hoping to see minnows. I avoided hollow logs and decomposing leaves so as not to cross a copperhead or rattler. I searched the overhead limbs for squirrels, thinking I might return later and shoot a few for Lishie's stew. And because of this wonderment, I ignored the one piece of advice Lishie had given since I was a young boy making tree forts: "Keep your head down in the woods." She knew I had a tendency to gaze at the canopy and trip over roots and into burrows.

And because of this, the claw, the knife, possibly the mythic liver-gouging nail of Spearfinger herself scraped along the arc of my left cheek, sending warm blood dripping from my face onto the ground as I bent over in pain.

"Shit!" I pressed my fingers to the gash. I turned in a crouched circle, searching for the cause. Nothing. No ominous owl. No erratic squirrel. No storied witch in search of careless children. Stunned, I sat down and pulled my knees to my chest so that I might gather my bearings before setting off again. When my heartbeat settled, I began to laugh. I laughed loudly with no soul around to hear me. Edgar, no doubt. Tsa Tsi's free-spirited monkey had paid me another visit. *That damn monkey!* I sat a bit longer until I heard what sounded like his familiar call. From the direction it came, I reasoned that he might be returning home to Tsa Tsi soon. The old man needed to know of Edgar's growing boldness before some hunter shot the poor creature out of spite. I decided to follow the bending branches before returning home. If he was going home, the distance would not be great. The last thing I wanted to do was walk myself right up to the fire line, but Edgar seemed to be moving away from the heavy smoke.

I had not spent much time on the slope of the ridge, had no reason to, really. There were tales of high waterfalls and cool swimming holes. The extended trip might be worth it if I could find a new pool beneath a cascade. I thought how nice it might be to bring Essie back with me one weekend. Show her a secluded fall—share another secret space with her.

Edgar called overhead again, farther ahead than I had expected. I still could not see even the bobbing of his tail, though. My foot slowed my pace, but I hurried as best I could. So much so that I came just shy of stepping squarely on an outstretched black snake, harmless but still good for a scare. I leapt awkwardly, unable to come to a complete stop in time. My left ankle buckled and I landed on my hands and knees in silt mud, startling a congregation of horseflies. Though I was still bruised from Lishie and bleeding from Edgar, my fall had only caused mild soreness in my ankle and muddied my hands and knees. Lishie would kill me if I wiped the mud on my church shirt or further stained my slacks. I looked around for broad leaves, but was relieved to find the waterfall instead.

It must have been twenty-five feet high from its base. It extended so wide across the mountain slope, fifteen feet at least, that I feared it might be home to a sleeping bear or panther. The base pool was clean and clear enough to reveal its shallow bottom. I dipped my hands into the cold water and rubbed them clean. I cupped my palms and brought the water first to my mouth and then across my face. The scratch on my cheek stung a bit, but then numbed from the coolness.

Refreshed and relieved, I stared into the waterfall before me. I thought back to my question to Lishie. *They ever figure out how Dad got through the wire to the enemy side so fast?*

Your grandpa used to swear that that boy would go in a cave and come out a waterfall clear on the other side of the mountain, she had answered.

Was this the falls? If there was ever even such a thing. I stared so long and intently at the rushing plummet, veiling a probable cavern behind it, that it turned before me into a fence . . . the fence, barbed wire delineated in the accumulated particles. I stared as I imagined my father must have done, knowing he had no choice but to penetrate it. Did he pause? Did he consider the danger? Did he wonder if he would return? And these weren't even the most important questions I had. Curiosity drew me forward, whereas a human call for help compelled him—if, in fact, the story was true. Darkness surrounding him, had he returned to dress, to retrieve a gun when no one else had even bothered to stir? Why had he not called to his brother for help?

I was not so bold as to traverse the unknown alone when given a choice. If I could ever convince Essie to return with me, I would bring her here. I would lead her to this sanctuary with confidence, knowing every rock and fallen limb to avoid. Together, we could enter the interior of the fall's cave if she wished. Explore together. Lighting our way. And maybe we too would exit on the other side of the world. If I were to go it alone on this day, no one would know where I was, unable to find me in the event of snake bite or cave-in, or if I fell into one of the dozens of unexplained bottomless pits lining the floors of mountain caverns. No, I was not brave like my father. And somehow, too, I managed to convince myself that Essie would miss me, and if I ever emerged, would be angry that I hadn't taken her on the inaugural journey, as she had me into 447.

I barely heard Edgar anymore, though I saw he had likely stopped at the waterfall's base to drink from its pool as well. His prints in the mud were unique among creatures of the forest, although smudged. I called into the cavern, "Edgar! You in there?"

Nothing.

"Edgar!" I edged into the mouth of the cave, careful to survey the ceiling for bats. "This your hiding place?"

Something rustled in leaves just ahead of me. I leaned in, balancing myself, ankle still throbbing, one palm on the clammy cave wall. Tiny drops of water dripped onto my head. "Buddy?"

Leaves rustled again, this time closer. I opened my mouth to call once again but was immediately silenced by a gust of wind that seemed to generate from the deep interior of the cavern. It sent leaves swirling, and specks of dirt nearly blinded me. I fell back and the gust washed over me with chilling force. I reached for a weak pine with both hands. It bent and my hands slipped down its trunk. *What the hell?* I pulled myself upright, nearly falling into the pool of water.

Mud and sticky pine resin caked my hands. I plunged them into the pool and splashed a handful of cool water across my face. My skin drank it in as though it, too, had been exhausted by the drought. Everything here was still mossy and lush—a stark and welcome inconsistency to the rest of Cherokee. I gathered myself and rushed off in search of the monkey.

CHAPTER FOURTEEN

Weekends at home seemed to lengthen each time I returned. It was a different monotony than that of the inn, filled with familiar faces, familiar chores, and Bud's familiar curses. I missed the inn—its anonymity, the beauty of such an opulent structure, Lee's jokes, and most of all—Essie. In truth, the only real draw home was Lishie. I worried about her, unsure if Bud was reliable enough to drive her to church or restock her firewood for the stove. After a few weekends of finding Lishie well fed and agreeable to accepting rides from long-time neighbors, I was content to remain in Asheville for the balance of the summer, mostly to spend more time with Essie. I did miss Cherokee when I was at the inn, enough to make me question if I'd ever find a place I was truly happy. Each held something for me that the other did not.

Instead of making the drive home after work on Friday and back to the inn on Sunday, I chose to remain at the inn seven days a week. Essie and I spent hours in 447, playing dominos, reading in silence, or day-dreaming out loud together. Occasionally, we joined the others on day trips off property if the weather was nice, but nothing more than a half-hour drive away. We retreated to the room so often that the evenings fused into one long moment.

There are snapshots of that summer, literal and otherwise, that refuse to fade, not because they are fantastic or even significant, but because they are elemental to what is now my existence—maybe what was Essie's, too. Essie was likely the most proper girl I had ever met and most certainly the most sophisticated girl from Cherokee. She fit into 447 like one of the first-edition novels we found there. And because she fit, I fit by association—adopted into some modern clan by the clan mother herself. Mind you, that is where the maternal instincts began and ended. Essie corrected no more than my grammar on occasion—quite the opposite, really. She led me to dangle on the edge of complete and utter failure and spin wildly in the awkwardness of it—dancing in delight at my blush.

"Go ahead, Cowpie. I'll spot you," she encouraged. And before I remembered who I was, I found myself upside down, attempting to walk across the length of the room on my hands. I crashed gleefully into the couch, unable to spare my breath from laughter's thievery. Essie too was unable to remain on her feet, overcome with amusement. She sank into the oversized leather chair and vibrated in a nearly silent wheezing laughter until the clearest expression of the word "Squirrel" eked out from her.

I sat straight up, imagining that a varmint had joined our evening reverie. She too sat erect, but she was blushing—eyes wide and hand over her mouth.

"Squirrel?" I repeated. "Where?"

Essie didn't answer. Her eyes fell. It was clear that I had not actually heard what I thought I had.

"Did you just?" She didn't move. "Essie Stamper! Did you just . . . pass wind?"

"Cowpie. Shut your mouth!"

"You did."

"Hush."

"You did."

"Cowney Sequoyah. One does not speak like that to a lady."

"Well most *ladies* don't speak through their backsides."

She fell into herself, hawing loudly. "I know, right? I couldn't help it. You got me so tickled."

"It sounded just like you said 'squirrel.' Or more like you said, 'squuuiirrelll—'" I couldn't finish. I convulsed in the joy of her humanity.

"Stop it, *Cowpie*. You keep this up and I'll call up a whole mess of squirrels—an out-and-out scurry."

Scurry of squirrels. Essie was always teaching me new words—most of which she likely found on the shelves of 447. My favorite word though, of all the fancy, sophisticated, high-falutin' words, was *Cowpie*.

I know it sounds strange that I would want an attractive girl like Essie calling me a pile of cow manure; but even cowpies attract beautiful butterflies—delicate and indifferent to the stench of refuse.

When I returned to the inn on the last Sunday that home had anything to offer me, I practically ran to find Essie and tell her that I had returned to the waterfall I promised to show her. I wanted to report where the fire had been contained and where a new outbreak had begun—and who was rumored to be the culprit. Whose home was in more imminent danger and that ours was safe for the time being. After parking, I weaved between the guests taking their morning strolls, headed straight for the dormitory, flung my bag onto my bed, and raced back out toward the main building.

Or at least I would have, had Sol not blocked the doorway of the dorm. He leaned his right shoulder against the wall, diagonally filling the frame, and took a long draw of his hand-rolled cigarette. The tobacco, sweet and stale, filled my overcharged lungs. Even in the dimness of the fading day, I noticed the reddened rims of his eyes. Only three things typically cause a man's eyes to be bloodshot, and I was relatively certain that Sol had never shed a tear in his life, or that a weekend off had caused loss of sleep. I bit my lower lip, a tip I had learned from handling Bud. It kept me from saying anything until I had at least weighed the risks.

"Letcha back off the rez, huh?" he smirked.

"Yeah, got a week off for good behavior." My lip slipped free quite easily despite the metallic aftertaste my willpower drew from it. I wanted to get to Essie and didn't have time to waste on his bullshit.

"Mmm. Looks like you brought back a set of balls with you." Sol righted himself, dropped his cigarette, and extinguished the embers beneath his heavy boot.

I refused him eye contact and clenched my jaw. *I don't have time for this shit.*

"Hey. Look me in the eye, boy." He craned his neck like a strutting rooster. "What? You gonna cry? Where you going in such a hurry, anyway?" He pushed my right shoulder so hard he almost lost his balance.

"Dinner," I managed to force out, without looking up.

"Too late for dinner. You know that. Gonna go find that pretty little squaw of yours? Essie, right?"

How'd he know about Essie? Had he catcalled her like the soldiers she spoke of? Her name sounded ugly on his lips. I shrugged.

"I'm talking to you, boy!" Sol's voice rose like an incoming thundercloud. He stepped toward me, grabbing my chin and raising it level with his. Amid the tobacco, a stale malt stench gurgled forward. The smell was so familiar it was oddly comforting. His tone had soured in the same fermentation as Bud's had early in my life. I didn't want to look, and yet at the same time I desperately wanted to stare into those hollow eyes, to show him that I wasn't scared. I was mad. Annoyed. Tired. But I was not scared. The realization of that absence of fear felt so foreign that it angered me even further.

I also knew, though I don't think I realized it until much later, that the moment two pairs of eyes meet is the very moment when each decides if those eyes are human, animal, or something entirely devoid of a pulse. If the other's eyes are not human, the fear will surely return.

Drawing in his rancid stench, I prepared my lungs to burst forth with every conceivable damnation I could muster, followed shortly by my best defensive, protective stance. For obvious reasons, I was never a runner, so I had become uniquely adept at blocking shots until my opponent tired.

"Sol . . ." I exhaled and, lifting my head, I grasped both his shoulders opposite me and pushed hard, knocking him back until he fell down the steps and onto the ground. For a brief moment it was as if I was watching a movie, that I was not the cause of his fall; but the release felt so good I allowed myself to be pulled back into the moment, responsible. There was no returning, no apologizing, and I was more than ready to keep moving forward regardless of what Sol might return with.

"Well, hello, gents. Didn't mean to break up social hour." A guard stared up at me, standing inches from where Sol lay.

I immediately recognized him as the soldier from the front gate, the very one who had greeted Essie and me on our first day.

"Not interrupting anything, am I?" The soldier smiled half-heartedly. I have never heard a rhetorical question so pointed. The guard,

Lieutenant Franks, according to his badge, stepped up toward the doorway and lit a cigarette he pulled from his shirt pocket.

"Can we help you with something?" Sol slurred, propping himself up. His face reddened, out of both rage and embarrassment.

"Nah, just making my rounds. Didn't even expect to find anyone here. Turning in early?"

I shook my head and took the opportunity to leave the barracks without a word, before Franks could leave me alone again with Sol.

I headed straight for the main building, entered the lobby without noticing who was or who was not there, ducked into the stairwell, and climbed my way to room 447. I was completely unaware if anyone saw or followed me. All I knew was that I had been diverted long enough from Essie and I desperately needed her honeyed perfume to drown Sol's lingering scent from my clothes, my hair, and especially from my boiling blood.

Weeks ago, Essie and I had devised a plan to hide the key in the closest wall sconce so that either of us could come and go as we pleased. When I reached the fourth floor, I turned the corner quickly and jammed my hand so hastily into the sconce that I nearly broke the bulb. My fingers fumbled around the fixture, but turned up empty. Essie had to be inside the room already. I moved to the door and jiggled the handle.

Locked.

I knocked softly twice.

Nothing.

My stomach knotted. *What if she wasn't inside? What if the key was lost or stolen? What if someone else was inside?* I knocked again, three times and this time louder. The door gave way so quickly I nearly fell inside.

"Geez! Give me a sec, will you?" Essie shook her head, hands on hips.

"Oh, thank God." I rubbed my face. "You like to have scared the—"

"Ah, settle down, Cowpie." Essie turned and flopped down on the couch, pulling a leather-bound book from the coffee table onto her lap. She folded that piece of stationery, the one I had seen her reading many times before, and tucked it in the middle of the book. "How was Cherokee? Still there?" Essie had long ago told me that home didn't hold much for her and she wasn't the least bit interested in returning if she didn't have to.

"Yeah." I settled myself, falling into the chair across from her. "Still there. But I have some stories for you."

"Oh?" She looked up from the book. "Do tell." Contriving sweetness, she cradled her chin in her palms.

For the next hour I spun my weekend visit home into such an engineered, fantastic tale it made Odysseus look like a joyrider. I resurrected earlier visits, fitting their joints so haphazardly my epic grew beyond anything of this world, ancient or otherwise. Essie lay on the couch, staring at the ceiling, and silently listened. Periodically, she would turn her face toward me, waiting on the next line, especially in the suspenseful moments. And, because it meant her looking into my eyes, I added a few suspenseful moments. I couldn't help myself.

" . . . stood on two legs just like a man, or I guess a woman since the cubs were there."

"'Cause she was a woman," Essie shrugged. "Bear clan for sure." Essie was reminding me of one of the original Cherokee clans and the Bear-men of our mountains. "Did you talk to her?"

"Well, hell, no, I didn't talk to her! She's lucky I didn't hit her or her cubs."

"I'd say you are lucky you didn't hit her or her cubs."

I smiled. "You know, I don't believe all those stories, but after seeing that yona and how mad she was at me, damn. I've only seen a look like that from Lishie. Don't know many animals that can strike fear like that." Essie laughed with me.

Despite her ever-changing analysis of the bear encounter, I was surprised to find that ultimately Essie was far less interested in the bears and the possible latest sighting of Edgar than she was the waterfall. She always asked about the waterfall.

"How tall? Could you drink the water? Where did you say it was again? Deep enough to swim? Any greens?" The questions trailed one after another. What I didn't know I made up so that she would not stop talking.

When I finished answering and exaggerating, rising to peruse the bookshelves as if I actually cared what was on them, she sat up and leaned over the couch's armrest. "So we're going, right? Maybe next weekend?"

"Where? Cherokee?"

"No . . . well, sort of. I mean to the waterfall."

"Oh, sure. I guess. I mean, if I can pull you away from this place," I mocked.

Essie sat back. It was as if she had abruptly awoken from a daydream. "Well, maybe not next weekend. I just want to go sometime." She hugged the leather-bound book to her chest.

"You have plans?" I turned to read her face.

"I don't know. I mean . . . Maybe." She looked away.

"Is it homecoming already?"

"No, not in Cherokee. I might have things to do here, though."

I gave her a disgusted look. "You do know they don't pay extra for weekend work, right?"

"I know. Not work. Just—"

"Just what?" *Was this a secret? An unspoken secret in 447?* My body cramped. I could still smell Sol on my clothes.

"Nothing. Don't worry about it. Have time for a game?" Essie moved to the shelf, brought out the box of dominos, and filled the empty shelf space with the book.

"Essie!"

"What?"

"You really aren't going to tell me what you're doing?"

Essie dropped the box onto the coffee table. "Cowney, you're not my father."

"But I thought I was your—"

"Friend?" Tiny wrinkles spread across her forehead.

I must have looked pathetic. Her face fell and she seemed to blink away the desire to respond cruelly, honestly. "It's nothing. Really not a big deal," she almost whispered.

Arguing, prodding her further on the issue was not a right I felt I had earned. I couldn't afford to give a girl like Essie any reason to avoid me. "Go ahead, set 'em up," I conceded, pushing the box of dominoes toward her.

We played until the awkwardness and early silence turned to excitement over smart moves and then to chiding each other's efforts. We played until the sun's light bled into the room en route to its evening resting place behind the mountains.

"Getting late, Cowpie. I will have to finish you off another time." Essie grinned. She stood and stretched, raising her arms to the ceiling and exhaling loudly. "I'll go first this time, but should be pretty quiet downstairs."

I moved toward the lamp, as if I intended to turn the switch and follow after her shortly. Of course I did not. "Okay," I agreed. "Be careful. See you at breakfast."

I waited until she closed the heavy door behind her and I could hear her footsteps progress down the hall and fade. I quickly located the leather-bound book, afraid that my mental image of where she had placed it among the others on the shelf would disappear before I could recover it. I pulled the book from the shelf and ran my hand across the cover before frantically exposing each of the pages until the piece of stationery fell to the floor. Its sudden fall momentarily gave me pause. In my hands was a piece of Essie that I was not entirely comfortable discovering. This was her secret and I had no right to touch it, expose it—let it drop to the floor carelessly. I placed the book back into its waiting holster, allowing it to edge out past the others just a bit so that I could locate it again quickly. Carefully, I unfolded the sheet and held it beneath the still-illuminated lamp. I wanted desperately to read faster than I was able.

"Loveliest Essie." The words framed the page. My body constricted.

I immediately located the signature. I needed to name my emerging enemy.

"Yours, Andrea."

Yours? Andrea? The name was familiar. I searched my memory— guests calling to other guests, guards reading off checklists. *Was this the son of one of the Italian diplomats?* I rushed back to the top of the letter for clues.

"I caught a glimpse of your amber eyes as you turned the corner and felt as if I might never recover from the heat that coursed through my body."

How could it be that a man—a boy, more accurately—from Italy wrote English so much more eloquently than I could even attempt to contemplate it silently? Even now, I'm not sure I have such words.

"Go with me to make cool this fire with a swim? I know of a place. The perfect cure."

His thinly veiled sexual references were embarrassing. His arrogance that the two could slip off was ignorant! *How could Essie believe in such a fool?* She wasn't any smarter than Bud, who thought I could build my own relationships with these foreigners. How could they not consider the risk? I wanted to tear the letter into pieces. I would have done it if I had known Essie would not find the evidence.

I sat down on the limp couch and folded the letter until it rested in the palm of my hand. *Or was I the fool?* I wondered. Had I missed my chance long ago to woo her simply by reciting trite, empty lines from forgotten film stars? Could it have been that easy? The tarnished mirror, askew, just above the fireplace, answered for me. I looked into the reflection, saw my workman's clothes and tired eyes, my out-turned foot that refused to align even while sitting.

My accent was not foreign to Essie. It must have sounded sickeningly the same as every other voice she'd ever heard in her young life. It didn't matter what Andrea said. It didn't matter in what language, tone, or context. Even as she read, she must have heard his difference, his exoticness, his uniqueness. Those were qualities of sound that Essie needed to carry her future away on singsong notes to some other place. My voice was nothing more than an echo.

Perhaps I could have forgotten the devastation of the note after a good night's sleep. Perhaps I never would have thought of it again after I tucked it back into its book and resolved never to ask Essie another question about her weekend plans. Perhaps it could become nothing more than another page of literature on shelves lined with fanciful stories, never to meet our reality. And still, had she told me about Andrea in her own words, in the sacredness of room 447, in the room where secrets are absorbed into the oak and dissolve into the plaster ceiling, had she told me after two "borrowed" cans of beer, through the cigar smoke we fanned out of an open window, I would not have believed her. And I believed everything we shared in 447. Words baptized in that room were the only words I had come to believe—believe in. But she had not told me. And I had not asked. And I tucked the letter back carelessly. I left 447 perhaps too early that evening, or too late. Or she had. And it didn't matter because all that seemed important in the whole world was that I rounded the bottom staircase at the very moment that truth was no longer optional.

His large, callous-free hands held her demure face and he kissed her in a way I do in only the deepest sleeps on the warmest nights. No man and woman in my world ever explored such forceful passion—unless, of course, it was made of fear and anger disguised as passion. And yet, neither had even reached the age of twenty.

"Essie?" Her name spilled from my lips. I immediately covered my mouth, but it was too late. The two separated quickly, both relieved I was not a soldier or supervisor and angry that I, insignificant I, had interrupted them.

"I'm—I'm sorry," I stammered. I started to walk away, but stopped myself. "Essie. Are you okay?" I still don't know why I asked that question. Of course she was okay. From the way their bodies were pressed against one another, she was better than okay. I was the one in crisis.

I looked desperately to Essie. She turned into his shoulder. I have never felt so much hate as I did in that moment. Years of suffering Bud's abuse, the glare of Sol's cold eyes, nothing, no one person had managed to dredge up the anger Essie's subtle refusal to witness had.

I shook my head and pushed the large wooden door to the main hall open hard.

"Whoa!" a muffled voice warned on the other side. "Easy," it continued.

Andrea kissed Essie's cheek and leapt up the stairwell, taking two steps at a time before the person on the other side of the entry released his grip of the door, allowing it to swing wide open. "You again?" It was Lieutenant Franks. "We've got to stop meeting like this." He smiled.

"I . . . I'm sorry, sir. I . . . I was in a hurry."

"Yeah, I can see that. You seem to always be in a hurry." Franks craned his neck to look beyond me at Essie, who had been frozen by his entrance and Andrea's exit.

"Listen, you kids need to get on back to the dorms. Doesn't look real good to find you both in the stairwells this late in the evening, understand?"

"Yes, sir." I nodded. "We were just headed out." Though I could not slow the pounding of my heart, his calm response helped me release the deep breath I had swallowed from shock.

Franks looked at us both as if he was trying to understand the relationship between and Essie and me just as much as I was. "Peter."

"What?" I raised my eyes to meet his. "Excuse me, sir?"

"My name is Peter. Lieutenant Peter Franks, but just call me Peter if no one else is around."

"Yes. Okay. Peter." I was eager to leave but felt as if I owed him more. "I'm Cowney Sequoyah and—" I turned to Essie, immediately disgusted again by the sight of her. "That is Essie Stamper."

"Nice to meet y'all." Peter nodded and then stepped aside, acknowledging a clear path through the open door. "Have a good evening."

I nodded in return and walked out. I did not wait for Essie to follow. I wanted to put as much distance between her and myself on the path to the dorms as she had already forced into our relationship.

I was just a boy then, and had no real insight into a woman's heart. I couldn't understand why we weren't an automatic fit for each other, a promised pair of sameness in this strange place. In the years since, I have learned that not all love is made of equal parts. There are more kinds of deep affection than we are sometimes willing to accept in society. I wish I had known then that she was more than any friend or girlfriend could be. What we had was deeper than a physical relationship and too big to be made simple with naming. It was everything and absolutely indefinable all at once.

CHAPTER FIFTEEN

I did not want to wake in the morning. I did not want to see anyone I had met last night. Not Lieutenant Peter Franks. Not Andrea. Not the version of Sol without Lee to rein him in. Not the real Essie. I wanted them all to be characters in a nightmare, washed away with the rising sun. But the morning murmurs brought forth heavy boots of mission-driven soldiers outside, Sol's final boozy snores grappling for a few more minutes of rest, and the clanging of bells too vigorous to inspire any reaction other than a blinded nosedive into the reality of the day. The morning brought smoke, which briefly caused me to believe I was back home. But damn, even if I had been home in the midst of an out-and-out inferno, it still seemed safer than being in a bed surrounded by luxury, military, and beautiful women.

Because I had to face reality unwillingly, I may, or may not, have bumped Sol's cot so hard as I walked past on my way to brush my teeth that he sat up with a start. It's hard to remember the details of such things. But I do know for sure that we both began the day with no desire to be breathing the same air. He cut himself shaving, ripping pieces of toilet paper into tiny temporary triage patches and cursing with each application. As for myself, though the morning sun brought hope for a better day, I had apparently gone to sleep with my hair still damp from sweat and placed my head in such an awkward position on the pillow that a peak of errant black hair jutted from the crown of my head as if I were somehow akin to a new half-breed of ruffed grouse.

The smoke proved to be benign, but it was evidence that fires had spread. I wondered if Bud found this fortunate—if he thought his hunting exploits would benefit. I couldn't worry about Bud, and Sol's behavior was quite typical, but worrying about both men still felt less daunting than addressing how to respond to Essie. I hesitated before entering the dining hall, fearful I would have to make an early-morning decision about her, about us. Should I greet her? Sit with her? Ignore her? Confront her? None of the options seemed plausible. A part of me wondered if she had dreamt the same horrible nightmare that I had or if, when I saw her, she could confirm for me that it had only been a delusion.

So, when I finally gathered the nerve to open the door and step through into the open hall, I was both relieved and disappointed to see that Essie was not there. The other girls that she would sometimes join for dessert if I left lunch early to return to work were there. They were exactly where they were supposed to be, according to this new summer tradition we had subconsciously developed. I hurried past their table, but felt the collective breeze of their whispers and the force of their stares. Perhaps it was the four winds that Preacherman had spoken of, but they breathed more death than life into me. I could sense, or at least I convinced myself that I could sense their inquisition: searching my face for Essie's whereabouts and then turning back to the door with an assumption that she would surely follow me through. As secretive as I had hoped my feelings for Essie were from the rest of the world, I also hoped that everyone would recognize our bond, our alliance, and come to depend on it as I had.

But Essie didn't follow, and the girls didn't ask. I scooped a small pile of plain oatmeal into a bowl, found a seat as close to a corner as possible, and shoveled bites into my mouth as quickly as they cooled. I guzzled coffee so fast that it nearly blistered my mouth. It probably would not have been a travesty if a burnt tongue had tempered my words.

Before heading out to find Lee and Sol, I paused for a moment to consider whether or not I should go to her dorm to check on Essie. I knew the trouble that would be caused if she showed up late for duty. *Had she overslept? Had she found Andrea again and was she still with him in the morning? Had he hurt her? Had another, less forgiving guard found them together? . . . Who was I to even ask?* That was the question that released me. I had no authority to ask anything but what was the next job I was expected to perform for the inn and its "guests." And so that is what I did. I left the responsibility of Essie to Essie and went to find Lee and Sol sharpening tools in the shed.

"'Bout time you rolled out of bed," Lee jabbed without looking up from the file in his hand and the spade lying across his lap. He greeted almost everyone in this manner on most days. I was grateful for some semblance of normalcy. Sol did look up when I entered, but his face was flat and expressionless. It was possible that our encounter the previous afternoon was not as memorable for him as it had been for me.

"Yes, sir. Always hard on a Monday morning," I replied to Lee out of habit. "What's on tap for today?"

"Better find a bandana to cover your face. We'll be clearing brush and this damn smoke just gets thicker."

"It'll clear with the morning fog," I offered.

Sol rolled his eyes. "Some kind of Indian prophecy?"

"Science. And fuck you!" I stared hard into him.

Lee shot out an upsurge of laughter. "Goddamn, son. What was in your oatmeal this morning?"

I shook it off and took an ax from behind the shed door. "Let's hit it then."

I spent the remainder of the day within twenty feet of where I had found the bone. Its mystery interrupted a near obsession with imagining where Essie could be or if Andrea was watching me, or exactly how much time I would have to spend in Sol's presence for the remainder of the summer. To avoid all of these things, these people, I chose to take my lunch in silence and return to the exact place of the bone. I built a bologna sandwich in the dining hall and pocketed a small red delicious. Keeping my eyes lowered, I managed to avoid Essie's table and her friends while both washing up and collecting my lunch. She may have been there. They may have been there, but I didn't want to know either way. We had made plans to play another round of dominos, but those plans were made before knowing she could make plans with anyone else. At least, before I knew it.

Outside, I sat on a stump above the spot where the bone had once been semi-buried. There was a part of me that wanted to talk to the bone, as odd as that sounds. Even though I knew the bone was no longer there— even though I knew it wouldn't talk back. I chewed slowly, listening to the laughter of the diplomats' children and the warning calls of mothers, an orchestra of languages, curt and simple, so clearly in response to the children's actions that I could translate every word into both English and Cherokee. *Careful. Stop. Not so fast.*

The guards watched everyone, even each other. Some lingered over the mothers, some over the children, some over the workers. They, too, took their lunch on the job and chewed like I imagined they unloaded their Brownings—reckless and rapid.

Twice I found myself edging close to the Japanese diplomats as they smoked cigarettes on the back veranda, speaking their native tongue but always within earshot of guards. I tried to pick up subtle clues to their language, perhaps pick up enough to casually approach them. I knew they understood English, as all diplomats should, but if I was going to broach the subject of bear medicine, then they needed to trust me, and language does much to build that trust. Yes, I had decided while eating lunch that first day alone that I had nothing, absolutely nothing to lose by brokering a deal for Bud. Hunters trade meat all the time. What did it matter who the buyer was and what otherwise useless part was being sold? It might even keep Bud off my back the next time I was home.

Unfortunately, the third time I angled near two Japanese men, I caught their attention. They nodded and I stood to address them directly. But nothing came from my mouth, not even a weak attempt at *ohayo*, the only phrase I had picked up. Their brows furrowed as they waited and then laughed off my awkwardness, turning to face the guards.

A guard called over, "Sequoyah, you need something?"

"No, sir." I bent back into the shrubbery and pulled nettle from the plants' bases, piercing my fingers through the heavy leather gloves.

For the entire week, I repeated the practice—minus interactions with diplomats. I spoke little to anyone other than to Peter occasionally and whatever spirit lingered from the hollow space once occupied by the bone. The smoke met us in the early morning and dissipated with the lunch bell. I watched it fade west—blacken with its retreat until the afternoon's work was illuminated with hot sun. I did not return to 447, though I wondered often if Essie did. I took dinner at the very last moment, much to the irritation of the women on dish duty, who had hoped to finish early at least one evening in time to join an impromptu barn dance or card game. I knew I would have to face Essie again, even if I could avoid Andrea. I would have to take her home at the end of the summer and it would be a long ride; but I couldn't face her just yet. I had nothing to say. I gave it all to an empty space, spilled into an echo of the bone.

I was fully intent on continuing this pattern of solitude the morning that Lee, sensing I needed a change, perhaps, diverted my plans.

"We'll be in the big house today, boys. Plumber is out sick or hung-over and they need us to come help out."

"I ain't no plumber," Sol grumbled.

"Me either." I agreed with Sol on one point at least.

Lee shook his head. "Not asking you to be. I'm not either. They just want us to come over and help clean up."

"Shit!" moaned Sol.

"Yep, probably some of that, too." Lee laughed as he put the tools on a bench and dusted himself off. "Better than being out in this smoke any-way. Those fires out your way seem to have gotten outta hand, Cowney. Heard tell Balsam's burning. We'd choke if we were outside all day. Let's get to it."

My oatmeal breakfast rose until it burned my throat. The inn's main building was the last place on earth I wanted to be. "You need us all in there?"

"Oh, hell yeah, he does," Sol interrupted. "You ain't getting out of this one."

"I wasn't trying to get—"

Lee rescued me. "Yes, Cowney. All hands on deck. If we divide up the work, we can be on to the outside chores by lunchtime."

Our work inside was just as Lee had described. Dripping water, over-flowing toilets, clogged drains. The problems were rancid, but not over-whelming. The issues were reserved to only a few areas and rooms. And while the military paid a licensed plumber for such tasks, they were sim-ple enough for our unprofessional skill sets.

The guards' break room: an overflowing toilet.

Two guest rooms, both with German occupants: a slow dripping sink that simply needed the faucet tightened before the water irreversibly stained the porcelain.

Six common rooms or unoccupied spaces: clogged showers that were to be snaked free of hair and soap buildup.

General cleanup: water, stains, damp nests of hair, paper, and human waste.

The building manager cut off water to some areas where the licensed plumber would be needed, but he assured Lee that that didn't mean we couldn't go ahead and take care of the cleanup. The sheer amount of congealed human refuse made me question just how many people we were living with. I never had a sense that the inn was at full occupancy, but this mess seemed to be the work of many. Perhaps it had just never been tended to after the paying guests left. Either way, I had to control my urge to vomit each time sprays of water broke free, sending particles of piss, shit, hair, and skin splashing against my body.

"Don't they have maids for this shit?" Sol grumbled as he mopped a pool of dust balls, red clay mud, and suicidal ants in the inn's prep kitchen.

"Yeah, but they're shorthanded, too. Plenty of other messes for them to clean up."

What did he mean by "shorthanded"? Had someone not shown up this morning?

Sol gave me a look. "Maybe those maids need to focus more on their work and less on their leisure."

"Seems to me like we all do," Lee reminded him. "Come on, Cowney. Sol's got this covered. I'll show you the next one on the list." He grabbed a toolbox and mop and handed both to me. I was grateful to Lee that he had removed me from Sol's sarcasm, but each time we moved to a new room, my heart pounded against my chest as if I might convulse into cardiac arrest at the first sighting of Essie's uniform, probably quicker if it were a glimpse of Andrea's scowl.

"What's wrong with you today, son?" Lee asked as we climbed the staircase I had so quickly escaped several nights ago. "You seem on edge. Everything okay back home?"

"Yeah. I don't know. I mean, sometimes this place is a little much for me."

"Work's too hard?"

"No, it's not that. It's just strange, you know. I mean every other guy my age is off fighting. The only ones here my age are in uniform." I followed him into the hallway of the fourth floor. We stopped in front of a large window looking over the mountains. "And I'm here cleaning up after foreigners we're supposed to call guests. It's just weird, that's all."

"Well, it's not forever. Just try to remember that. Shoot, aren't you even off to college in the fall? Isn't that what I heard?"

"Yeah, maybe. Still not sure."

"Oh, you like cleaning up shit that much, huh?" Lee nudged my shoulder.

I smiled halfheartedly. "Ah, I don't know. Not sure I belong places like that."

"Well, son. I can promise you one thing. None of us belong in a place like this either." He walked down the hall with me trailing after him.

"It's this one. He pointed to a guest room. No one is staying in here anymore. Rumor is, they got traded for an American diplomat. Got to go home."

"Home? To D.C.?" According to the little news I had heard, all of the diplomats and nationals staying at the inn had been bused down from Washington, D.C., but I felt sure they would not be allowed to return until the war ended. How odd it was to consider someone deciding where your home is or will be for you, especially if you have never set foot on the land before.

"Doubt that. Just heard the soldiers talking the other day. They said home. Who knows what that really means." I could relate.

Lee unlocked the door and showed me slick tile floor and damp carpet. "I'll leave you to it."

It wasn't until I heard Lee's footsteps disappear down the hall that I was able to orientate myself to exactly where I was. Had Lee and I ventured two more rooms down the hall, we would have been standing in front of 447. My chances of seeing Essie just doubled. I considered closing the door to the guest room behind me as I worked, but mold permeated the carpet and the stench was too strong. I resolved to work swiftly and quickly get back downstairs.

Twenty minutes or so into the job, I thought I might just make it out without confrontation. I should have known better.

"Sure got yourself a mess there, don't you?" It was Peter making his rounds. Essie never mentioned that guards made rounds so close to room 447. Likely she knew that bit of information would deter me for certain.

"Yeah, could have been worse. It's mostly just water."

"Good." He reached out and handed me a key. "Can you return this

113

to your boss for me? He let me borrow some tools from the shed. Tell him I will get them back to him shortly—just as soon as we finish shoring up the fence line. Won't take long. Really appreciate it."

I tucked the key in my pocket. "Sure. Will do."

"Mind if I take my break here?" Peter asked as he flopped down on the bed and lit a cigarette. Sweat ringed his collar.

"Not my place to mind where you go," I responded, wringing the mop outside the open room window.

"So, you said your name was Sequoyah, right?" His pronunciation had gotten better since his first attempt at the gate.

"Yes. Cowney Sequoyah."

"Like the alphabet guy?"

I pulled the mop back inside and faced Peter, surprised by his knowledge of the originator of the Cherokee syllabary.

"Yes, that's right. How'd you know that?"

"Well, it's not often I hear the name. I guess it just sticks. Plus, I mean, it's not every day that someone just up and creates a language."

"Syllabary," I corrected as gently as possible. "We've had a language forever. He created a system of writing. A syllabary."

"Still damn remarkable, don't you think?" Peter sat up on the bed and ashed his cigarette in the tray on the nightstand.

"Oh, yeah. Of course." I closed the window and laughed a little, thinking about what I knew about Sequoyah. "You know they say he was insane. Wife burned his papers twice."

"Figures. Women have such a hard time recognizing genius." Peter and I laughed together. I think it might have been the first time I truly breathed all morning.

"Ah, don't mean to hold you up from your work, Sequoyah." Peter extinguished his cigarette. "Let me help you out. Maybe get you to lunch early." He pulled up the towels I had laid on the carpet to soak up the moisture, opened the window again, and wrung them out of it in the same way I had the mop.

He told me about the girls he had dated and why he joined the army and how he'd give anything to see more action, both with the girls and the military. I didn't have to nod or tell him how much I understood how he felt. He would glance at my foot periodically as he spoke. Not in a demeaning way. Not in the way others did that made me feel uncomfortable. It was almost as if he were calling for an "amen," and my deformity was that unspoken response.

When we soaked up all the water we could, I tucked the wrench back in the toolbox. "Thanks for the company." I shook his hand.

"Anytime. This routine gets pretty boring and I'm just trying to stay out of trouble."

"Don't guess you guys have to worry too much about that since everyone else here is trying not to get in trouble with you."

"Yeah, but some of these guys, some of the guards, they make their own trouble when bored."

This must be what Lee and Sol were talking about, I thought. "You mean with the girls?" I asked, walking with Peter into the hall.

"That's one way," he acknowledged. "Say, who was that girl you were with that one night?"

My stomach sank. *Why was he asking? Was he just making conversation or had he decided to make his own trouble?*

"Essie?" I asked as if it were really a question.

"Yeah, Essie. Who is she?"

"What do you mean? She works here."

"Well, I figured as much. I've seen her around plenty. I mean, who is she to you?"

"She rode over from Cherokee with me. I mean, we know each other, kind of."

"So, friends?"

"Yeah, I guess so. Sort of."

"But let me guess. You'd like her to be more?"

"Peter—"

"Oh, I'm sorry, Cowney. Didn't mean to pry. It is just, well. I know that look. The way I saw you two that night."

I walked over to the window and pressed my palms into the sill. "Girls like that are not meant for me."

"She have a boyfriend?"

Peter was the first person that whole summer who I felt like I could tell about Essie. I had just really met the man and yet I wanted nothing more than to spill everything I knew, thought, dreamt of. But he was still a soldier and Essie was still a servant. And Andrea was still a "guest."

"I don't know."

"Don't get the wrong idea. I'm not interested for me, just so you know. I'm married." He pulled a wallet from his back pocket and pulled out a photo. "And this here's my baby girl."

A tiny, bundled baby, eyes wide, stared back at me.

"Beautiful," I offered.

"Yes, sir. I'm a lucky man."

"I bet you miss them."

"Yes. Every. Single. Second. Just try to pass the time as best I can."

"Any advice on how to do that?"

"Not much. Maybe take up a hobby. Get out as much as you can. You fish or anything?"

"Yes, but don't know where to go 'round here."

"I wouldn't mind showing you sometime. Me and some of the guys go out on weekends sometimes to the French Broad."

"Say, you wouldn't have access to a canoe, would you?"

He shot me a crooked smile. "As a matter of fact, that's one of my favorite ways to pass the time. The inn had practically a whole fleet in storage. I figure it's better to use them than let them sit there and rot."

I smiled, too, thinking how even the smallest of revenges, doing something Essie had wanted to do so badly without her, felt empowering. I thought for a moment that I would show him room 447. We were so close to it, no one else was in the hall, and if someone did come, I was with a guard.

But I did not get to make that decision. The stairwell door down the hall flew open, crashing against the wall, and a fumbling private came around the corner. "Sir." He nodded to Peter. He then turned to me. "Are you Cowney See—See—"

"Yes, I'm Cowney Sequoyah."

"Lee asked me to fetch you. A call came for you." He handed me a note.

I felt nauseous as I read. "I have to go," I told Peter.

"Everything okay?" Peter asked.

"No, no, I don't think it is."

"Anything I can do?"

"No. Thank you." I turned to leave, but looked back at Peter and dug the key from my pocket. "You'll have to return this yourself, though. And thanks for your help."

"No problem," he called after me.

I read the note one more time, just to make sure that I was truly reading what I thought I was. "Come home . . . Lishie . . . not long . . ."

I rushed from the property with such speed that nothing seemed to move in real time. The note drove me, drove me so quickly that I remember nothing about packing, speaking with Lee, or being in the car the two hours home to Cherokee, to Lishie. I prayed. I remember that. Prayed I would make it back to her before she was gone. I conjured every drowsy word I could possibly recall from church meetings with Lishie, from summer revivals and deep-water baptisms. English, Cherokee—it mattered not. Somewhere along the way, I dug deep into my pocket and pulled forth the mother bear's scream.

CHAPTER SIXTEEN

When I arrived home, I washed my hands in the sink. I breathed in the scent of the lye, anything to delay entering her bedroom. I had been in such a rush to get home, but now I was nearly paralyzed. I rubbed my hands until they warmed to a bright red, threatening to bruise. When I could no longer stand to hear her distant cough, I reached for a dishrag, knotting my hands dry. That is when I first saw it. Blood. Tiny drops of deep crimson blood in perfectly wrought circles by the sink. I imagined how she had coughed into the basin, washed the murky spittle down the drain, cleaned up her own mess as best she could.

Hallowed be thy name . . . Dust to dust . . . The hand of the Lord was upon me . . . Amazing grace . . . that they may live . . . ga-lv-lo-i . . . a-gi-ni-shi . . . a-gi-li-shi.

I called her Lishie because my mother had and since my mother had, my father had. And when my father had, Lishie referred to herself as such. In truth, I didn't have a lishie, not in the Cherokee sense. Not a maternal grandmother. Not one that I knew. My Lishie was my father's mother and should have been called a-gi-ni-shi, if we're speaking in the strictest sense. But there was nothing strict about our family tree. I guess I always just thought that my mother needed Lishie more as a mother than she did her own. It was Lishie who brought clean linens to sop the blood from my birth. There was no room in that story for any other mother.

Bud came through the door carrying a load of firewood. "'Bout time you got here." He shoved the logs into the stove.

"How is she?"

"I wouldn't have sent for you if she were well," Bud grumbled.

"I know. I just—what should I be prepared for?"

"You haven't been in yet?"

"No. Just washed up."

Bud pushed the last log inside and wiped his hands on his jeans. His eyes welled and he turned away. "Can't prepare yourself for things like this. Just go see her. She's been asking to see you."

Lishie's modest cabin seemed to stretch as I made my way to her room. There were others with her. I heard muffled voices. Preacherman's for sure. Myrtle's maybe. I felt my body shrink. I could also tell others had been there before me. The scent was there.

Grease

Lilies

Tobacco

Vanilla

Fresh dirt

Pine sap

"Lishie," I whispered, easing open her door.

"Come in, son." Preacherman stood and opened the door wider. "She's resting now."

Lishie's face was pale and someone had combed her wiry gray hair out long and straight. It outlined the rise and fall of her shoulders. I hadn't seen Lishie's hair unfastened in years. She wore it beneath a bandana like the other ladies when she went to town and either braided it tight or coiled it into a bun when at home. She always had it braided so quickly after washing it that I forgot what it looked like loose. A quilt was pulled to her chin and her black King James sat on the table beside her, illuminated by the oil lamp's flame.

"What happened?" I turned to Myrtle, knowing I'd get the uncensored truth from her. She and Lishie had known each other for as long as I could remember and carried on like sisters more than some sisters I knew.

"Not completely sure. Bud found her, thank goodness."

"Why's she here then? Shouldn't she be in the hospital?" I fumbled to understand.

"She refused to. Plus the fire's so close to the hospital, can't hardly breathe in there. And . . . well . . ." Myrtle shook her head.

"Doctor said there's nothing else they can do for her, Cowney," Bud continued. "She needs rest and they sent home some medicine with us, but—"

"She'll be okay?" I looked at Bud with more hope than I had ever afforded him. "How long has she been asleep?"

"There's no way to know how she'll be. She's been asleep since we got her home," Bud answered. He approached me as if he were going to touch my shoulder, but let his arm drop before we touched.

And then a silence fell on the house like I hadn't sensed in many, many years. And I realized that I did remember (if that is the word) far more than I ever thought I had about my father, about his funeral, about each anniversary of his funeral, about Bud, about . . .

Grease
Lilies
Tobacco
Vanilla
Fresh dirt
Pine sap

I remembered that there was also yelling. There was Myrtle tending to Lishie and Preacherman warming everyone's coffee. There was Bud and there was a jar of homemade liquor. And then there was Bud and there was yelling. There was Bud and Lishie and there was more yelling. And there was a tiny version of me and darkness beneath a heavy quilt. I was an infant one moment. I was three the next moment and five the next. It was as if the pictures had been stored in my blood only to slowly develop over the years until my brain found the words for them.

It was one mess of a memory that pulled me from the present so quickly that I did not wait for Lishie to wake or for Preacherman to offer coffee. The memory coursed through my veins, chilling and constricting the vessels. I passed by Bud and the fumes of his breath. I walked down the ever-expanding hall to my room and dove beneath a heavy quilt.

I could not stop the images from coming. I folded my pillow over my eyes, but could not shade them from the scene.

"He was your brother!" Lishie was pleading with Bud. "Please, for his sake. For the boy's sake."

"Is that who you are protecting? Or are you just protecting yourself?" Bud

turned up a mason jar to his lips and then flung it against the cabin wall. It shattered into large, sweepable pieces, and also into tiny pieces that bit the pads of feet, shredding skin and drawing blood.

"Bud! I'm trying to keep this family together." I could hear Lishie's voice as clear as if she were still in the room with me. But it was a younger, softer voice.

"Is that what you were doing when you cashed that check from the army?"

"It's for the boy—"

"The boy? The boy? Call him who he is!" Bud stormed.

"Cowney," Lishie whispered. I remember that for sure. The sadness of my name.

"Yeah, Cowney. Your boy, right?"

"If I have to raise him to be." Lishie stood her ground.

"Like you raised me or like you raised my brother? Careful now," Bud warned. "The result is very different depending on which you choose."

"I raised you the same." Lishie was crying now.

"But we weren't the same."

"No, that's right, son. You're right. He wasn't as strong as you. I had to be gentler with him. We all did. But I still raised you both to be family men."

Bud reached for a set of keys on the kitchen table and left the cabin.

Lishie cried and cried.

And her cries morphed from memories into my own beneath the quilt. Whether or not these words were spoken in this order, in this fashion, in this temper, it doesn't matter. Their truth persisted, even through years of silence. Even through the thick smoke outside.

I waited until I heard Preacherman announce he would return after Bible study and Myrtle say that she was going to fetch dinner from home and bring it back in an hour or so. I waited until I no longer heard Bud moving about, until I figured he had found a place inside or on the porch to pass out for the evening. I crawled out of my bed, still in my work clothes, and drug myself back into Lishie's room. She was still sleeping, so I crawled beneath her quilt and wrapped myself around her body. She breathed deeply, signaling a welcomed recognition, but did not speak or open her eyes. I smelled her lye soap hair and tried to block out all other smells.

Until exhaustion overcame me, I thought of the last few visits with Lishie. I remembered how she had started taking afternoon naps and added two new medicine bottles to her cabinet. I remembered that she had paid a local boy to bring her a basketful of dandelions, more than typical to treat an occasional bout of heartburn.

Dammit, Lishie. She knew and she had spared me. It had not been the first time she had shielded me from the pain of heartache. She had been doing it all my life. As my skin warmed hers beneath the blanket, I wanted to take the pain from her, absorb it into my own body. I was already deformed, crippled, imperfect. What was one more affliction to me?

That night I spoke to Lishie, though only through my dreams. It felt so real; sometimes I still wonder if it wasn't. Maybe I spoke in my sleep and she responded in hers. I told her about Essie and Andrea. I confessed how I felt for Essie in ways I had never felt for anyone before. I told her how afraid I was for Essie to know, to respond. That night, in my dreams or otherwise, Lishie asked me if I remembered how to make her pound cake. Did I remember the proportions and how to mix the wet ingredients and dry ingredients separately until just the right time? Did I remember how finicky sugar was in general? Like when we made Christmas peanut brittle? If you heat it, it burns so easily—hardening into a sticky, bitter brittle. You must always watch sugar closely, even if you're not heating it on the stove. Keep it stirred up, adding your flavor to it slowly. It seemed like a delusional fever dream, piecing repetitive memories together into a moment. Why would Lishie rise from her deathbed to share recipes with me?

Thinking about it now—shit. If that ain't love advice, I don't know what is. It didn't make a lick of sense the first half dozen times she said it, especially the time I dreamt about her saying it; but it sure as hell does now. I only wish I recognized it in time to ask her what to do when there was no sugar in the cupboard to spare, when it was rationed in times of war.

CHAPTER SEVENTEEN

In the morning, I was in my own bed, wrapped around myself and within a sweat-dampened quilt. I was helped there at some point in the night, but was too tired to resist or notice who led me. Likely, it was Myrtle and Preacherman, as they were both in the kitchen when I stumbled in looking for a strong cup of coffee. My eyes cleared only to see the blur of Myrtle's. She did not even wait to hear "Good morning."

"I'm sorry, son."

I fell into a kitchen chair.

"Early this morning . . . In her sleep. Peaceful."

"It likely was a blood clot or aneurysm." A new voice spoke, rising from the living room. Dr. Pritchett had been called. And now he was being served coffee as if he had just come by for a neighborly chat. "She passed quickly. She was getting older, son. She'd fought this off quite a while already." He spoke calmly, practiced.

"Fought what off?"

"Death," Bud intervened. "Death. We're all fighting it off." He was angry and already loose-tongued. Bits of cornbread speckled his white T-shirt as he crammed the remaining piece into his mouth between words. As early in the morning as it was, he had already begun sweating. I was not as mad about his insensitivity as I was that he felt he had a right to be angry.

"Her heart had been giving her trouble for some time, Cowney. That along with other complications that come with age. Sugar and blood pressure. It just all finally caught up to her," the doctor continued.

I looked around at all the people in the room. *When had they arrived? When had Lishie left? How could so much have changed while I slept?* I attempted to speak. "But I didn't—"

Myrtle tried to comfort me. "Your lishie wasn't the kind of person that is going to burden her grandson with that sort of worry."

I pushed the kitchen table away, shaking the breakfast bowls and plates, and ran to Lishie's room. She was exactly where I'd left her. The covers were straight and neat around her body. Her face was even paler than before, graying to the hue of her hair. Someone had folded her hands onto her lap like she was sitting in her Sunday pew awaiting Preacherman's call to worship.

I whispered her name, desperately hoping that she would share the secret with me, open her eyes and smile as if she had just played a trick on everyone else. "Oh, Lishie. No. No. No. Please, Lishie." I draped my arms across hers and buried my face against her shoulder. "I can't—" No more words came, only tears, followed by a throbbing head.

Myrtle came in with a cup of coffee and helped me into a bedside chair. She was wise enough not to speak for some time. She watched as I spoke without words to my Lishie, punctuating each regret, each promise, with salty marks.

I felt so guilty that I hadn't stayed. If I had known . . . I would have written down everything she told me. What more could she have said to me? She knew more about my father, I had no doubt. I couldn't fathom why she wouldn't tell me. Maybe she thought I couldn't handle it or that it didn't matter anymore. I wondered who would tell me the stories now. *How long are you supposed to boil the bean bread before it turns to mush?* She had always been the only one.

When my breathing calmed, Myrtle offered, "Why don't you get some air, child? Maybe sit on the porch and I will bring you some breakfast? Smoke ain't as thick this morning."

"I'm not hungry. But, yeah, maybe I will get some air." A new resolve came over me. There were plans to make, and I quickly remembered that I was the only one to make them. The inn's work seemed ridiculous compared to the work that needed tending here. Bud would likely absorb into himself; Myrtle and Preacherman would help, but it wasn't their place to see to this. I took a deep breath, kissed Lishie's forehead, and walked out to the porch.

Though I should have been, I was somehow unsurprised when I found old man Tsa Tsi sitting on our porch, hands on his knees, looking to the trees. I sat down beside him, rubbing my eyes. "Good morning," I offered weakly.

"Sunale," he returned. He turned to look at me briefly, then back to the trees. "I'm sorry about your lishie."

"Thanks. When did you hear?" I wondered if they had awoken Tsa Tsi even before me.

"Oh, just this morning. I came by looking for Edgar and met Preacherman on the steps here. Wouldn't have bothered y'all had I known she was ill."

"You're not bothering us." I leaned back on my hands and tried to breathe in the morning air. "How long has he been missing?"

"Not sure. It's hard to know. Couple of hunters said they think they heard him last week, so I wasn't too worried. But sometimes people like to think it's Edgar when they're scared in the woods. It's better than thinking something else is tracking 'em. I haven't seen Edgar myself in a good month or so." Tsa Tsi shook his head. "Some kind of master I am." He turned to me again. "I can't rightly remember the last time I saw that monkey. Ain't that terrible?"

I nodded, more for myself than him, and trailed my eyes over the treetops as he had been doing, beginning to search the branches myself.

Tsa Tsi sat up and pulled a Skoal can from his pocket. He jammed a wad deep behind his lip, then offered the can to me. I took a small pinch. I had tried it before, but was never partial to chewing tobacco. It smelled too much like Bud.

"You know I used to sit on this very porch with your dad?" Tsa Tsi rubbed his fingertips, flecked with bits of tobacco, together. Their roughness made a soft swooshing sound. He crossed his legs high and tight, causing them to appear even more thin than normal.

"Oh, yeah?" On another day, I would have shown more interest, but I couldn't muster the energy to hear more ghost stories so early in the morning, especially this morning.

"Yeah, before the war. Shoot, long before you were even born. Used to sit right here with him and Bud both. Lord've mercy. Those two boys were wild in their youth." He wore a faint smile, as if we were traveling into a place of peaceful remembrance.

"Really?" Thinking of my father and Bud being young and wild made me feel even older than I was—like I had somehow surpassed that phase in my own life. Maybe it was still ahead of me, but it didn't feel like it.

"Yeah. I've never seen two brothers so close. Lots of brothers are close, but those two did everything together." He nodded. "That's a special kind of bond."

"Hard to believe that now," I muttered.

"Why's that?"

"Don't see much of my dad in Bud."

"How old were you when your father died? Four or five months?"

"Not even that."

"Yeah, things look a lot different when you are around to see for yourself."

I turned my face toward him. "You telling me that my father was a bastard like Bud?" The anger was welling again and I did not want it to overflow onto Tsa Tsi.

"Lord, no!" he protested. "I'm just saying Bud's not always been like you see him. Used to be a real fine young man—wild, but respectable. War changes people."

"Sorry, Tsa Tsi. It's just real hard for me to believe that."

"I know. I'm used to people not believing me." He smiled. "Heck, how many people you think believe I have a pet monkey?" We laughed together. "Those three were just about joined at the hip before you came along," Tsa Tsi continued.

"Three of 'em? Who?"

"Your dad, uncle, and mother. They grew up together and Lishie had taken in your mom like one of her own. Everybody always knew your mom would marry one of 'em, but I figured she'd find a way to marry them both."

My stomach churned and I was unsure whether it was his words or the tobacco juice escaping down my throat.

Tsa Tsi read the disgust on my face. And smiled. "You know, you might want to give Bud a chance. I know he's hard. And you sure as hell have to wait until he's on the level, but he's not evil." He uncrossed his legs and leaned on his knees. The air felt hotter, wetter. Morning birds rhythmically called to each other.

"Not sure I believe that either."

"Your lishie loved him. Your mother loved him. And your father especially loved him. You might try to see what they saw." He let his hands slide back and stretched his back erect with a groan.

"Lishie and my father had to love him. And I have a real hard time seeing how my mother would even like the man that led the father of her only son to his death if she'd been alive to see it."

"That what you think?" Tsa Tsi stood and leaned on a post, spitting into the dust below.

"That's what I know." I scooped the tobacco from my lip and flipped the wad onto the ground.

Tsa Tsi sighed. "Well, I better go find this damn monkey." He started down the steps, then stopped and turned to me. "Again, I'm sorry for your loss. She was a good one."

I nodded. "Thanks. Good luck finding Edgar. I'm sure he'll turn up." I thought about telling him where I thought I'd heard him last, but knew it wouldn't help after all this time. I wasn't mad at Tsa Tsi for what he had said. But it crawled all over me, and I needed more air than the porch was offering. We'd have to tend to Lishie's sittin'-up and burial soon enough, but first I needed to shed a least a layer of my feelings. I knew just the place to do it, too. I called back into the cabin through the screen door, "Be back shortly!"

Myrtle hurried to the door. "You okay, son?"

"Yeah, I just—"

"And where the hell you headed now?" Bud's heat stumbled up the steps behind me.

"Out."

"We've got arrangements to—"

I didn't let him finish. I took off in a sprint, or as close as I could come to a sprint, through the woods.

I did not have Edgar's overhead leaf-turning to follow this time, and I was approaching from a totally different direction, but there was no question where I needed to go in that moment. Even though I had only been there a couple of times (several fewer than I had told Essie), the waterfall seemed far more familiar and consoling than anything home had to offer now. I ran faster than was wise on unfamiliar terrain, especially given the awkwardness of my gait. I stopped three times to gather my bearings, but finally found the rushing water, the enigmatic cave, and the cool basin pounded by the cascade's force. My skin was slick from sweat and the heat sweltered around me the deeper I went into the woods as the morning humidity rose all around. But I could feel the cooling breeze floating on the surface of the water, so instead of stopping and wading into the water or beneath the falls, I pulled off my shirt in mid-run and splashed into the pool, falling to my knees on the muddy bottom. My pants absorbed the water and began weighing heavy on my legs. I fell onto my back and dipped my head into the water. I drew air deep into my lungs and pushed it back out again, trying to breathe four directions of wind back into a life, and this time that life was my own.

I might have lain there the remainder of the day had I not had an overwhelming feeling that someone or something was watching me from just beyond the water's cascade, or perhaps even inside the cave. I sat straight up and craned my neck to see what or who might be behind me, but I could not see anything. I stood, having to pull my left foot into proper supporting position as the mud made me quite unstable. My heavy work pants were made even heavier by the water. I tried to bleed the water from them by squeezing the sides, but had little success. Slogging my way out the water, I kept a careful eye on the cave.

A thick oak log had fallen and made a makeshift bench by the pool. I backed over to it without letting the cave out of my sight. I didn't hear anything except the waterfall. But my gut ached with the feeling of another presence that had no other place to hide except the grotto. The sun was starting to warm the deeper part of the woods where I was, and my body was already losing the coolness it had retained from the water. I shook my head. I needed to dry out the pants before trudging back home in them, so I peeled them from my legs and laid them beside me on the log as the sun made its way through the tree leaves onto them. At least I was wearing boxer shorts. I figured that I had an hour or so before someone came looking for me. I just hoped no hunters were still out from the night before. I slid down the curve of the log and rested my back against it. My eyes stung. I closed them, inhaling deeply, and opened them again on the exhale.

That was the moment that I heard the first break in the water. Its rhythm had been so consistent, if not monotonous, but now there was a different pattern of splash. I froze, straining to see if this emerging mass of fur was the same mother bear that Lishie and I had seen, but I couldn't tell and there were no cubs around. It was entirely possible that the cubs were inside the cave, but this bear behaved unlike most mother bears. He moved with no concern for anything or anyone else around. He pulled his head back from beneath the falls and made his way around to the pool. I saw a large patch of matted fur on his left flank as he turned toward me. I wondered if a hunter had shot him or if another animal had attacked him.

Thankfully, he ignored my presence. He struggled over to the water's edge and bent down to drink. Periodically he raised his head and looked off into the distance, but he didn't seem to be on the alert. After some time, he pulled his body into the pool with his front paws and sat in the mud. The clear waters churned with a mix of blood and silt. He appeared to gather even more strength and began to thrash in the mud, rolling onto his back and digging his head into the water.

I have seen bears most of my life. I've seen them walk on all fours, stand like men on two legs, and swim across lakes. I've seen them resting and asleep. But this was the very first time that I had ever seen a bear wallow in mud as if he were a farm pig.

I reached for my pants and glanced at my shirt nearby. If I were going to flee, this would be the moment, when Yona was too preoccupied to notice. Thankful that the waters must have washed the "man" off of me, I realized there was a decent chance that he did not smell me so nearby. I was optimistic, but not certain. I pulled my shirt on and fastened the buttons. There was no way that I would be able to pull on wet pants without fumbling, so I clinched them in my hand, hoping I could find a safe spot on the way home to squeeze back into them.

Fear set me back down as soon as I began to rise. The bear stopped his roll and rose onto all fours in the pool. He shook his body as a dog would, sending water flying. He huffed a deep breath and then sauntered out of the water and climbed back toward the cave with no sign of a limp. I struggled to glimpse his left flank again, trying to see the extent of his injury, but saw nothing.

As he entered behind the waterfall, I watched as the cascade purged the bear's blood and agitated mud from its pool. By the time the bear disappeared, the water was completely clear. I had a strong desire to follow the bear. I wanted nothing more than to go with him into the cave, figure out if it was his home or just a resting spot in his likely large self-proclaimed territory. I wanted to examine his leg, understand if it had truly healed in that moment as it had appeared to. I wanted to journey with him deep into the cave and see if we came out clear on the other side of the Smokies.

But that was an adventure I was not destined to make. The wind blew, tree limbs danced, and I was distracted by what sounded like Edgar. I resolved to follow the bending limbs as long as they led me in the general direction of home and leave the bear to walk on alone. I stood and ran as quickly as I could back toward the cabin.

When I reached home both my morning tears and saturated work pants were dry. I had almost forgotten the heavy feeling of the cabin's porch and the almost smothering heat of its interior. Familiar and less familiar faces swarmed inside, heating pots, pouring coffee, chopping vegetables, and slicing cakes.

Grease
Lilies
Tobacco
Vanilla
Fresh dirt
Pine sap

"Cowney." Myrtle pushed her way past the women in the kitchen, her wide hips relentlessly clearing the path. "I'm glad you're back. You and Bud need to make some decisions."

I nodded. I knew Myrtle was trying to be helpful, but every word from her mouth twisted my heart tighter. "Okay," I said. "I need to wash up first."

"He's in with Lishie."

Knowing that simple fact motivated me to wash and dress quickly. Lishie needed someone else watching over her, anyone other than Bud.

Myrtle facilitated every detail of Lishie's sittin'-up, service, and burial. Bud and I nodded through the selection of dress, color of bandana, the quilt that she would be wrapped in, and the simplicity of a pine box from a Bryson City lumberyard. We chose passages from Ezekiel and Psalm 121 because we all knew Preacherman would read them anyway. When the choices became difficult, Bud deferred to me, not out of apathy, but out of deference. I accepted the permission gracelessly. It came so unexpectedly.

"Who will the pallbearers be?" Myrtle looked to Bud, who immediately turned to me.

"Whatcha think, Cowney? Obviously us, but who else?"

I suggested a couple of men from church, he offered the names of two cousins, and the decision was made.

"You boys need to think about a tombstone or some kind of marker. Maybe have someone to carve dates. As long as you know where the grave is, it should be fine. Tombstones are expensive."

"I've got some money saved from this summer," I offered.

"No," Bud interrupted. "You should use that money how you intended to. I'll find the money for a proper stone for her, no matter what I have to do."

I was so exhausted that I didn't even notice this change in Bud until Myrtle proclaimed, "Os-ta. Okay. I think that is all. Thank you both. Lishie would be proud of you boys."

I turned to Bud and saw that a look of peace was spreading across his sober face and that he was looking at me. As difficult as it was to accept, I think Bud was actually proud, and proud of someone other than himself.

The day continued with a constant stream of deliveries, both of people and of the essentials of death. Each one accompanied by its own distinct smell.

Grease
Lilies
Tobacco
Vanilla
Fresh dirt
Pine sap

Myrtle and the other women had dressed Lishie and tucked her hair neatly into a new red bandana Tsa Tsi brought from town. He, Bud, Preacherman, and I had lifted Lishie's stiff body into the fresh pine casket lined with the quilt from the foot of her bed. She had always been my soft place to land in life; feeling her heavy rigidness in death seemed unnatural. Lishie had always held me in comfort. To hold her, any part of her, now felt like detached manual labor and made me nauseous. Myrtle had taken the quilt from my bed, unwashed of my night's sweat, and tucked it around Lishie's body and beneath her arms, folding her hands once more on top. The casket was lifted and moved to the center of the living room for the entirety of the night. I stood beside it, hands clutched in front of me, for several hours until I lost feeling in my feet and my head pounded from greeting those who came to pay their respects.

As the sun fell behind the mountains, the screen door screeched open in steady rhythm. Folks were getting off work, or leaving fields, or bringing by the remnants of that evening's supper. My exhaustion led me to an unsteady rocking chair by the fireplace, still close enough to the casket. Mourners would greet Lishie's body, shake my hand, and find a warm plate of food. Bud and Myrtle milled about, carrying on thankful gestures and sighs and hugs and back pats, depending on whether it was Myrtle or Bud offering. I must have dozed off periodically, because I do not remember half of the people churning through our home that Myrtle commented on later. I do, however, remember the moment the screen door creaked open so slowly that it sounded like something shattering. And I remember how she peered around its edge, cautious and nervous. And I remember the tall soldier, still in uniform, standing behind her, propping the door open further so that she might be encouraged to enter.

She was beautiful, and I hated that she was beautiful. Her loveliness splintered the sadness of the home, leaving threatening shards at my feet. The two entered the living room, attracting the unabashed stares of everyone in the room. I half expected Lishie to sit straight up in her casket to take in the odd sight.

It's hard to describe what the sight of her made me feel. I had far from forgiven the coldness she had shown me at the inn. The image of her and Andrea still haunted me so deeply that I thought it was slowly becoming a part of me. Seeing Essie Stamper standing in my living room was surreal. She entered my past uninvited. It was all well and good that Essie had come to know the Cowney I wanted her to know; I had carefully shielded her from the Cowney that my father and my mother had created, that Bud had created, that a twisted left foot had created. But now she was here to see the Cowney that Lishie had created, and I needed her to see him, too. Everything that happened at the inn suddenly seemed so unimportant, but I recognized how utterly weak it would have been of me to embrace her like nothing had happened, like she could treat our friendship with as much disregard as she wanted if it was convenient for her. I was tired—too tired to show her my hurt, and yet too proud to welcome her with anything other than a cold stare.

Peter moved past her as she froze in front of the casket, staring at the floorboards. "Cowney, I'm sorry for your loss," Peter began. "We're sorry." He turned and nodded to Essie. She looked up nervously and produced a half-hearted smile. "She wanted to come and . . . well, I knew she didn't have a ride. I hope you don't mind."

"No. Thank you." I reached out and shook Peter's hand. "I'm sorry. I left in such a hurry that I didn't realize I was leaving her stranded."

"I can stay the evening and take her back in the morning, or I can come back after my next shift to fetch her?" he asked me, as if I were now responsible for her. Realizing this, he turned to Essie. "What would you prefer?"

She began to speak, but I interrupted her. "I'll take her. If it's okay with Lee and Mrs. Parks. I will bring her back after the funeral."

"I'm sure it won't be a problem. I'll make sure Mr. Jenkins and Mrs. Parks know your plans." I could tell Peter felt uncomfortable in the room as he waved off my offer for him to sit, eat, or have a cup of coffee before he left again. He only scanned the room, as if deliberately trying not to see it, glancing sharply to his periphery without moving his head. "No, thank you. I appreciate it, but it's best I get back on the road." He shook my hand another time. I was relieved he chose to leave. He stiffened an already stiff room.

"I told him I could hitchhike, but he wouldn't hear of it," Essie said, sitting on the hearth beside me.

"Thank you for coming," I responded. "You didn't need to—"

"I know. I wanted to." Essie turned to me and laid her hand on my shoulder. She searched my eyes. "Cowney. I am so sorry. I know how close you were to her."

I tried to speak, but my throat tightened. Essie was likely the sixtieth person who had offered condolences that day, but hers sounded different to my ears. It wasn't the words. The words were the same. I didn't want to cry in front of her. She still did not deserve that from me after all that had happened. I wondered if she understood exactly what she had done or if everything, every emotion, resided within me alone. I wasn't sure she was really sorry about what she needed to be sorry about. Sometimes it's just something people say when they don't know or don't want to say anything else.

"Who do you think you are?" Our awkwardness was broken by a commotion on the front porch. We walked toward the screen door. I heard Bud's voice first, but it was in competition with another man's.

"Do right by that boy." The white man flung a pointed finger in my direction. He looked familiar, like the kind of familiar you know from photographs or crowd scenes.

"It's none of your business." Bud turned his back to the man. "Who called you anyway?"

"Someone's gotta speak for your brother."

"You have no right—"

"Why? You think you have all the rights to him? Shit. You've always thought that, haven't you?"

"Get the hell off our property."

I wanted to quiet Bud, remind him of the solemnity of the day, but it was clear he was too far gone, maybe had already started drinking again.

"It's not your place to tell me to leave." The man was walking over to me now. I sat back in the chair. "Son, you can tell me to leave. It's your house now, too."

"Mister, I'm sorry. I don't even know who you are."

"I served with your father and your uncle." The man shot a glare at Bud, who had lit a fresh cigarette. "I just wanted to pay my respects, see if you need anything. I ain't blood, but if you ever—"

"Oh, go on." Bud blew the command out with the smoke.

"Son, you call if you need anything." The man pulled a card from his wallet and handed it to me. He nodded to Essie and walked down the steps, as Bud turned and went back inside, allowing the screen door to slam shut.

I followed Bud into the kitchen and tried to appear calm by pouring a cup of coffee. "And what the hell was that about?" I whispered.

"Just another white man that thinks he knows everything," Bud mumbled.

"He said he served with you and Dad."

"He did."

"Was he there when—"

"Yeah," Bud acknowledged. "But he doesn't know what he thinks he knows. I'd like to know who the hell thought to call him."

"But he knows something." I held out the card he had given me. "Maybe . . ."

Bud grabbed the paper from my hand and held it up to the butt of his cigarette.

I knocked the card and cigarette from his hand. Coffee splashed, searing my skin.

Just another secret I will never know, I thought and left the half-charred paper where it had landed in the sink.

I stood silent in the kitchen looking defiantly at Bud, who refused me eye contact. I held the cup of coffee in my hand and let its heat nearly burn my hands.

"Let's get some air." Essie was beside me. Her whisper broke my gaze.

I agreed, more willing to leave with someone who had blatantly and swiftly broken my heart than stay with the man who had slowly and selfishly broken my will.

I set the cup on the kitchen table, plucked the scrap from the sink, and tucked it into my pocket before Bud could notice. I ushered Essie out the front door. Mourners in the living room certainly took note of the scene, but were too polite to stare or interrupt their vigil.

Essie was likely unfamiliar with my area of the woods, and she had already taken the first step, so I motioned for her to follow me. I knew exactly where I was going, even though night shadowed the forest before us. Had I not been so tired, emotionally and physically, I probably would not have chosen to lead a young woman through dark woods to the waterfall and the cave beneath it that housed an injured black bear. But this was my choice. No one could advise me or betray me there. Essie had to trust in me on the journey, even if I could no longer trust her. After replaying the image of her and Andrea a million times in my head, I wanted to replace it with an image of my choosing—of Essie and me at the water.

"Where were you?" I gathered the courage to ask as we made our way down the beginnings of a trail I hoped to wear away between the cabin and the waterfall.

"What do you mean? I had to finish my shift—"

"No. Last week. I didn't see you at breakfast."

"Oh. I didn't make it to breakfast much." Essie dug her hands into the pockets of her cotton dress and feigned interest in the treetops.

I sniffed a laugh. "Well, I know that."

She must have been comforted by my laugh and shot me a look. "Okay, Cowpie. Didn't know you were keeping up with me."

My face warmed. "Well, I mean after—"

"Geez, I had to follow you all the way back to Cherokee to find you. Where have you been? I must have checked 447 a dozen times. You owe me a rematch in dominos. Don't think I'm going to let you crown yourself champion that easily."

I smiled. I couldn't help it. I wanted to be cold, reserved, indifferent, but I never could be any of those things with Essie. Maybe I *had* made too big a deal out of the whole scene, the letter. Maybe we had just missed each other after all and she wasn't avoiding me. I couldn't stand it anymore. I stopped and grasped her elbow, turning her so that we faced one another. "You know I kept putting you off, right? Bringing you here." I looked up at her, my smile subsiding as hers grew.

"Yes, I know! Why?" From the curiosity in her eyes, I knew she had no inkling of how I really felt, and in that moment, with Lishie now gone, I needed someone still living on this earth to know how I honestly felt. I think I needed to hear myself say it, too—to admit I still wanted to believe loving someone was a possibility. "Tell me."

"I was afraid I would kiss you." The words didn't sound like mine. I couldn't pull them back, as badly as I immediately wanted to.

The pause that came next grew a canyon between us. I so desperately needed to hear her say: *I wanted you to kiss me, though. I want you to kiss me now. Hard and long, soft and sweet. Kiss me like I am the last person you will ever kiss.*

A breathy sigh rose from Essie's chest. And I couldn't distinguish whether it was a sigh of pity, like when someone sees an injured animal limp away, or if it was a sigh of relief and release—that she was somehow grateful that some boundless truth had finally been revealed.

But I couldn't bear to wait for her to distinguish. I opened my mouth to deny or twist or do whatever I had to do to change what I had just said.

Essie placed her hand on my arm. "Cowney, I'm sorry that I didn't tell you about Andrea. I thought I was protecting you."

"Protecting me? From what?" I thought I knew what she meant, that she was protecting my heart, though I had no intention of admitting that to her.

"Protecting you from the soldiers, management. I know I'm not supposed to be with a guest, and we both know if I got caught, I'd be gone. And we both know they'd send you home as well if they found out you knew about it."

I had not expected her to say that, to think that was the only thing she should protect me from. I was surprised at how it saddened me that she could so easily ignore my feelings. And still, it was an easy excuse for her. It made her reticence look courageous.

"You should have told me." I pulled my arm away and faced her eye to eye.

"I know. I'm sorry. I just—I just wasn't even sure how long it would last. And I do care about you. You're my best friend. But Cowney, I want you to know it's worth it."

"Worth it? Worth nearly getting us both fired?"

"I mean—that is why I wanted to keep you as separate from it as possible." Her eyes dropped from mine. "So it wouldn't affect you. I just mean it's worth it for me. I've never felt this way about anyone. I'm sorry—it would have been lovely to kiss you at the waterfall. I'm sure of it, but I think this place is meant for another girl—a really lucky girl."

I knew she was telling the truth about Andrea. She likely hadn't felt that way before. But the words of Andrea's letter were still fresh for me and I knew, out of jealousy or not, that this relationship was most certainly not a "first" for him. At that moment I knew that I needed to set aside my own broken pieces. It would not be long before hers would mingle among them and there was nothing either of us could do to stop that. I needed a friend and she would likely need one soon as well.

We made it to the waterfall just before nightfall. Clouds and the returning smoke periodically concealed the moonlight. Dusk rustles reminded us that we were far from alone, yet still inconsequential to the life of the forest. Tiny pops of lightning bug bulbs dotted our path. I chose not to tell

Essie about the bear, fearful that she might be too scared to stay. I would not be able to explain to her how I knew that the bear was no longer inside the cave. I just knew somehow that we were the only two beings there.

We swam, fully clothed, under the moon's watchful gaze, which fought its way through the stubborn overcast, and we reclined on the same log where I had that morning. My work clothes were still filthy from earlier, as I hadn't had time to pack any clean clothes, so I didn't mind the opportunity to wash them as I swam. Essie's summer dress skirt floated up periodically with the water's ripples, forcing her to modestly pat it down. As the moon glowed soft in the distance, we talked about family, the inn's gossip, my attempt to speak Japanese, and our theories about what Bud and the stranger had been arguing about back at the cabin.

"There's one thing I've learned," Essie offered. "There's something about war buddies that ties them together forever. It's not friendship, exactly. It's almost like they're bound by blood or something."

"You know many of your brother's buddies?" I asked.

"Sort of." Essie shrugged.

"What do you mean, sort of?"

"He sent a letter not long after he left. He mentioned a few guys, where they were from, how swell he thought they were. So, I guess I kind of picture what they look like, you know. But I've never met them. Probably won't."

"He's not serving with anyone from home?"

"No. He was at boarding school when he enlisted. Guys from all sorts of different reservations, but none from home. In fact, he didn't mention that anybody else from school was in his unit either."

"He'll probably come rolling in here with them when it's all over. Heck, couple of them may even give old Andrea a run for his money once they lay their eyes on little sis."

Essie blushed. "I don't expect so." She looked down at the ground.

"Why not?"

"He's not coming back here."

"Oh, gosh, Essie. I didn't know. I'm sorr—"

Essie looked up again. "Oh, no. It's nothing like that. He's not dead or anything." She laughed. "That sounded terrible. I just mean that he already told us that he wasn't coming back from school either. Said he was moving to a city when he graduated. Chicago, maybe."

"I see." I scooted my feet in the dirt. "Can't blame him, I guess," I said.

"Yeah. I guess."

"It's just so hard to get by around here. No matter how hard you're willing to work. Shit. Between the two of us, Bud and I can barely afford a headstone for Lishie."

"Are you going to have to use your school money?"

"Don't know yet. Bud's got this plan, too. He wants me to try to sell bear parts for him."

"Why you?"

"It's who he wants to sell to. Thinks the Orientals, the Japanese in this case, would buy them for a pretty penny. Use them for medicine or something."

"What do you think? I mean, we're not supposed to even really talk to the guests, let alone trade with them. Is that why you're trying to speak Japanese?"

"Yeah. But I wouldn't even have pursued it if this hadn't happened."

"You be careful. After all those stories you told me about missing children and bones, I can't help but wonder if someone didn't just cross the wrong path at that place."

"Ah, I was just storytelling," I assured her.

"There's always at least an ounce of truth in storytelling. Sometimes I wonder if you haven't seen more than you tell me."

"Me? I'm the absolute last person to know anything. I mean, look at what you've been getting yourself into."

Essie blushed. "Yes, but he's the only one I've spoken to. I don't know. I just trust him for some reason." She paused for a moment to knead her toes into the ground. "Anyway, I get it. I can see why you'd take the risk. You really should make sure you can still afford your schooling."

"You want to stay around here? I mean after college. Or you heading straight to New York?"

"I'm not sure. And I don't think I'll be going to college either. So yeah, probably I'll be around . . . Well, unless Andrea has other plans." She raised her eyebrows.

I forced a smile. "Why do you not want to go to college? I thought that was your plan, why you were working at the inn and all."

"It's not that I don't want to; I just don't think I can. Since my brother left, my family . . . Well, the money is just not there to send a daughter to college. And while I appreciate a little pocket change this summer, it won't likely cover the cost of books, let alone tuition."

I wondered if Essie was telling me the whole truth. I wondered if meeting Andrea had changed her mind about college. Both reasons were plausible. "Well, hopefully this summer will do it for me. I can't wait until I don't have to see that son of a bitch Sol anymore."

"Really? He's been giving you a hard time still?"

"Yeah, he's just a fathead. Thinks he's better than me or superior because he's white, but he has the same job I have. I don't think even Lee likes him as much as he pretends to."

"Oh, Cowpie, don't worry about Sol. He keeps giving you a hard time, you just ask him about Carol."

"Carol? The redhead you work with?"

"Yes, that's her. Sol has a real crush on her. Haven't you noticed him following her around in the dining hall? He's like a silly puppy dog."

We laughed together for a bit and let the air easily fall into a peaceful silence. Stars occasionally darted through the parted canopy, and we tried to keep count of unspoken wishes we were both collecting. I'd never seen so many falling stars in one night's sky; then again, I can't remember spending so long in patient wait looking upward.

As the morning descended around us, I knew that I needed to get back, but as each minute passed, I became more and more resistant to move. Essie could tell from my sighs and increased fidgeting.

She broke the silence after some time. "What's bugging you, Cowpie?"

"I don't want to go home. Too many people. Bud's probably got a whole list of chores for me by now."

"What is it between you two?"

"He's hated me since the day I was born."

"Now, I find that hard to believe."

"It's true. If Lishie were here, you could ask her. I think he blames me for both Mom and Dad dying."

"How so? Didn't you say that your mom died just after your birth? You couldn't have helped that. And your father, Lord have mercy. That was war. That certainly was not your fault."

"I know. I didn't say it made sense."

"Maybe you just remind him of them. I mean, look at how he treated your dad's army buddy. Seems like he has a real problem with reminders of his past."

"I guess that makes sense. You know he wouldn't even write to Lishie during the war? After the funeral, he wouldn't even talk about what happened to Dad. Wouldn't answer anybody's questions."

"What kind of questions did they have?" Essie asked.

"Just details, you know. I mean, I guess we know the basics but . . . I just can't picture what they say happened."

"Why not?" Essie scowled inquisitively.

"Something to do with the shots and who was where and why."

"That sure does seem like more than 'nothing,'" Essie prodded.

"The guy he was trying to save was a sleepwalker," I began. Essie leaned into me, really listening to the words I formed, piecing them together from memories of Lishie and the letters. She listened as I told her everything I knew. When I finished, she leaned back on the log and nodded.

"The army recovered the two guns?"

"Yes."

"Now I know why you have questions and why Bud's not saying much about it."

I wondered if she thought the same as I did, but was afraid to confirm my own questions with her suspicions.

She didn't wait for my prompting. "You said he was a sleepwalker? The soldier in the barbed wire, right?"

"Yes," I nodded, knowing now that she was thinking the same as me. Sleepwalkers don't carry guns and they don't survive gunfire waiting to be rescued.

She shook her head and sighed deeply. Heaviness blanketed us both. We didn't speak again for a long while. Instead we rested, exchanging harmonized breaths.

CHAPTER EIGHTEEN

Here is what I remember of Lishie's funeral:

Grease
Lilies
Tobacco
Vanilla
Fresh dirt
Pine sap

Except this time, this ceremony, I remember one more thing: Essie. I remember her sitting beside me. I remember turning my face toward her when the sunlight pierced down over the grave, temporarily blinding us all. I turned toward her instead of Bud, who sat on my left side. And as I choked down tears that seemed to rise up from my gut, my chest heaving in the struggle, I remember Essie taking my hand in hers.

We buried Lishie that morning high on a hillside, beside my father and my mother, beside two open spaces awaiting Bud's and my bodies. There were no other graves around. I thought of what Essie told me about her mother not getting to choose who she was buried next to. I thought too of Watkins Cemetery, close to Bryson City. How other Cherokees elected to continue to share the cemetery with whites, blacks, and those of their own blood. Graves side by side. How those of each respective community came on Decoration Day at some unspoken agreed-upon hour so that they could honor the graves separately. I thought of how their souls would mix all the same. How their blood and bones and flesh would dissolve and evaporate together. I wondered if Essie might choose to bury her mother there, just for spite. I wondered where I would choose to be buried if I could. Would it be among the purest of familiar blood on this hilltop, or could I make one last attempt to improve my bloodline in shared soil?

This hillside cemetery was not so much formal grounds, like the churchyards of neighboring towns, as it was a return to unspoiled earth. A lost traveler might one day even mistake it for a collection of nondescript stones haphazardly placed in the middle of nowhere in particular. Birds chattered on perimeter limbs as if disturbed by our intrusion. But as Bud knelt down, still clutching the shovel he had used to cover the casket with dirt, and the ladies in boldly colored headscarves sang "Amazing Grace" in our language, I had never felt such a holy order surround me. Bud's shoulders shook as he sobbed, head lowered. His grief was startling. It overtook my own so that I was left to stand in awe of this shared loss with a man I felt I had never shared anything with before. Other than the singers and Bud's wet gasps, I heard no human voices until Preacherman's words came into focus, "For dust thou art, and unto dust shalt thou return."

As we walked back down the hill, Bud came up behind me and grabbed my right shoulder, almost causing me to trip into Essie, who led the way. "We need to talk, Cowney."

"I know," I responded, still trying to make my way down the hill. "But I need to get Essie back to Asheville soon." Essie turned, hearing the mention of her name, but chose to walk faster, offering privacy for Bud and me.

"She can wait. We have a lot of decisions to make." Bud released my shoulder and walked beside me.

"I thought we'd made all of the important ones."

"Cowney, you can't run away to Asheville from this and hope everything just gets sorted out."

"What? Run away from what? From you? From that old cabin? From Cherokee? I think all those things will be just fine without me."

Bud turned and blocked my path. "Cowney. Dammit, son. Listen to me. There are other things we need to talk about. Things you need to know." He was sweating heavily and breathing hard.

"What? Your damn bear huntin'? I'm not going to be your errand boy. I tried. Ahh. Never mind. It can wait until the summer ends." I brushed past Bud. "Tell you what. I promise that we'll talk before I leave for school."

"School?" The word froze Bud.

"I'm going this fall." I reminded him that Lishie sent off for the applications before she could confirm that I could not enter the service, her insurance that she would not lose another boy to war. But even as I said it, school was beginning to feel like an impossibility. I still didn't even know how I could afford it. I left Bud standing alone and walked home.

Back at the cabin, Essie waited for me on the front porch steps. "Cowney, I really can find—" she began.

"No. Just give me a second to pack some things. We'll leave shortly."

"Okay." She smiled, resigning herself. "I'll go ahead and make us some sandwiches for the road. I don't want to stop on the way if we can help it. I'll meet you at the car."

I packed a clean set of clothes Myrtle had prepared for me, knowing I only had work clothes at the inn and that I would not be back to Cherokee on any more weekend visits until the job ended. I packed two books, *The Great Gatsby* and *The Sun Also Rises*, considering I might leave them in room 447 or trade them for two already on the shelves; and I pulled the bone, still wrapped in its bandana handkerchief, from my bottom bureau drawer. I did not pack it in the suitcase, so I could easily show it to Essie as we drove to Asheville.

Bud did not protest as we pulled out of the driveway in the Model T. I imagined he would spend the day there, thanking well-wishers and cleaning up half-eaten dishes. I imagined that Myrtle would help also since Bud was never much one for cleaning house.

I looked briefly into the side mirror and watched him trudge up the porch steps and disappear through the open door. Then he and the cabin were lost to me within the blanket of smoke. Lishie was lost to me. Never again would I find her there, darning a quilt or stirring a pot of beans. Never again would she wait for me to return.

CHAPTER NINETEEN

The weeks that followed my and Essie's return to the inn seemed like time rewound, with only a few minor changes. Essie and I continued to retreat to 447, where I placed the bone on the fireplace mantel in a place of honor. I was so thick with grief over Lishie, I found myself holding vigil with the bone. So far from her grave, I needed somewhere to speak to her in private, stolen moments. Staring at the bone in 447 afforded me that short-lived solace. Essie found me there more than once, red-faced and bleary-eyed. Her interruptions were just about the only thing that motivated me to numbly carry on through daily tasks. She continued to see Andrea, who had at least stopped staring at me every time I passed, though he rarely spoke more than a few words of greeting when Essie was around, and not at all if she was not. In a strange way, I missed the hard stares from Andrea. At least they were a sign that I posed some sort of threat to him and his relationship with Essie. I liked believing he might be jealous. I wondered what she had told him to quell his suspicions and what he would think about our time in the room together. Was I less to her as well? I also worried that she would bring Andrea to the room, that he might even stake his claim there; but I was too afraid to ask, too afraid to start an argument and unbalance the peace we had created.

Lee and Sol continued to be Lee and Sol, and I drew fierce power in the name of Carol when Sol fell into a mood or got drunk. Peter joined Essie and me for some of our meals, especially breakfast, when the other soldiers weren't up yet to invite him to their table. A time or two, Essie and I discussed taking Peter to the room, but thought better of it. He still had one foot in each world, theirs and ours, and we decided there was not much to gain from showing him. He would likely have to report its existence as a matter of security anyway.

Essie was ecstatic when I told her that Peter could wrangle us a canoe. I did not tell her of my original intention of going without her to make her jealous. A few days after my return to the inn, Essie, Peter, Carol, and I made our way to the confluence of the French Broad and Swannanoa Rivers.

When we arrived at the designated spot, I snapped the first picture of the outing—my three companions for the day standing side by side with paddles raised. Peter and I unloaded the canoes and the girls spread out blankets for our pre-race picnic.

"Okay, we've decided our teams," Essie announced.

"Girls versus boys," Carol said as she placed strips of bacon onto a slice of bread.

"Well, that's not fair!" I interjected.

"What are you saying, Cowpie? We can't handle the big bad river by ourselves?" Essie mocked.

"That's not it at all." I shook my head. "It's not fair that the two of you get to be together. We all know you ladies cheat!"

"How you figure?" Carol asked.

"Oh, don't play innocent, Carol. We all know you broke poor Sol's heart when you went out with that townie last week. Once a cheater, always a cheater." I shielded my body from the inevitable fists headed my direction.

"Well, sorry. It's done. Put on your big-boy knickers!" Essie jibed.

"Yeah, and hold on tight!" Carol added.

It's not important who won that day, at least as far as I am concerned. What is important is how free we felt—so far from the fences of the inn. Before that summer not a one of us knew each other. I can't even say Essie and I really knew each other. And I think if we had stayed at the inn, we never would have really known each other either. I mean the kind of knowing that comes with neutral land. None of us were in *our place*. We were all just visitors. There was no inside knowledge, and as much as I teased Carol, no one had the advantage. The girls' boat was lighter. Our collective arm strength was greater. Nature's rapids decided the outcome for us.

When we had raced twice, losing both times to the less than humble ladies, we lay on the bank talking for hours. The sun warmed us, eventually forcing us back into the river to wade waist deep.

I took so many photos that day that the film stopped just like Lee said it would. Back at the inn, I ejected the film and tucked it into my suitcase so I would be sure to have it for development the next time I returned to town. I walked Essie back to her dorm in the fading light. The air had cooled, sending goosebumps across my sunburned forearms.

"You meeting Andrea tonight?" I asked, trying to be casual. His name still shredded every nerve in my body.

"Yes. He promised a picnic dinner on the grounds." She ascended the steps to her dorm then paused, turning to face me.

I looked at her, confused. I couldn't believe she'd be so bold.

"I know. We'll be careful. I think he has a place picked out in the tree groves, near the fence line. The guards will be at dinner in the hall before the evening shift. We'll still have to wait until dark, though . . . and eat pretty quickly. But I'll let him figure all that out."

Essie seemed to always allow Andrea to take the lead, make the plans. She never allowed anyone else the same responsibility.

"I think he might ask me to go with him."

"Go where?"

"Back to Italy, silly," Essie smiled, reaching down to jab my arm.

"Oh, really?" I couldn't look at her when I spoke. I didn't want to see her excitement.

"Can you imagine? Italy. It must be beautiful."

"Well, probably was at one time. Not sure how it will look after the war."

"Italy has to be lovely. Of course, any place is better than Cherokee."

She might have been right, but I couldn't help feeling defensive. I had spent the whole summer running away from Cherokee, trying to find a way never to be stuck there, and yet to hear her say this, well, it felt sacrilegious. I wanted to tell her not to speak that way of our home.

"So you're definitely going if he asks?"

"I think. I couldn't even imagine him leaving without me."

"So you're sure you're not going to college?"

147

"This just seems more likely."

I was beginning to hate how sickeningly optimistic Essie could become when talking about Andrea. Nothing else in the world brought out such naiveté in her, and those moments were probably the only ones keeping me from falling so deeply in love with her that I couldn't make my way out again.

"I hope you're right, Essie."

"Oh, Cowpie. You truly can be such a rain cloud." She shook her head. "Don't you worry about me. I'll be fine." She paused for a moment before reaching for the door. "Say, how about I fix you up with one of the girls?"

"Oh, no!" I protested.

"Well, you need to find you some kind of distraction before the summer ends. Otherwise you'll go back home to chasing monkeys and avoiding Bud."

"I guess you do have a point." I shrugged. She took a step back down as I stepped up, allowing her to kiss me on the cheek as had become our routine. Oh, how I prayed for poor aim just one time!

That evening, I lay on my cot unable to sleep. I knew it was just about time for Essie to sneak to the fence line with Andrea, and the image of him spreading a blanket on the grass and proposing their future agitated me. Lately, it was unusual for me to struggle falling asleep, as the day's work in the heat was exhausting. What was more of a challenge was staying asleep.

Lishie visited my dreams most nights. Sometimes they were comforting, as if nothing had changed between us. Sometimes they were terrifying, accusatory even. She would plead with me to save her life but no matter how I tried, I could not. I never dreamed of Essie, probably because she was still a part of my reality. But I did dream of the waterfall and the wounded bear, and sometimes I dreamt of the mother bear and heard her scream. Those were the nights that I awoke in a sweat. The sound was so real, so deafening in my ears that it took several minutes of wakefulness for the ringing to dissipate.

The night that Andrea met Essie by the fence line, I was dreaming mother bear dreams as my mind fell in and out of consciousness. I tried to shake myself back into reality, but presence of mind was losing badly to the physical exhaustion of my body. The bear would be rooting by the roadside at first, like she was digging up grubs or roots or something, and I would find myself outside the car watching her. When I turned back to the car, Lishie would be gone. I'd turn again to the bear and ask, "Where'd she go?" The bear would look at me like I was stupid and then rise up on two legs, screaming so loudly that my whole body shook, so violently that when I awoke from the fear, my cot still vibrated. I lay there for a few moments until I realized that I could still hear the scream . . . except that the scream was not a scream, it was a siren . . . and the vibrations were coming from the heavy boots of soldiers running across the pine floorboards.

Drill? I wondered, though I hadn't remembered the guards responding so alertly to drills in the past. I sat up in my cot and looked at the workmen who were also awake, confused.

"What's going on?" I called to Lee, a few cots over.

"Not sure. The siren woke me up."

I got up and walked outside just as Peter rushed by. "Lieutenant. Franks!" I called to him. "Lieutenant! What's going on?"

"Must be about the guest that went missing," he stopped to whisper. He likely saw the fear on my face because he quickly confirmed for me, "Not Andrea. It's a young girl, a daughter of one of the diplomats. They must have a lead. That's all I know. Go back to sleep," he instructed and then continued toward the other gathering soldiers. I hadn't heard of a missing girl, besides the vague rumors I heard prior to coming to the inn. But when I thought about it, the guards had been acting unusual. This hadn't been the first siren. I imagine the powers that be were in no great hurry to admit they had lost a prisoner.

"What'd he say?" Lee asked as I returned. All of the workers were looking at me now.

"A little girl is missing. One of the guest's daughters."

"Oh, there'll be hell to pay," Sol grumbled sarcastically. "God forbid something happens to one of those brats."

"Shut up, Sol," Lee scolded him. "You boys try to get some shuteye. Nothing we can do and I'm sure this doesn't mean we get a holiday in the morning."

I lay back down and closed my eyes. I pulled the pillow around my head, but only managed to slightly muffle the wail of the siren. I remained in that position for nearly an hour, I guess, until the siren wound down and I dozed off, waking what seemed like only minutes later to the sound of Lee's alarm clock.

With the first clang of tiny hammer hitting the brass bell, I sat straight up and swung my feet onto the floor. Along with the other men, I dressed and headed for the dining hall. Periodically, the siren would blare and subside again.

A guard in front of the dining hall met us. "Good morning, gentlemen." He spoke to us as a group. "As you are probably aware, we are on high alert this morning. You are not in danger, but please let me remind you that when you hear the siren, you should consider yourself on lockdown wherever you are. If you are outside, please proceed to the nearest building until you are released."

Who's the prisoner now? I wondered as I made my way past him into the dining hall. Essie was not inside, though her friends were. Carol avoided eye contact, but the others made note of my entrance. "Where's Essie?" I mouthed to one of the girls.

She shrugged and whispered a worried "We don't know."

I pushed back from the table. The morning breakfast smells were nauseating. *Had they found her and Andrea while they were looking for the girl? They wouldn't have expected guards.* I decided that I had to go look for her. I made my way to the inn's main building, trying to concoct a plausible reason for doing so should one of the soldiers swarming across the property stop me.

I climbed the large rock steps and entered the front entrance with as much false confidence as I could muster. Surely Essie would be with Mrs. Parks if she were in trouble. I turned in the direction of her office. I had no idea what I was going to say if I found Essie there, but I wasn't going to leave her alone, as surely Andrea had. I made it only halfway down the hall before I saw her. Essie was alone. I was grateful. Likely the other drama of a missing child had taken more of everyone's attention. When she saw me, Essie took off in a sprint toward me. My heart leapt, grateful she was relieved to see me.

"It's okay." I reached out to embrace her. "Are you okay? What happened?"

She stopped short of my arms and looked at me. Her eyes were red with tears. "You read it, Cowney. I know you did." Her face was sharp and exacting.

"Read what?

"My letter. I wasn't going to say anything when I noticed it was put back in the wrong place. I thought I could trust you. First you go and read my personal . . . I can almost forgive that, but then you share my secrets? How could you tell them—"

"Okay. Okay." I tried to calm her with my voice. "You're right. I shouldn't have read it, but if you think I told anybody—"

"How did they know where Andrea and I were? That I would be with him? Did you set us up? Could you really be that jealous of what we—"

"I never said a word to anyone . . . I mean, Peter knows about you two, but no one else unless it was one of your girlfriends."

Essie shook her head and then stopped cold, raising her eyes to mine. "Oh, Cowney. I was mad. I thought you had—" Essie's eyes flooded with tears. "I told them about the—" Her voice shattered. "I didn't think they were connecting you to this. I didn't know a girl was missing. They were asking if we'd seen anything out there. And I remembered what you told me. I just told them about the—and then they—I mean, it was a child and they said you might . . . It was too late for me to explain."

Even all these years later, I will never forget the way her eyes met mine. How they grew as if she thought they might form around me in some protective encasement. There was guilt there, but the kind of guilt that ripens from sorrow and innocence, still dewy from the realization. She was altogether responsible, yet by no definition was it intentional. And at the very moment that I was recognizing this, so was she. Her mouth remained closed because, I imagine, she knew it caused what was about to happen to me, and what was about to likely happen to her. My skin grew cold.

There was no time. She had told the soldiers about the bone; that was a certainty. Had she also confirmed my attempts to carry out Bud's business? They would fill in the blanks themselves: one missing child plus one bone plus one brown-skinned day laborer equals conviction, both in the judicial and the spiritual sense. If they even bothered to separate the two.

I nodded, closing my eyes briefly in order to avoid hers.

She leaned forward as if she might speak, but I turned away before she could. No one, certainly not Essie, could protect me now. I had never been in trouble, not with anyone other than Bud. As soon as I knew that I couldn't do what the other boys could, grow up to serve as my father and my uncle had, my sole duty was to keep my head down and bring home a decent wage. Now her words stripped all of this away. Committed it to the forgotten.

I heard people talking down the hall. English voices. Not the guests. The guests, by now, had a sixth sense about the rhythms of the inn. They slid quickly behind the large oak doors when the pressure grew and the soldiers began to churn. I had seen this only a couple of times before, but their movements were divergent on "lockdown days," the only days I was expected inside the inn myself. A distinct siren roar and the guests were out of sight, out of mind.

And now, the loud speaker sounded its warning again, an unscheduled demand for retreat. I wished I'd thought to do the same as the guests, or that I even could do the same as the guests, and found an alcove of respite. I intentionally spent as little time as possible inside these walls, thinking that would serve me well. So, at this moment, the irony was thick. The long hall spreading out before me was disorienting.

Of course, I could have stayed. I could have waited for the questions, the accusations. I could have taken a breath, prepared my responses. We almost always have choices in moments like these. But I don't remember choosing. I don't remember options, other than which way to run. So my body ran, with or without my mind—with or without my heart.

I was moving too fast to read the directional signs, though the room number ranges would have meant nothing to me. I could find my way out in the open air or find 447. Both options seemed unlikely as the buzz of voices converged from every angle.

"I saw him go this way," the first discernible voice bellowed.

"Step it up. And you two, head to the main gate!" boomed from farther away.

I ducked into a recess and crouched out of sight of the hallway, bringing my knees right up to my chest. I was struck with the thought, odd as it may sound, that I was no different than Edgar—far from home, crisscrossing a foreign landscape, running from something or for something, neither of which I knew. Was I as free as Edgar or as tamed as Edgar?

From where I squatted, I could see the sun break through the clouds and stream through a series of lead-lined, poured-glass windows framing the alcove. I was on the second floor. Two more up and I could reach the room. Two floors down and I could run the maze of the basement, a space I had entered periodically for storage supplies, where there would be fewer eyes and a hope of making my way outside. If I were seen, then I would have to make a third choice. But for now, no one, save Essie, could confirm that I was running from anyone. There had been no eye contact, no shouts of "Stop!" or "Wait!" to indicate they knew I had seen them.

I wondered if Essie might meet me in 447 or if she was still standing as I left her. More than anything, I did not want to include her any further in this moment. I didn't want to consider what the guards would do if they found us in a room together. Conspiracy is far more criminal than whatever it was they suspected me of. I hoped that Essie had gone to the room to wait, though I feared she had most likely sought consolation from Andrea. That was far more likely, in fact. Still, the secret room didn't breathe—there was no alternative exit without the likelihood of running into a guard. Once I entered, or we entered, there was no leaving until nightfall. I could not stand the thought of being trapped alone, or worse yet, being trapped with the one person who betrayed me in the one place I thought we would always be safe.

Peering out from the protection of a corner wall, I watched as two uniformed guards raced past me toward the end of the hall. They moved with such single-mindedness they did not notice me. I located an EXIT sign only a few feet away. A louder murmur was closing in. I darted across the hallway, flung my body weight into the door, and almost tumbled down the staircase when the door opened far more easily than I expected. As much as I wanted to run down the stairs, I was careful to mute my steps and pause before exposing myself to the open landings and then, finally, I reached the basement.

I made my way through an open door into the cool, dim light of the inn's dual cellar and bomb shelter. Hazy light seeped in from the high slit windows bordering the ceiling. I felt as if I were walking into a wet blanket, slowing my escape to a standstill. I smelled the sharp twang of peeled onion remains buried inside three large trashcans. The earthiness of potato peelings mingled among the translucent membranes, and my subconscious mind questioned if I had actually wandered into Myrtle's kitchen.

All this because of a bone, a trinket of boredom-born obsession. Not only was I now likely a suspect of some heinous crime, but also Essie and I could never again return to who we were to each other. I wondered if she regretted sharing our secret or was grateful that it had distracted the authorities from her and Andrea's secret.

In truth, had Essie begun to slip away weeks ago? Each time she uttered Andrea's name, I could almost see the divide between us grow. My stomach ached. *Had she given them my name to save Andrea? Was this an effort to prove some sort of loyalty? How safe was anything I had told her?*

Those thoughts were unsettling, but not as much as the final question that purged me from the basement. *How safe was anything she had told me?* I could not be caught because I was not sure I could protect Essie's stories if questioned by the guards. I was not as strong as the POWs Bud talked about, not as strong as my father. I waited a moment on the top step leading out to the exterior storm doors, listened for any sign of life on the other side, and slowly inched the cellar door upward. More daylight peeked in; I blinked as my eyes painfully adjusted.

I could hear a bird: such a sweet, simple chirping it nearly convinced me that it had all been a bad dream. If I could just drench myself fully in the sunshine waiting outside, I would awaken in a kinder, simpler world. I pushed the door further, barely enough to squeeze my body into the open air.

No one direction was better than the other. There was no escape. I might have been standing in a Smoky Mountain resort, but it was no more than a prison camp wrapped in periodic strands of barbed wire and trigger-happy sycophants. Each edge of the property was just as exposed as the next. It was time I prepared myself to be questioned. I needed to make sure my story was clear in my head, even though every ounce of it was truth. It had to be clear to the soldiers. I reasoned that it might be useful to appear to be working if caught. It would be difficult to explain why I was not inside the inn during the lockdown siren, but perhaps I could formulate a story around finishing my work. I eased back into the basement, searching for my alibi. There were brooms, rakes, and shovels. I found stray two-by-four boards and broken light fixtures. Each item seemed unrelated to any work I could possibly be doing or else too closely resembled a weapon. I reached for a rake, a tool practically useless in the summer months, but my eye was suddenly drawn to a glisten in the far left corner of the room. Three silver paint cans were haphazardly stacked upon one another. Dried drips of white paint stained the sides. I grabbed a can and brush.

I made my way back to the exterior steps and eased the door open as carefully as I had the first time. I set the bucket and brush just outside, then slid out the doors, slowly lowering them behind me. My view to the shed was still clear, so I hurried toward the west end of the property, to the place where I had first found the bone. The soldiers would most likely secure the property exits, leaving this area to the last of their checks. I had to go quickly, but not suspiciously, because if seen, I could not appear to be running. The guilty run.

I used the great oaks peppering the property as protection. I clung to each one of them as if they were life preservers. The air vibrated with the siren's pulse, but all other sounds were drowned, with the exception of my footsteps and pounding heartbeat. The grounds were pocked with shallow holes where shrubs had been redistributed or rodents had burrowed. I had learned early on where they were, but now I seemed to stumble into every one. The bucket swayed in my hand, and I prayed the lid was fastened tight so as not to leave a trail of paint behind me. As soon as I could see the brush pile, a marker I had chosen to leave when I first found the bone, I checked my periphery and shot toward it. I knelt beside the nest of branches and bark, setting the paint can and brush beside me. I sifted through the loose wood, running my hand across the rough, veined bark. I hoped both that I would find more bones and that I would find nothing. *What evidence would prove me innocent? Maybe I could unearth a grave marker or woodland creature's skull—anything that would complete the story for the soldiers before they completed it on their own.*

In short order, I recognized the absurdity of the scene I had created. There I was, kneeling at the edge of wilderness accompanied by whitewashing tools. Military guards swarmed like bees all around the perimeter. I was a wayward child playing in his yard while the tornado siren warned of impending doom. I could almost hear Bud's disgust closing around me. *Can't even keep your mouth shut and mind your business. Have to go and piss off a buncha white folks with guns.* A gray squirrel almost knocked me over in surprise as it leapt from one branch to the next above my head.

I pulled aside a large rotting log, causing a family of three tiny field mice to dart toward the fence line, as desperate as I to save their own lives. Their exit exposed a small hole, and inside I could almost—

"Stop what you are doing and stand up, slowly," Lieutenant Peter Franks's voice was clear, close, and unsteady. "Stand up, Cowney."

I reached for the paint can, causing Peter to pull out his sidearm and point it.

"Okay, Lieutenant. Easy. What's this about?" I stood slowly and raised my arms. I was a poor liar, but Peter seemed too nervous to distinguish truth from fiction.

Peter walked toward me. His right foot caught in one of the many hollows and he struggled to regain his balance, eager to keep his gun aligned with my chest. "Colonel just wants to ask you some questions."

"What about? Can I put my hands down now?" I hoped my confidence would outweigh his apparent influx of authority.

"Yes . . . but leave the can." Peter pointed at it with his gun. "It's about the missing girl. That's all I know. You need to come with me."

"They haven't found her?" I hoped ignorance might put him at ease, but I immediately regretted it since he surely knew everyone on the property was now aware of the reason behind the siren's continuing alarm. "Okay. Okay. Just put that thing away." I walked toward Peter, still showing my palms, careful to maintain eye contact.

He nodded. Peter's eyes briefly hinted at reluctance, but Lieutenant Franks quickly took over. He holstered his gun and grabbed my right elbow, escorting me back toward the inn.

Peter and I walked in silence, both doing our best not to arouse the gazes of the workers or guests. As we neared the main entrance, Peter grasped the back of my right arm and began leading us toward a row of army vehicles.

"Where are we going? I thought you said that Colonel—"

"Keep your mouth shut. Colonel's busy right now. We need to take you to a secure location until he returns."

"Secure location? What are you talking about?"

I shook my head and chose not to speak to Peter until we returned to the inn, entering the main building together. White curtains inched open as I was led beneath the guestroom windows. Peter had radioed ahead, so by the time we reached the inn's lobby, several soldiers greeted us, heavily breathing and sweaty. They seemed to share in some sort of communal victory. The alarm had wound down to silence in my absence, and maids emerged as if no time had passed, utterly indifferent about beginning their work again. Another soldier flanked my left side, and two more fell in behind us. We walked down the west-wing hallway and into a small lounge.

"Sit here and the colonel will be with you shortly," Peter robotically offered.

I did not share Peter's definition of "shortly." I sat in that room, too terrified to move, for several hours. I was not offered food or water, not that I could have brought myself to consume anything other than fear. I wanted to cry. I wanted to scream. I wanted to scream like the mother bear and silence the voice in my head. *Why had Peter done this to me? Why had Essie done this to me?*

As cold as Peter had been, my stomach still grumbled with disappointment when he left the room, effectively signing me over to an ever-changing rotation of three nameless uniforms standing in the back of the room and a higher-ranking uniform yet to arrive. I sank deep into a maroon leather club chair facing a dormant stone fireplace. Above the fireplace hung a grand, regal portrait of General Andrew Jackson. President Jackson, others would likely rather say, though I'll always see him as a leader of war rather than diplomacy. He glared outward, toward some unknown point of interest high above my head. Along with my seat, two other matching chairs and a small, similarly finished couch surrounded a rectangular coffee table made of cherry wood. The table was bare, except for a book and the twinkling shadow figures cast from the chandelier fastened from the ceiling above it. Tall bookshelves lined the walls, showcasing colorfully leather-bound volumes of science, law, and literature. I scanned the titles and authors, hoping one would be familiar, but knowing that would be unlikely. The room was pristine, yet still smelled of dust and old paper. This space was intended for drinking and bullshitting before the army took over. I imagined it was still often used for those purposes, though I doubted I'd be offered a shot of whiskey on this day.

A uniform cleared his throat.

Another cracked his knuckles.

The third passed in front of me, under the resolute gaze of Jackson.

A clock ticked from high on the bookshelf.

157

My mouth went dry. My shirt grew wet from sweat.

Finally, the door behind me creaked open. I heard the shuffling of papers and the three uniforms snapped to attention, then disappeared beyond my periphery, presumably out the now open door.

"Mr. Sequoyah?" It was the colonel's voice, calm and deep. "Did you hear the warning alarm today?" He walked around to face me.

"Yes, sir. I'm sorry, sir. I assumed it was a drill and I was behind in work this morning."

"Is that so? And were you also aware that a child has gone missing?"

"I'd heard something of it." Half truths were easier to cover.

"Something . . . Hmmm." He paused, staring curiously into my eyes so directly that I couldn't resist looking away. "Listen, son. You are going to have to be more specific. What exactly *do* you know about the missing child?"

I felt my face flush. "Well . . . I heard it was a little girl . . . a guest's daughter. Heard she just up and disappeared a couple of days ago. That's all I know. I didn't connect the two. The siren and the girl. Why was the siren just now—"

"You're here to answer questions, not ask them." The colonel turned away from me. He unbuttoned his front shirt pocket and pulled out a cigarette and a lighter, shaking his head. He lit the cigarette and inhaled a long drag. "Cowney. I know that is not all you know. We've scoured this place in here"—he waved the cigarette around his head—"but I have a feeling that little girl is not in this building. And if she is not in here, well, she certainly passes through where you are assigned to work. One thing I know for sure. You can't trust a goddamn Indian. So don't think for a minute I'm just going to take you at your word."

What I wanted to say was: *And how come your men didn't see her? It was their job to see her!* But I didn't say that. I just sat there and hung my head. I knew I looked guilty. "Sir, I don't know anything," I barely whispered. I raised my eyes to meet his as he faced me again.

"Now, Mr. Sequoyah, I understand you're a good worker. You mind your own business for the most part." He was pacing now. "But we're talking about the missing child of a foreign diplomat during wartime. Now, I also understand that your affliction keeps you from serving your country with your peers, but there are other things you can do to be of service. I want you to think real hard about the last few days. I want you to remember *everything* about those days. You don't want this to turn into some international incident, do you?"

"No, sir."

"Tell me about the bone."

I thought about denying I knew anything of any bone. But then I thought about Essie. She had clearly given them some information, and my denial would either land me further in trouble or place blame on her. At least he wasn't asking about my attempt to sell bear parts, not unless he thought the bone was bear. "I found a bone when I was gathering branches on the property."

"And you didn't think it was important to tell anyone in authority?"

"No, sir. It was earlier in the summer."

"Know a lot about bones do you, son?"

"No, sir."

"See, from where I sit, it sounds mighty convenient that even though the army is just now hearin' about this bone you found on this property, you claim to have had it for quite some time."

Given his lean, I knew I had to ask. As much as I didn't want to utter her name even within earshot of these uniforms, I had no choice. "What did Essie tell you? She knows how long I've had it."

"She told us you showed it to her just the other day for the first time."

"Well, yeah, that's true, but I told her about it a long time ago. If it had anything to do with that missing girl, don't you reckon it'd be more than just a bone? There'd still be flesh. The bone was clean. You said she went missing just a couple of days ago. That's not even enough time for a body to decompose."

"I'm going to warn you just this once to use a little more respect when you refer to the child. She is the daughter of a diplomat, you know."

"I don't mean any disrespect. I'm just saying that it doesn't make sense that the bone I found has anything to do with this."

"Any reason why your *friend* would have thought you with a bone was important for us to know about? You give her any other reason to suspect you might be involved?"

I had been launched into a nightmare. "No."

"Have you made friends with any of the diplomats? Maybe got a little chummy with some of the folks on your break? Tried picking up a new language in your spare time?"

I shook my head defiantly.

The colonel rose, picked up the remainder of his cigarette, and took one last drag before extinguishing it. "I see." He nodded at me. "I see." He walked toward the door behind me. "Wait here and don't move. We have much more to say to you."

I did as I was told, moving only to rub my palms down my thighs, trying to dry the sweat that now flowed uncontrollably and to shift to the couch to avoid the sunlight piercing my eyes through a slight break in the curtains. The door closed softly behind the colonel, only to burst open again minutes later. I heard two hurried sets of footsteps enter and move toward me on both sides of the couch.

CHAPTER TWENTY

Over the course of the next several hours, a steady flow of men in uniforms proceeded to question me. I tried to speak as little as possible, but found it difficult to control my tongue. I succeeded fairly well until Peter returned. He came to sit with me while the others took smoke breaks, or lunch breaks, or whatever it was time for in the world of those who could choose. I lost track of time.

"Peter," I pleaded. "You know I had nothing to do with this."

He didn't answer, just paced the room.

"You said the girl has been missing for a couple of days, right?"

No answer.

"Well, why are you just now looking for her?"

Peter stopped and turned to me. "They've been looking. There were a lot of theories at first, but yesterday evening, a guard found a purple ribbon. That's when they thought there might be foul play. You know we have to consider everything."

"So how do you go from a ribbon to worrying about a bone?"

"Cowney, it's not me. I'm just doing my job. You've been seen talking to guests before by other guards. And good Lord, Cowney! Trading with the Japs?" *So she had told them about that.*

"Okay, how do *they* make the leap?"

"They didn't until they found Essie. Cowney, she was with Andrea again. After hours. Out near the fence line. Guess they realized more was going on than they knew about."

"Did you tell them about Essie and Andrea?"

161

"No. I mean—I just kept my mouth shut. Did as I was told. They would have found them anyway."

"And Essie told you I had something to do with the missing child?"

"Listen, Cowney, you've been a good friend to me, but I can't say anything else."

I could almost see Essie offering every bit of information that she could to protect Andrea, to protect her future with Andrea.

"Don't be too hard on her, Cowney. Those guys can be pretty convincing. She didn't accuse you. Just mentioned the bone, from what I understand. And how you thought about selling gallbladders. They've not found much on that, though. She must have thought she was helping."

"Peter, I know exactly how convincing those guys can be. I'm the one who has been sitting in a room with them all damn day."

"Alright. That's enough." Peter grew cold. "I'm not even supposed to be talking to you." He turned back toward the window and resumed his pacing. I didn't like this version of Peter. Even his face seemed dimmer, emptier than before.

"Is Essie okay?" I asked, ashamed that I still cared.

"Yeah, they cut her loose as soon as she gave her statement. I haven't seen her, but Colonel hasn't mentioned her anymore."

"And Andrea? They cut him loose, too?"

"Sent him back to his room. Probably going to speak with his father about catching him out on the property so late."

"But he's no longer a suspect?"

"I don't have any reason to believe that he is."

"You have reason to believe I should be?" I asked pointedly.

Peter breathed deeply. "Cowney, we just want to find the girl or find out what happened to her. The Feds are asking questions and Colonel Griggs is furious."

I rubbed my face with my hands and dropped my feet back to the floor. I reached for a book lying on the coffee table, the cover of which had been torn off. Peter shot me a quizzical look as I flipped through the pages, hopeful there were pictures, charts, or illustrations of any kind to give me a single moment's escape from the reality of the situation.

The door was slung open, startling us both.

"That will be all for now, Lieutenant." Colonel Griggs waved off Peter. Peter did not look at me as he exited the room.

"So, Mr. Sequoyah. We need to see the bone now."

My skin felt hot. Essie might go to 447 with Andrea—then they would be caught together . . . not that that should even matter. It would be her mess to clean up. The soldiers would close the room forever, or worse, open it for their own pleasure, exploring it as if it were their own. It would become their discovery of literature, amusement, and artifacts. They would likely nail golden numbers, "447," into the wooden door, ordering it among all of the other doors already under surveillance. "It's not much. I just ask that when all this is over and you know that the bone has nothing to do with the girl, you will return it to me. It's worthless, but well . . . I don't know. I just want to hold onto it."

The colonel's frown broke. "If your story shakes out and the bone means nothing, we will return it. But let's not get ahead of ourselves, okay?"

I nodded and proceeded to tell the colonel every detail of how to find the room, the key, and the bone inside.

The office had no fan, and though the curtains were drawn fairly tight, with the exception of the seam incapable of shielding off the piercing thin line of sun, the air grew thicker by the minute. I unbuttoned the first two buttons on my shirt, and then feared that the colonel would take this as a sign of guilty nervousness, so I buttoned them back. I stood and paced the room, eager to churn some semblance of air, but only achieved working up more of a sweat. For several moments I just stood and stared at the godlike portrait of Jackson and studied every detail of his garb. I looked hard into his eyes, which refused to look into mine. *Was a general higher ranking than a colonel? Essie would know.* For the life of me, I could not remember. The only soldiers I really knew were my father and Bud, and neither of them held any significant rank, as their service was short-lived. Jackson looked tired. His skin was gray, stretched across his high cheekbones, his wild hair popularly considered distinguished due to its graying sophistication. I thought of how he had betrayed John Ross, a distant relative of mine, as Lishie told it. How Ross saved his sorry life at the battle of Horseshoe Bend, and Jackson repaid him with the same kindness Hitler was now affording the Jews. Maybe they left me with Jackson on purpose, had given him the orders to finish me off.

No fresh air entered the room until the door was heaved open again, and two soldiers flanked the colonel as he entered in a huff.

"Sit down," he ordered.

I couldn't understand why he looked so angry, why he had not brought the bone in with him. His hands were empty. I did as I was told, sitting back on the couch. The two soldiers stood on each side of me and looked straight ahead. Peter was not one of them.

"Now that you've wasted our time, Sequoyah, let's cut the bullshit. Where's the bone? I know you people do all kinds of godforsaken things with human—"

"What?"

"Is it part of some sort of sacrifice or conjure or some—"

"Sir?" I practically whimpered. "I don't understand. I told you where to find it."

"What you did was send my men and myself on a wild goose chase while you had some extra time to figure out the next lie you were going to summon up. We went to the room you sent us to. Hell, the goddam key was exactly where you said it was. But there was no bone. We turned the place upside down."

"It should have been there, Colonel. I left it on the mantel. It has been there for weeks."

"There was nothing on the mantel, son. It's time to come clean. You can't keep this up."

"I swear," I whispered, and my voice rose from my core. "I swear!"

The colonel shook his head.

"Colonel, I can honestly tell you that I have no idea where it is. But I also know that you won't or can't believe me. So, please, let me make a phone call."

The colonel laughed. The sound echoed coldly throughout the office, maybe throughout the entire inn. I could feel the tears rise again. "A phone call. Sure!" he cackled. "Go right ahead. Call anyone you want to, but who the hell do you think you're going to call? I've seen your file. You've got no family. And it seems as though that friend of yours, that Essie, isn't too keen on helping you."

"Yes, sir. You are probably right. But please, let me make one call and you can keep me here as long as you like. Ask me whatever you want."

"Oh, we are going to do that anyway. Seems like you forgot this is wartime, son. Not like you get to lawyer up on this one. But . . ." The colonel stuck out his lower lip as he pondered the request. "I don't see harm in it. Maybe whoever is on the other end of the line can talk some sense into you. Go ahead, there's a line out over there." He pointed to a phone on a corner desk in the room. "You've got five minutes."

As the colonel closed the door behind him, I pulled the card from my pocket and unfolded it. The name had faded, but was still legible. The other information was clear somehow, even though it was a stranger's name. Faded ink spun itself into my only lifeline.

> Jonathan Craig
> BG—U.S. Army, retired
> Special Agent
> Federal Bureau of Investigation

I dialed the operator and read off the number listed at the bottom of the paper. My heart felt as though it had ceased beating as I listened to the tonal ring. One. Two. Three. An "Ello" interrupted the fourth chime. "Elllooo?"

"This is Cowney. Cowney Sequoyah."

"Are you okay?"

"No—" The tears welled again. "No, I don't think I am."

"How can I help?"

His response immobilized me. He hadn't asked what I had done or how much trouble I had caused. He just wanted to help.

"I'm at the Grove Park Inn. I've been working here this summer and there's been an incident and they think I . . . There's a missing girl . . . diplomat's daughter, and they think I might have something to do with her—"

"You sit tight, son. I'll be right there. Don't say another word to them." The phone clicked.

When Brigadier General and FBI Special Agent Jon Craig walked through the door after what must have been less than an hour later, the colonel's face turned the same dull shade as Andrew Jackson's. I did not know the first thing about Craig, save two very important facts: he had served with my father and he wanted to help. The only other important detail in that moment was that I desperately needed his help.

I was still new to all of this army protocol jargon, so I expected Craig would salute the colonel or vice versa, but that is not at all what happened.

Craig spoke first. "Griggs, you asshole. What in the hell are you doing?"

"Sir?" the colonel responded, confused by the presence of the general. "I . . . we . . . Mr. Sequoyah is—"

"What's this about a missing diplomat's child?"

I was taken aback by Craig's knowledge of the situation. Perhaps because he was a current agent or perhaps the men out front told him. Peter surely would if he had seen him on his way in.

"We're handling it, General."

"Looks like you're harassing a kid to me." Craig crossed his arms and frowned.

"Sir—"

"What evidence do you have to hold him?"

"Testimony of another worker."

"That Essie Stamper?"

"Yes—"

"The one you found with an Italian diplomat's son after hours?"

"Yes, but—"

"That's enough, Colonel. That's all I need to hear. If that is all you have, I will be taking this boy with me."

"But—"

"Don't worry your pretty little head," Craig snapped. "Consider him in my custody until things get sorted out." Craig turned to me. "Get up, son. The colonel's done with you."

"Now, you just wait—" Griggs reached for my arm.

"I don't think you want to put your hands on a civilian, Colonel." Craig stepped in front of me. He nodded to me to make my way toward the door. Softening his posture minimally, Craig continued, "Colonel, I'm not about to make this situation any worse for the bureau or the army than it already is. When you have a good reason to talk to him again, I will bring him in myself." Craig turned and met me at the door. "Let's go, son. Best we get you off property as soon as possible."

CHAPTER TWENTY-ONE

I followed Jon Craig down the hall as if I had known him my whole life. Whether it was the heat, the barrage of questions I had just faced, or the stress of it all, I am not sure; but whatever it was, it left me in a foggy state and I desperately needed someone else to lead the way. I was grateful to be able to follow Craig. As we approached the main entrance, a semblance of awareness was shaken loose.

"Wait!" I think I startled Craig with my abruptness.

"What is it?" he questioned.

"I need to take care of a few things first."

"Okay, but we need to get you out of here before Griggs changes his mind."

"I understand, but I need to at least tell my boss and need to grab my car keys from the dormitory."

"We'll leave a note at the desk for your boss and you won't need your car keys; but if you need to grab some clothes, you've got time for that. I need to make a call anyway."

"What do you mean I don't need my keys?"

"I'm driving you to Cherokee. Well, at least to the next county. Hopefully, your uncle will meet us there."

"Bud?"

"You have another? I sure as hell would call someone else if I knew of somebody."

"No, I mean, Bud probably won't come get me."

"Let me handle that. Anyway, if he won't meet us, I'll take you the rest of the way if I need to."

"But my car. I can't just leave my car."

"They won't let you take it, Cowney."

"Do they think I will run?"

"Probably. That and if they keep it, they know you'll come back for it."

"It may be best anyway. Essie would be without a—"

"Wow. Now that's something. Essie? That's the girl that ratted you out, right? That's what I was told."

"Yeah." I hung my head. "I know. But I can't just strand her here."

"She'll be fine. Go get your things. We'll leave the key up front here, too."

When I returned to meet Craig with my sweetgrass suitcase and duffle bag, I scribbled a quick note and handed it, along with my car keys, to Mrs. Parks. Craig didn't love the idea, but agreed that it was better than handing it over to the colonel.

"Did you get ahold of Bud?" I asked, unsure of the answer I wanted to hear.

"Yes. He's meeting us near Clyde."

"Okay." I nodded. "I'm ready."

"Good. Me, too," he agreed.

When Craig's car safely passed through the gates of the estate, I rolled down my window, allowing new air to finally fill my lungs. "Mr. Craig?"

"Yes." He focused on the winding drive down to the main road.

"How'd you know Lishie had died?" I had to know who had called him, how he managed to hear and make the trip to Cherokee in time for the sitting-up. It was obvious he was a busy man. I couldn't imagine that a man I'd never seen my entire life would just drop everything to express his condolences in person within the same day of a person's passing.

"I didn't," Craig responded, a hint of regret in his voice.

"Then why were you there?"

Craig smiled as if recalling a fond memory and turned to me briefly before focusing back on the road. "Lishie called me a while back. I hadn't talked to her in a very long time, so I'm not sure how sick she was when she called. She sounded older than the last time we spoke."

"What did she want? Why did she call?"

"She asked me to come talk to Bud. She always worried about him. Was afraid he was getting money some way he shouldn't. She also wanted me to meet you. Said you were about the age your dad was when we served together. I told her I would stop by, but I had no idea what I was walking into."

"So you and Lishie have kept in touch since—"

"Ever since your father sent the first letter home from the war. I saw him writing to his family and asked him about y'all. He told me about you, showed me the picture they sent him when you were born. And he talked all the time about Lishie and your mother. Of course, I knew Bud. After your father died, I wrote to Lishie. We corresponded until after the war and then when I was sent to Asheville to work, I looked her up."

"How come she never told me about you?"

"I can't answer that, Cowney. She's the only one that could have told you that."

"Maybe because Bud doesn't seem to be your biggest fan." I let out a short laugh.

"Well, that certainly is true. But don't be too hard on Bud. He's been through a lot. That's one of the reasons I wanted to talk to him at the sitting-up. I've been pretty hard on him myself."

"When was the last time you saw Bud before Lishie's funeral?"

"The day he shipped out back home." Craig squinted, the sun bearing down hard on us as we topped the first of many hills.

"Lucky you."

Craig seemed to ignore my last remark.

"You hungry, Cowney? Craig reached awkwardly behind him and retrieved two Cheerwines and a bottle opener from a cooler. "This do the trick?" He smiled and handed me a bottle.

"What's this?" I took the bottle from his hand and eyed the label.

Craig swerved carelessly as he popped the metal cap from his bottle and then reached over and did the same for mine. "You've never had Cheerwine?"

"No, sir. I don't think I have ever even seen it."

"Well, I just don't believe that. It's made right here in North Carolina. Salisbury, I think. Gatling gun, Krispy Kreme doughnuts, and Cheerwine. The best of everything right here in our backyard."

Craig's backyard was not mine, as much as he apparently thought so. Still, the fizz and sweetness of the soda revived my body. Craig regained a steady line on the road and nodded to his briefcase at my feet. I pulled a sandwich from inside. "Want half?" I offered.

"No, thanks. Eat up."

"So you just keep a cooler full of sodas on your floorboard?"

"Nah, I was headed to do some fishing this morning."

I looked out the window and thought about saving half of my sandwich anyway. I was doubtful there was even any food in the house. Myrtle might come check on me if she heard I was home, but that would likely be it. I couldn't count on Bud to take care of anyone other than himself. Eventually, my hunger and road daydreaming must have overcome any worry of future hunger because long before we reached Clyde, the sandwich was reduced to tiny crumbs in my lap and the Cheerwine vanished from its bottle.

"You heard much about your dad?" Craig broke the silence. The question was almost startling, as I had preoccupied my mind with thoughts of the waterfall.

"Umm . . . not really. I only know what he looks like from the photo Lishie had of him in his uniform." That wasn't the whole truth. There were bits and pieces peppered throughout my mind, mostly disconnected specks from many different accounts. In that moment, I remembered one other thing as I tried to look back into my past. I remembered his gray skin—another constructed memory, of course. He must have been in the casket. His eyes were closed. His skin was so gray. I didn't tell Craig this. He surely didn't want to hear *that* about his friend.

"Must be hard not knowing him, huh?" Craig nodded, turning his head to look out his window periodically. "Must be real hard some days."

"Yeah, I guess so. I don't know. Sometimes I think I just got used to it. Didn't know anything else. Might have even been better that I was so young. Less to miss."

"At least you had Lishie and Bud."

I thought back to my father's gray skin and pulled my memory back as if retracting a zoom lens, struggling to see more. From my faux memory's angle, I could make out Lishie standing beside the casket, younger then, her hair still black, crying . . . no, weeping . . . violently against Bud's

170

shoulder. In another moment, they seemed to melt into each other, pouring themselves into an intertwined heap on the planked floor. I couldn't remember another time when I had seen them embrace. Maybe that is why I created the scene for them.

"Yes, sir. At least I had someone to take me in."

"Does it bother you if I talk about your father, Cowney?"

"No. I mean, it's hard sometimes, but I like to hear stories about him. Do you have any stories?"

"Oh, yeah!" Craig smiled, laughing heartedly. "I've got some pretty good ones. I'll have to tell you them when we have some more time."

I was disappointed. I thought we had plenty of time for a story or two.

"I'm not sure when that will be, so I think there are some other things I should tell you while I can." Craig's tone grew serious. He arched his back, as if to stretch it.

I sat silent, bracing for whatever might come next.

"I don't mean to lay a bunch of heavy stuff on you, son. I know you've been through hell already today."

"It's okay," I reluctantly offered.

"You were the last thing on your father's mind when he died."

Something about that thought unsettled my stomach. "With all due respect, Mr. Craig, how could you know that?"

"Well, now, I guess you are right about that. There's no way I could know for sure what he was thinking in that moment, but his love for you, the love he had for your mother, that is what led him to do what he did."

"How do you figure?" I could not mask the annoyance in my voice.

"I'm not sure what you know about your father's death, so let's back up a bit here."

I wanted to tell Craig that backing up was a damn good idea; but then again, this is what I wanted. I'd spent my whole life looking for the truth. I didn't get to cherry-pick it.

"What do you know?" he pressed.

I told him what Lishie had told me about the soldier at the fence, the sleepwalker. Maybe Craig, though unclear about my father, would know more about the sleepwalker. I turned to him, trying to read a response from his face.

"And did she tell you that we heard a shot? That's how we first knew that your father and the man were at the fence."

"Yes, that's right," I agreed, nodding.

"Does Bud ever talk about that night?"

"No. Not to me. I don't ask him either." I looked out my window. "Why? What's he going to say that Lishie hasn't already told me?"

"I imagine he'd tell you about some of the terrible shit we did to the Indians in our unit."

Craig had my attention again.

"Like what?"

"Now, you have to remember that most, heck, none of the men had ever served with nonwhites before, and most had never even met an Indian." Craig searched my face. I offered him nothing other than a clenched jaw. "Army didn't know what to do with folks like your dad and uncle. I guess they figured they were white enough. Not like there were enough of 'em to start their own colored regiment or anything. Likely some Indians from other places were sent to existing colored regiments, but at least not the fellas from boarding schools, far as I can tell. You probably know more about that than me." Craig was losing focus, both on the point of his story and the road. The car's right tire skidded on damp grass and he swerved back onto the road. "Sorry about that. Where was I?"

"Men weren't used to Indians," I prompted.

"Right. So, some of the guys used to take the bullets out of the guns belonging to the Indians at night. I know how crazy it must sound to you, but people do some crazy shit during wartime."

"Why would they do that? That doesn't make any sense. Who on earth would that make sense to, no matter what time it was?"

"Some of the guys worried that the Indians might rebel, shoot them in their sleep."

"You've got to be kidding me!" I groaned. "Rebel?"

"Yeah, you should've heard some of them talk. They'd say things like, 'It's a full moon, the natives will be restless.'"

"And they were serious?"

"Serious enough to remove bullets from the guns of their fellow soldiers in the middle of a goddamn war."

"Did they know?"

"Who? Your dad and uncle?"

"Yeah. Did you tell them?"

Craig sighed. "No. I didn't know until much later. I have to think that your dad and Bud knew. They weren't idiots. They probably didn't see the point in making a fuss about it."

I shook my head. That was all I could do. Craig focused on the road, likely too embarrassed to continue; at least I hoped he was embarrassed.

Until it hit me. And it hit hard.

"Wait. The shot. You said you heard the shot. That night at the fence. You heard a shot."

"That's right, Cowney." Craig sighed again.

"But it wasn't the sleepwalker, was it?"

"Do you know any sleepwalkers that carry a loaded gun? A gun at all, for that matter?"

"But there was a sleepwalker?"

"Oh, yes. That part is true. I can't believe he didn't get himself killed well before that night."

"So, my father had a gun."

"Yes."

"And he fired the shot?"

"Yes. I believe the first shot. Then all hell broke out." I could see from his look that Craig knew how unacceptable this answer was after what he had just told me.

"And he had been asleep, right? I mean they found him half dressed."

"Now, I can't be sure he had been asleep, but he had been in his bunk. I was playing cards with the other guys. He and Bud weren't with us."

My heart began to race as we passed the county line sign. I only had a few minutes. "They found two guns. The army found two guns at the fence, didn't they?" I asked as if I didn't already know the answer deep down.

"Yes, that part is true also, Cowney. Two guns and no bullets in them."

Tears rushed up from what felt like my very gut. I fought to choke them back down. "Was . . . the enemy . . . firing?" I continued, my words breaking into pieces as they fell from my mouth.

"Yes. After the first shot, the enemy, or what was left of 'em, began firing. I don't know if they even knew how close they were to us until they heard the shot. And we sure didn't know they were that close until we heard theirs. It's not like you'd see in the movies. The war was almost over, Cowney. This wasn't a major battle."

173

"But the other gun . . . It belonged to one of the—"

"It was an US Army–issued revolver. They both were," Craig answered before I could finish my sentence.

I searched his face again. "There he is." Craig pointed his index finger over the steering wheel. Bud stood next to his newly resurrected truck.

I followed his finger and nodded. "Yeah, that's him . . . but—"

Craig drew a deep breath. "Cowney, I know that doesn't answer all your questions. If you're like your dad and uncle, you're smart enough to have a lot more questions. But I'm telling you all I know. There were three people at the fence line before the enemy fired a single shot. Two of those people are dead and the other one is sitting in that truck over there, waiting to take you home. I recommend you find a way to ask him your questions if you ever want to know the answers."

I sat back and slid deep into the seat. I looked at the truck as Craig pulled off the road and toward it.

"But sometimes the answers are not the ones you want to hear," Craig continued, turning the wheel. "Sometimes you have to decide if you want truth or peace."

"I want both," I replied softly.

As the car came to a stop and Craig shifted into park, he said, "Well, son. I wish you luck 'cause that man right there is your only chance at both."

I nodded and thanked him for the ride and food.

"No problem. I'm glad you called. I'll keep my ear to the ground and make sure we know what the colonel is up to. Once they clear you, and they will, I will get word to you and give you a ride back to Asheville."

"You think they'll let me come back?"

"Don't see why not. Long as your boss needs you, they'd likely have you back before trying to hire someone else this late in the summer. Plus, they have your car. They'll have to let you have that back."

"I sure hope so. Don't really want to spend the rest of the summer here, I don't think. And I still need a paycheck. There's no work here."

"You'll be fine, son. You call me if you need me in the meantime. Tell your uncle the same, though I know better than to hold my breath for him to call." He smiled and helped me unload my suitcase and bag from the back. I shook his hand before climbing into Bud's truck and watching Craig make a wide U-turn back onto the main road.

As I settled into the cab next to Bud, I wanted him to speak first. I had grown comfortable with that arrangement. He'd growl something about the gas money he'd spent having to pick me up in Haywood County. I'd offer an insincere apology. He'd accuse me of getting myself into trouble because I was too stupid to keep my head down and mouth shut. I'd nod all the way home.

That's how I wanted it to happen, but it did not unfold that way, not this time. Bud steered his truck back onto the main road without a word. He didn't glare at me or huff out of irritation. He drove as if we were just driving to the store. In fact, he was more relaxed than he had been running errands with me as a young boy.

"How much did he tell you?" I asked, desperate to break the silence.

"Not much," Bud offered matter-of-factly.

"You mad?"

"I don't know enough to be mad, except for interrupting my day."

"Yeah, sorry about that. Mr. Craig said he could—"

"I think we've asked enough of Jon for one day, don't you? Hand me that thermos, will you?" Bud nodded at a large green Stanley thermos sitting on the passenger side floorboard and against my seat. "Loosen the lid."

I did as he asked and he took a long drink of what smelled like strong coffee.

"How'd you know to call him anyway?" he asked, passing the thermos back to me for the lid.

"He gave me his number at Lishie's—" For a moment I forgot that only I knew the note had not been destroyed.

Bud shook his head. "Persistent. Well, probably best you did call him. Nothing I could have done for you here. Still, I wish you wouldn't have—"

"So he did tell you what happened? That I got into some trouble, but it wasn't—"

Bud sat up straighter in his seat, continuing to stare forward out of the windshield. "What? Wasn't your fault? You know that doesn't matter in a white world. I guess you'll have to find some other work around here."

"I didn't get in trouble with the inn. My manager, Lee, he's a good guy. He'll hear me out when I get a chance to talk to him about it."

"Who the hell sent you home, then?"

I wished Craig had told him. I wished he'd explained the details, the

175

reasoning behind the suspicion, and how ridiculous the whole thing was. But Bud probably wouldn't have listened to him anyway.

"The army. Well, kind of. I mean, they didn't send me home, but Craig thought it better if I go home for a while."

"Craig still giving orders, I see."

"No. He was trying to help. Army thinks I had something to do with a missing girl."

"Missing girl? Do you?" Bud's head swiveled, allowing him to check for truth in my eyes.

"No! Nothing! It's all a misunderstanding."

I could see Bud's eyebrows furrowing as I spoke. His mouth gaped open. "Jesus, son! Did you get busted in the mouth?!"

"What?" I exclaimed. "What are you talking about?"

"Your mouth. Look at your mouth!"

I rolled my window down and craned my neck so that I could look in the tiny side mirror. Bud was right! My mouth was stained red. But it wasn't blood. I covered my face with both hands and attempted to respond to Bud through them. "It's . . . not . . . blood!" I chuckled. "It's . . . Cheer . . . Cheer . . ."

Bud reached over and grabbed at my left arm. "Speak up!"

"It's just Cheerwine. I drank a Cheerwine on the way."

"Good God, boy!" Bud blurted and then fell into laughter with me. "You look ridiculous! Like some kind of goddamn vampire." He shook his head, unable to not smile. Seeing his smile made his face seem brand-new to me.

"Yeah, I guess I do. I didn't know it would do that." I rubbed my mouth on the inside of my shirt collar until my lips were raw and my collar damp.

"I was beginning to think you had caught tuberculosis from those guests."

"No, different kind of guest at the inn now."

"Yeah, I guess so." His voice evened. "So who was the girl?"

"The one missing?" I clarified.

"Yes. She a prisoner or maid?"

"Child of one of the diplomats. That's why it's such a big deal."

"I guess that's why Jon wanted to be involved, too."

"Not sure he exactly wants to be involved. That was more my fault."

176

"So why do they think you have anything to do with it?"

I couldn't believe that Bud and I were having a conversation about this. *Was he willing to hear my side of the story?* I treaded lightly. "I told Essie, that girl that came when Lishie—"

"Yeah, I know Essie Stamper."

"Yeah, so I told her about this bone I had found on the property. Anyway, she apparently told them I had a bone and they made some messed-up kind of connection to the missing girl."

Bud nodded. "They needed a body and you provided the first piece."

"I guess so. That damn colonel had me in a room for hours asking questions."

"You didn't get caught trying to sell those bladders, did you?"

"No. Don't think so. I mean, maybe that's part of it, too. Some guards saw me trying to talk to some guests, but I never got a word out about 'em."

"Good. You still have the bone?"

"It was gone when they went looking for it."

"Gone? How the hell's a bone going to grow legs and just walk away?"

"Beats me. But I told them exactly where to find it and when they looked, it wasn't there."

"Did you look for it yourself?"

"No, they wouldn't let me."

Bud cupped his chin with his left hand and cracked his neck. "Sounds like someone wants to make it look like you had something to do with this."

"Yes. Exactly. But I don't!"

"That doesn't matter, Cowney!" Bud corrected me. "You think anybody gives a shit about you? You think anybody gives a shit about Indians except other Indians? Hell, no, they don't! They've been erasing us for two hundred years." He looked disgusted.

And there was the old Bud. The one who didn't care what I had to say. He grabbed for the thermos and opened it himself this time, keeping the steering wheel steady with his knees. I stared out the window. "No, I guess not," I conceded. "Guess not."

"Sooner you learn that, the better off you'll be." Bud slid the thermos back onto the floorboard.

I would have sat in silence the remainder of the ride had he not taken a coughing fit, cracking down his window, desperate for fresh air. "Dammit . . ." he barked. I looked at him, struck by the violence of his coughing. He held the steering wheel with his left hand and cupped his mouth with his right. I had already noticed a small bandage on his right hand when he took the thermos from me, but now, with his forearm extended across his chest and his rolled sleeve pulling back further, I could see a large, pus-stained bandage on his arm and sloughing skin outlining the adhesion.

When his cough subsided, I turned away again. With my back to him, I asked out of curiosity, not necessarily concern, "What happened to your arm? That's a large bandage."

"Nothing. I mean, I got a little cut, but this damn gangrene . . . Can't seem to shake it. Should've had it looked at. Got caught between some trees falling, slipped, and between falling limbs and a rusty saw blade, got ripped up pretty bad. Would've been alright if it hadn't gotten infected, though. It's just acting up and my sugar doesn't help. Nothing seems to heal anymore."

"You should take better care of yourself," I said coldly.

"I do the best I can. I don't get to run off to a resort for the summer."

"Yes, Bud. That's right. I've just been playing badminton with the Vanderbilts and Roosevelts. That's exactly what I've been doing all summer."

"Just saying, maybe you should go a little easier on a veteran still feeling the effects of war."

"Yeah, I'll never know what that's like, will I?"

Bud shook his head. "I'm done talking about it."

And apparently so was I because we sat in silence for the remainder of the drive. We had started the trip with so much promise. I might even have gotten answers about my father from Bud. But that moment had passed before I could hold tight.

When we arrived in Cherokee, the dirt roads were busier than normal. Bud focused on steering and cussing while I continued to sit mute. As we passed by the string of tourist shops downtown (teepees and sale signs elbowing for attention), Bud rolled his window back up. "Where you want to go?" he asked matter-of-factly.

"What do you mean?" I attempted to read his expression. "Home."

"Okay, but just so you know, there's probably no food or firewood there."

"I'll be fine," I lied.

"If that's what you want." Bud turned the wheel, hand over hand, steering the truck onto a side road toward the cabin. "I'll bring a few things over this evening."

"I can go to the store later."

Bud stopped the truck and then began backing up.

"What are you doing?" I shouted.

"Taking you to the store. You don't want to have to walk, do you?"

Bud pulled in front of the trading post and I got out before he had time to give me his list. I only had a few dollars in my pocket and figured Bud didn't have any.

Tsa Tsi was sitting outside the trading post on a bench whittling as I walked up.

"Si-yo," I greeted him.

"Si-yo," he responded. "You back already?"

"Hopefully not for long."

"Alright," he nodded. "Didn't happen to see Edgar over your way, did you?" he asked, looking almost hopeful. "He's been known to wander all the way to Buncombe County, you know. And these fires, they've got me worried."

"No, sir, sorry. I'll be sure to let you know if he shows up while I'm home, though."

Tsa Tsi nodded and continued to scrape his pocketknife down a long strip of wood.

Inside the store I bought a quart of milk, a small sack of flour, a jar of dried pintos, and half a dozen eggs. I gave Jones, the clerk, the wrinkled dollars from my pocket, and he agreed to let me pay the balance when I got my final paycheck from the inn, assuming I ever got one.

Tsa Tsi was gone by the time I left the store. When I climbed back into the truck, Bud eyed my purchases. "Why'd you get eggs and milk?"

"To eat," I responded sarcastically.

"You know I've got chickens and a cow. You're wasting your money."

"It's my money to waste."

"Well, now, that's the truth." He nodded. "But don't think you aren't going to help out with the milking while you're home. You owe me for the gas I wasted picking you up." Bud toggled the gear into reverse and we made our way to the cabin. When he parked, I grabbed the groceries, opened my door, and pulled my bags from the truck bed. Bud did not get out. I think he started to speak, but I slammed the passenger side door and made my way up the cabin steps before he had time to stop me. Rocks and broken branches crunched beneath his tires as he turned the truck and left down the drive.

Inside, the cabin was still. The floors had been swept and everything was neatly stacked and arranged. Lishie had been such a slight woman, but her absence was all consuming. I put away the groceries and dropped my bags inside the door to my room. Sleep consumed the afternoon.

I think I had been home a few hours when the phone rang, waking me from a nap that was quickly turning to a deep, full-night's sleep.

"This Cowney or Bud?" Gail, the evening switchboard operator, asked.

"This is Cowney, Gail. Who you need?"

"Call's for you. Hold on while I connect you."

There was a click and then I could hear Craig clearing his throat on the other end. "Listen, son. We've got some trouble."

"What's wrong?"

"Well, as soon as I got back to the office Griggs called me."

"Did they find the bone?"

"No. Still can't find the bone . . . but there's a soldier, think his name is Franks, that keeps making a fuss about letting you go. Keeps insisting Griggs question you more. I think he's really gotten into Griggs's head."

"Why, you reckon? I've never done anything to him. He's a—" I stopped short of mistaking anyone for a friend.

"Don't guess you have to. Probably trying to make a name for himself." Craig paused a moment. I could hear him taking a deep breath. "Cowney, he's telling them that he thinks he saw you playing with that little girl a few days before she disappeared."

"What?" I howled into the phone. "I don't know the girl. I may have seen her playing outside a couple of times, but that's all."

"I know. I know. But, well, it's his word against yours."

"What am I going to do, Mr. Craig? I have no idea where the bone is. Essie's already sacrificed me for her boyfriend. Now Franks is just plain making stories up. What's happening to me?"

"I wish I knew, son. Are you sure there is nothing else you can tell me about all this?"

"Sir . . ." I was too frustrated to offer more.

"I know. I know. Cowney, trust me now. I believe you. I may be the only one that does, but we are going to get this cleared up."

"How the hell are we supposed to do that?" My anger grew too quickly to quell it.

"I'm not sure, but we are going to start by finding that bone. If what you say is right, someone had to take it."

"Think it was Franks?"

"Maybe. Doubtful, though. You know, Cowney, you have to accept that it may have been Essie. It's just that she's the only person who would have known where to find it, right? I'm sorry to say it. I know she's a friend."

"Not sure I would call her that now."

"Well, let's reserve judgment for now and hope they do the same. Listen. I need to go. Got to get back to work. You try to rest. I'll call you soon as I can."

"Okay," I agreed. "Thank you."

"Don't thank me yet, son."

The phone clicked.

The cabin was too quiet. I couldn't reconcile how Franks had befriended me and then, only days later, jeopardized my freedom—maybe even my life. I found the coffee kettle high on a shelf, the wrong shelf, and filled it with water. I lit the stove beneath it. I opened the coffee canister, but it was empty. Someone had even washed out the residue. I turned the stove off and poured out the water. I was hungry, but too tired to cook. I walked to Lishie's bedroom. I don't know what I expected to find, but whatever it was, it was not there. Her bed was made; a new quilt, one that had likely been packed away in her trunk at the foot of the bed, was spread across it. I knelt by the bed, burying my face in the quilt. It did not smell of Lishie. It smelled of cedar. The smell, perhaps the absence of her smell, burned my eyes. I let the fabric absorb my tears.

I stood and pulled the quilt back, exposing bleached white sheets. I picked up the pillow and held it to my chest. I inhaled deeply. Lishie had been washed from it as well. I put the pillow back and remade the bed. *This is no longer her room*, I reminded myself and closed the door as I left.

My room, however, was just as I had left it. Apparently Myrtle, or whoever had taken care with the other rooms, had settled on leaving mine in its natural state. I guess she or they knew I would be returning.

I pulled my suitcase onto the bed and began unpacking its contents. At the very bottom I found a small roll of film. I smiled, thinking of the images that were likely on it: 447, the impressive grounds of the resort, our canoe race on the French Broad, everyone posing goofily. My smile faded quickly as I thought about how those faces would look different to me now. I resolved to take the roll into the trading post the next day to have it developed. I would have to kill a few squirrels on the way in so I would have something to barter, but I felt confident that I would be able to make a trade. For some reason I can't explain, those pictures seemed more important that anything I could purchase from the trading post. I wanted to make a square deal for them. As I rolled the film canister between my fingers, envisioning what was held inside, I thought that I might just add three new items to my wish list: a proper headstone for Lishie, my own camera (used would suffice), and a new roll of film.

I fell asleep that night hungry and otherwise empty, allowing hand-picked Asheville memories to fill the void in my dreams. I did not care that I might not be wanted back; I would go no matter what. There was nothing for me in Cherokee. Not now.

In the morning, I quieted my stomach with a scrambled egg and set the beans to soak. Before leaving, I grabbed my 12 gauge from beside my bedroom door, somewhat surprised that Bud had not already "borrowed" it while I was gone, and found an old, empty corn sack should I have any luck hunting on the way. Though the mist still hung low on the mountains, weighted down with smoke, it looked as though the sun was about to make its permanent entrance for the day. The chill was quickly subsiding. I was glad that I wouldn't have to worry about rain even though we desperately needed it to slow the fires. I did not want to ask Bud for a ride into town and if I asked anyone else, I'd have to explain why I was home in the first place. As I made my way down the drive, I considered going to the waterfall again first, but thought better of it. It would take some time to get the film developed and I needed to get it to Jones as soon as possible, just in case I was able to return to the inn quickly. I had no idea when to expect a call.

The walk into town took me close to an hour. I did stop and pick blackberries, though I could not manage to keep any for later; I was far too hungry not to immediately eat each one. I also managed to shoot two squirrels, and cleaned them by the river. Downtown Cherokee was practically deserted when I strolled into the trading post.

"Morning, Cowney. Two days in a row. I feel honored," Jones greeted me. He was a gangly young man whose Adam's apple ran the length of his neck as he spoke. With the exception of his bright, blue eyes, he always looked as if he had just woken from a nap.

"Don't get too excited. Last time I was here, I put half my order on credit."

"Now that is a fact, but you're good for it."

"You develop film here, right?"

"Sure do," Jones confirmed.

I handed him the film canister. "How long until I can pick it up?" I asked, expecting it might be quite some time.

"Well, I don't have any other orders right now. Tell you what, I'll work late tonight and get 'em done for you by tomorrow. Come by around lunchtime."

"Really? Are you sure?"

"Yeah. I enjoy it. Kind of a hobby of mine, I've been doing it so much lately."

"I'd like to learn how to develop film sometime."

"Not sure I'd be a good teacher, but I can try. Have to do it before the fall, though."

"Why's that?"

"I'm heading off to college."

"Oh, yeah? Where to?"

"Black Mountain. I'm going to learn more about photography. That and probably a bunch of other stuff."

"Why'd you decide to go there?"

Jones slid a pamphlet across the counter. "Here. Read this. This is why I decided to go. No mention of math or grammar. Says you get to choose whatever you want to take. Direct your own learning, or something like that."

I took the pamphlet and studied the photos. None of the faces looked like people from our area, Cherokee or otherwise. I couldn't see Jones there, let alone me.

"What about you? You thinking about heading to school ever?" Jones asked.

"I'm still not sure."

"Well, you ought to at least check out Black Mountain."

"I probably can't afford anything like that."

Jones's face fell. "Well, there are lots of good schools. I hear some places even offer assistance for Indians."

"Someone must have told Lishie that, too. She was always talking about that, even after I came home from junior college early. We'll see, I guess." I shrugged and stood back from the counter. "Thanks. I'll try to get back tomorrow sometime. If I can't catch a ride, it will depend on the weather. I don't want to carry them back in the rain." I turned and walked toward the door.

"Hey, Cowney," Jones called after me.

I turned back toward the counter without answering him directly.

"You know, I was thinking. If you want to stick around town for a bit, I mean, if you don't have anywhere to be, I can probably get these done in a few hours for you. It's just one roll."

"Really? That fast?"

"Yeah. I mean, I may need another mess of squirrel soon for it, though." He smiled.

"You've got a deal!" I returned his smile.

"Keep an eye on the place a few minutes, will ya? I'll get these started."

"Sure thing."

I browsed the store a bit, turning over jars and cans for prices, running my hands over the tightly knitted fabric of picnic blankets and slick reeds of river cane baskets. Maybe it was the fires that were keeping people away, but the store was nearly empty the entire time Jones was gone. Since the Great Smoky Mountains National Park opened not long ago, people came to the mountains in droves; but no one wants to be outside surrounded by forest fires—and the smoke that came in such suffocating waves. The one notable exception was a turtle of a woman—white fluffy mop instead of hard shell. Her dawdling shuffle across the dusty wooden floorboards and exasperated sighs—as if life was far too much for her—drew my curiosity.

"Anything I can help you with, ma'am?" *Maybe I could make Jones a sale.*

"I sure hope so. Doubt it, though. Doesn't seem like anybody around here knows the first thing about customer service." She sighed heavily again, setting her large, bulging pocketbook on the front counter. "I collect baskets. I need a quality one. And mind you, I know what they're worth, so don't try to pull the shit y'all pull with tourists. Plus, I'm in a hurry. Making my way to Kentucky next for a real Appalachian buttocks basket."

"Okay." I blushed, taken aback by her direct language and unfounded accusation. "What kind of basket are you looking for here?"

She contorted her chubby face until it looked like an anemic prune. "Indian. Why the hell you think I'd be in this godforsaken place otherwise?"

"Yes, ma'am. River cane? Honeysuckle? White oak?"

"Cherokee."

"Yes, ma'am. There are different types of Cherokee baskets."

"I mean a real one. I want an authentic one. I am a collector."

"Yes, you mentioned that, but . . ." I looked around and eyed a cane purse. I recognized the maker immediately by its smooth lines and perfectly angled rim. I should say, I recognized the family immediately. I wasn't sure which one, mother or daughter, had done the weaving, or which one, father or son, had whittled the drop handles. "Here. This is what you want." I handed the basket to her.

She flipped over the white tag, exposing the red-inked price. "I was not born yesterday! This looks like it came from a department store. I want one a Cherokee woman actually made. It's the lack of imperfections that give away a fake."

I had to agree with her there.

"Thanks, Cowney." Jones waved to me as he closed the storeroom door behind him. "Did you make me some money while I was back there?"

"Nope, not a dime. But I didn't cost you any either." I caught a glimpse of the tortoise exiting, her white head shaking in disgust.

"Well, I'd say that's fair enough," Jones laughed. "Still, can't believe how slow it's gotten around here. Usually things pick up in the summer, with tourists nosing around and all."

I ran my hands through a bucket of corn beads. "So you'd say that Black Mountain College is probably more expensive than a state school, right?"

"Yeah, quite a bit, unfortunately."

"I hope you don't think I'm prying, but how you plan on paying for it?"

"I made a deal. Told the old man that I would not volunteer for service and stay here and help run the store as long as I could. Course, if I were to get drafted, well, then I'd serve, no question. The old man doesn't pay me, but promised to send me to school anywhere I could get in and wanted to go."

"That sure does sound like a fair deal. Well, thanks again, Jones. I'll be back to pick them up before you close."

"My pleasure, Cowney. I hope you get some good ones out of the batch!"

I walked out the door, the bell ringing overhead.

While activity in town was far from its normal summer hum, it was steadily busy in spite of the smoke. I wandered the streets of Cherokee as if I were one of the summertime tourists, stopping to watch men in colorful feathers play Sioux in front of shoddily made imitation teepees. I watched Cherokee women haggle with white women in white dresses and big floppy hats over the prices of baskets, pottery, and jewelry. Later in the day, I watched young boys careen headfirst into the Oconaluftee River, splashing their summers away. I smelled steaming hot dogs and popped corn until my stomach ached from hunger. I took a nap beneath a large oak tree by the river, trying to fill my emptiness with sleep.

When I returned to the trading post, Jones was sweeping the front porch and speaking with Tsa Tsi.

"Oh, there he is!" Jones greeted me. "I was just telling Tsa Tsi here that I think you got some great shots of Asheville."

"Well, that's good to hear. I guess it was worth two gray squirrels then."

"Hope so. Let me go get them for you." Jones leaned his broom against the storefront and went inside.

"So, whatcha up to today?" I asked, sitting on the bench next to Tsa Tsi.

"Oh, not much. Just watching the clouds go by."

"Any word on Edgar?"

"Nope. Startin' to get worried; he's never been gone this long."

"Well, I'm sure he'll turn up."

"Hope so. Hope he didn't decide to run off with some carnival. He's a big fan of cotton candy, you know." Tsa Tsi smiled. His hair seemed whiter than I remembered and he ran his fingers through it so that half of it remained standing on end.

"Okay, here you go!" Jones announced as he came out of the store. "Hope you like them."

I couldn't exactly remember what shots were on the film, so I elected to take them home and look at them in private.

Tsa Tsi's expression as I stood to leave was far from approving. "Not going to share a peek?" he pried.

"Oh, well. I don't know."

"Come on, you let that one see them already." Tsa Tsi pointed at Jones, who was quite amused.

"He developed them!"

"So. Didn't you know I was an art critic? Let's see if you have potential."

Jones shook his head and went back into the trading post with the broom.

"Oh, alright. We'll look at them together." I sat back down on the bench beside Tsa Tsi.

The first two pictures were of the canoes we raced down the river. They sat side by side in the tall grass. Then came the picture of the four of us standing in front of my car, taken by another guard who, I remember, had looked fairly put out with the whole scene. I flipped past it quickly, not wanting to not look at Essie's and Peter's faces any longer than I had to. The next was just of Peter sitting in one of the canoes, still in the tall grass, but he was pretending to paddle nonetheless.

"Who's that fella?" Tsa Tsi asked, stopping me from moving the picture to the back.

"That's Peter. Lieutenant Peter Franks."

"He your friend?"

"He works where I do . . . where I did. Wouldn't exactly call him a friend."

"Looks goofy."

"Yeah." I smiled. "He's a little goofy."

We continued to flip through the pictures, sifting through images of the inn and its grounds. I had taken a few of the buildings in downtown Asheville. Tsa Tsi stopped me with each picture and told me his own personal story of visiting Asheville. Where he had eaten, what he had eaten, how much gas and indigestion it had produced for him.

"Oh, now there's a picture." Tsa Tsi took the photo from my hand. "That little Essie Stamper?"

I nodded. "Yes, that's her." Tsa Tsi held an image of Essie, high on her toes in mid-twirl. I had taken it the day I caught her dancing by herself in room 447. Her straight, dark hair was flung around her face, her eyes lost in the spinning motion. Essie's mouth was closed tightly, without compromising her expression of sheer serenity. The skirt of her baby-blue maid uniform rose on one side, swept up in the twist of her long body. A moment later, after I had captured the image, she nearly fell in surprise and went about beating my arms with her clenched fists, trying to resist the urge to laugh at herself the way I was. These were the moments that had entrapped me, had convinced me that I saw her the way no one else had and made me believe that she had seen my true self as well. I both loved the picture as testimony to our unique friendship and wanted to rip it up.

"She's turning into a real beauty," Tsa Tsi remarked and handed the photo back to me. I didn't respond.

"She come back with you this time?"

"No, she's still in Asheville."

"Mmm," Tsa Tsi replied. "Wouldn't leave her there too long if I were you."

"Left my car for her."

"Not your car she needs, son."

I smiled awkwardly and brought forward the next picture.

"Where's that?" Tsa Tsi asked.

"Gosh," I responded. "Not exactly sure. I don't think I even took this picture. I think it's of the grounds." I flipped through the next three photos. None of them looked familiar. I remembered I had left the camera in 447. Essie must have borrowed it. I looked back at the pictures she had taken with more attention, curious to see what she found beautiful, worthy of capturing at the inn.

There was one of a flower garden, one of the exterior facade of the Grove Park's main building, one of Andrea sitting on the dining hall steps smoking a cigarette. I came to the final photo and stopped. It was Essie and Andrea sitting on the grass, smiling, posing. Andrea had his arm around Essie. Carol must have taken the photo.

Then something else caught my eye. Something in the far corner of the photo. I squinted to better see the faded outline of the fence in the background. There was a break in the wire pattern that so tediously wrapped the property—an undeniable hole. Metal was peeled backward. I had never seen even the slightest flaw in any of the perimeter fencing before. The impenetrability of that border took precedence over every chore Lee assigned, and there was no way this would have gone unnoticed for long, but we were never assigned to fix it.

"Who's that fella?" Tsa Tsi asked. I had been so focused on the fence, I started to answer, "I don't . . ." but realized that Tsa Tsi was looking at the man. "I mean, it's Andrea. That's Essie's boyfriend."

"He looks goofy, too." Tsa Tsi laughed.

"Yes." I nodded. "I think so, too." I quickly gathered the photos together and tucked them inside my knapsack. My mind raced between the trading post and the inn, between the fence line and the faces, between those clear and smiling faces and those turned from my gaze. I gave him one more nod and said good-bye to Tsa Tsi. He waved and reminded me to keep an eye out for Edgar. I promised that I would, but wondered if maybe he had left Edgar alone for too long. Maybe Edgar had gotten used to being alone and had just resolved to stay that way. I wondered if that might just happen to me, too.

CHAPTER TWENTY-TWO

I called Craig as soon as I returned home and told him about the photograph.

"That's real good, Cowney. Real good. Give me some time and I'll be in touch."

I was at home almost two weeks, all told. I tried not to think too deeply about the pictures I had seen, the images of the inn and its people, still unsure of exactly what was showing up in the photos and what was just a trick of the lens. In the mornings, I made my way to Bud's house, milked the cow, and gathered eggs before he could drag himself from bed and pull on his boots. I preferred working in solitude as I was not eager to speak to him, but if I helped with chores, I knew he would not complain too loudly if I took a small portion of the milk and eggs for myself. On Sunday, he offered his truck so that I could drive myself to church. I accepted the use of his vehicle, but drove into town instead to trade firewood or a few of the eggs from Bud's chickens for necessities from the trading post. I also wanted to sit on the front porch and talk with Tsa Tsi or whoever wandered by. Most often, I chose not to speak at all, but I didn't mind listening. Listening was easy. Sometimes Jones joined me on the porch when business was slow and we talked about what college might look like.

"Plenty of girls. That's all I know," he mused during one visit.

"Yeah, different girls," I clarified.

He laughed. "The kind that don't know us yet."

"The best kind!" We both laughed at the potential promise.

Whether it was because of that particular conversation or something that had been weighing on my mind for some time, on my next visit to town, I was inspired to bring two college application forms I had hidden away beneath my bed for several months. Lishie had sent for them without mentioning a word to me until she handed them to me. To this day, I don't know how she knew to get them. Likely someone from church had helped her.

I waited until all of the customers left the trading post before I pulled them from my knapsack and laid them on the counter in front of Jones. "Think you can help?" I asked.

"You haven't sent any yet?"

"No, but, you know, I wasn't in a big hurry. Need the money first."

"Well, I guess it's never too early to apply for admission for the next semester. They might want to offer you a scholarship."

"Doubt that. Anyway, I thought while I have some time, maybe I could get them filled out and just send them in when I'm ready."

"Well, let's get started," he said and motioned for me to join him behind the counter, pen in hand, so that we could both look at the questions together.

"Bacone." He read the name on the first letterhead. "Sure you didn't mean to send off for bacon instead?"

I smiled with him. "Bacon might be more useful to me."

"Nah. You'll see. Anyway, let's get you in and then you can decide if Bacone is right for you or if you should stick to breakfast meats."

"Fair enough." I pointed to the other letter. "That one is for Milligan College."

"Where are they located?"

"Bacone is in Oklahoma. Milligan is in east Tennessee, near Johnson City."

"Well, Milligan certainly is closer."

"True, but Bacone is like a prep school for Indians, from what I hear. I know a few folks from Cherokee who are there already."

"So you have done some research?"

"No. I mean, not a lot. Just what I hear from folks."

"Is that why you sent off to these two schools?"

I was too embarrassed to tell him that Lishie had made the decision, so I just nodded.

Jones read aloud the questions and I responded quickly to the easiest ones, the biographical questions such as birth date and address.

"Do you have the credits in these courses that they list?"

"Yes. Yes, all of them except Latin."

"You can take that your first year. They just need to know what entrance exam to give you."

I didn't like the thought of testing. I had never been a strong test taker, but figured that was the least of my worries at the moment. As Jones read, I also realized how different questioning is when one is not presumed guilty of a crime. Jones asked and took my answers at face value. Though sometimes he asked me to clarify a response, he was ultimately just recording my truth. The colonel had done nearly the opposite. He and his men asked and then chose to record their own truth, simply signing my name to it.

"You'll need a letter of reference. Do you have one yet?"

"No, but I thought I could ask Lee, my boss at the inn."

"That sounds like a good idea. When will you see him again?"

"Not entirely sure."

"You could always call or write him for one. Anyone else you might have as a backup plan?"

The emptiness of my mind frightened me. I had never considered who could and would speak on my behalf if needed. I couldn't think of a single person, other than Lee, who would be able to offer a recommendation of my character and work ethic. *Had I really lived all these years and not identified even one potential advocate or ally? One that hadn't either used me or sacrificed me to save themselves?* Maybe I could ask Miss Marjorie. She saw enough in me to ply me with books every chance she got. She talked to me like an adult about them too—even though I'd been still in high school.

"I might be able to ask one of my teachers or the headmaster."

"Okay, not a bad idea. Do you think one of them will be able to give some examples of your accomplishments or your ethics? Anything like that? I don't know too much about your school. From what people say, sounds like you guys were responsible for farm chores, too. That'd be good to include. Play any sports? Have a coach that might—"

I looked down at my left foot and then back to him. I didn't need to speak.

"Oh, right. Sorry. Well, think on it a bit. I am sure you will find a good person. You can always ask your preacher. He's probably written a dozen or so over the years."

Jones and I continued to fill out the questions, deciding I would also need more time to think about what my personal statement should say. He agreed to read over it for me before I mailed the whole package. When we answered every question I could in the moment, I folded both applications into their respective envelopes and thanked Jones for his help.

"Wish I could do more," he offered. "I'm sure you'll find the right home in the end."

Those were not the only two envelopes of importance that I held in my hand that week. On one of the days I had elected to walk into town to go swimming in the river, I decided to stop by the post office and pick up any mail Lishie may have had stacking up since her passing. Other than the college applications, a few US and tribal government mailings, I never had mail. So I was particularly surprised when the postmaster handed only one envelope over the counter and it had my name on it.

"Bud's been picking up your grandmother's mail. But this came for you today," he informed me. "Had extra postage on it, so it must be important."

I looked at the return address:

I. Jenkins

Asheville, North Carolina

It took me a moment to recognize Lee's name. I smiled, remembering his unusual given name, Iliam, and was grateful he had chosen Lee long ago. I thanked the postmaster and tucked the letter in my knapsack. I wanted to wait until I was home before I opened it, but I was far too curious to wait. Instead I walked to the riverbank and opened the letter as I sat with my bare feet in the river. The sun beat down so ruthlessly that I removed my shirt, tying it to my belt loop, and let the beams further deepen the maroon of my shoulders and auburn of my chest. I tore jagged edges into the letter, disfiguring my name and address on the front. I read quickly:

Cowney,

I'm not one for letter writing, so I'll be brief. The army has informed staff that they are transitioning out of the current "guest services businesses" and need us to finish our work a few weeks early, including all repairs on our list. I need you to return ASAP or inform me of your inability to do so, so that I might hire short-term labor. Please call the Grove Park immediately as I do not have your phone number and am tired of dealing with that Colonel S.O.B. who refuses to give me any information about you.

Sincerely,

Lee

I could hear Lee's voice in the letter, his intolerance for drama and detestation of the arrogant faction of the soldiers at the inn who seemed unaware of his own service in World War I. I smiled as I read the letter again, verifying that I understood the request. He wanted me back. I needed to get back as soon as possible. I wanted to finish a job. I wanted to prove that I could actually do something I had set out to do. The entire summer was filled with false starts and faded hopes—I wanted to believe there would be at least one person who I wouldn't let down and who wouldn't let me down. Lee was that person. Did Essie's face flash through my mind? Of course. I immediately felt ashamed that it did, but it was as if I also needed her to see that I had not just run away like a guilty or defeated man.

I grabbed my shoes and socks and ran a good half mile before the unpredictable rocks stung my feet enough for me to stop and dress properly. In hurrying home to pack with such excitement, I nearly forgot two important details. What would the colonel do if I came back, and how the hell would I even get back to Asheville without a car? I still hadn't heard anything from Craig since I told him about the picture. The questions waited to bum-rush me until I'd already made my way into the cabin, pulled my bag from the high closet shelf, and slung every piece of clean clothing I owned into it. As I sat on my full duffle in the middle of my bedroom, another detail weighed down on me. Lee had said that the job was cut short. That would mean that pay was also cut short, no doubt. Would it even be worth it to return? I did not know whether I should start searching for the inn's phone number to tell Lee not to expect me or if I should look for Craig's number for a ride back. I still needed to tell Bud either way. I sat my bag by the front door and returned to the living room. I fell onto the couch. My father's picture in his uniform stared at me from its perch on the fireplace mantel. He didn't smile. He looked proud, chin up and resolution in his eyes. "Handsome," Lishie would say.

I wondered who had taken this photo of my father. Of course, it had to be an official army photographer, but I wondered if he spoke with my father, told him to pose a certain way, or if my father had chosen his own image, chosen how he wanted to be remembered. I walked to the bathroom and washed the day's dirt from my face. I looked into the mirror. I could see my mother. Wide eyes, slight mouth. My father's look of certainty was not there. *Would I ever grow into it? Would those eyes narrow and focus later, when I had seen enough? Would my chin rise when I had a family of my own to have pride in?* I went back into the living room without looking at my father's picture, turned down the gas lantern in the kitchen, and returned to my bedroom to read until I could fall asleep.

The fires lingered so long that summer I had grown accustomed to their residue. But that night, there was an unavoidable thickness. When I finished the book I'd had no intention of finishing, the smell of smoke was so intense inside the house that I was compelled outside. The moment I opened the door, I realized the fire was no longer lingering. It was raging and rolling and headed straight for my doorstep, far more threatening than the smoke had been the morning Preacherman and I watered down the front yard. I now felt the literal heat from nearby flames. There would be no time even to draw water.

I ran back inside and began throwing nearby clothes into my bag before I realized my real problem. I had no car. I would have to leave on foot. Not having seen actual flames, I had a false sense of time and took advantage of it to gather pictures, both new and old, and one of Lishie's quilts. I also pulled one of her bandanas from her dresser drawer and tied it tightly around my nose and mouth, drawing in her scent until it brought tears before I descended back into the smoke.

The woods were so drained of moisture that the tops of trees in the distance burned with ashy embers. The fire was jumping treetops, which I had never seen happen before. I had two options: head toward the road and hope someone would pick me up, or head for the waterfall and hunker down in the water or, if need be, the cave. If anyone else was evacuating from our holler, they were likely long gone. And so few people knew I was even home, save Bud. I'd long ago learned not to wait on Bud to save me. The road also seemed directly in line with the fire's movement, though I admit it was hard to discern through the smoke and dark of night. The question had become where did I want to die rather than where could I continue to live. The answer was clear. I bundled the quilt under my arm, clutched the suitcase of clothes and memories, and headed into the woods away from the heat.

Bud's rickety old pickup truck spun within seven feet of my path. "Get in. We don't have long."

Without question I climbed into the cab and gave God silent gratitude for my uncle. Probably the first time I had ever done that. I tossed my suitcase into the back bed to lie atop a cushion of bear and deer hides. It was almost as if Bud inherently knew which splits to avoid, an impossibility in the darkness. And then, after only five minutes in his truck, I understood. He knew because he knew where the fires had started.

"Pull over."

"Have you lost your mind?"

"I want to get the hell out, Bud. Pull over!"

"Are you kiddin' me? I'm trying to save your goddamn life."

I grabbed the wheel and pulled hard until Bud's only option was to stand on the brakes, forcing us into a rut. Flinging open the passenger side door, I gathered my things as quickly as I could, but Bud had managed to push his way outside and intercept me at the back of the truck.

"How could you?" I managed to whisper.

"What? How could I what?"

Unable to coax any new words outward, I felt as if I was waking from a dream and acting in delirium. All evidence that I once believed I might have of his guilt melted and puddled beneath my feet. If I moved, I felt as though I would slip in it and fall into a ruined heap. I shook my head, forcefully dislodging my eyes from his. "You set those fires."

"For fuck's sake! You don't understand a damn thing," Bud shouted. "Get your ass back in the truck. We don't have time for this shit."

And I did. Without question, with little hesitation, I crawled back in because I knew it was my only option. If I ever wanted to know the truth, I had to let Bud drive.

In the morning, I was awakened by the phone's ring in Bud's house as he snored in the other room.

"Cowney?" the operator, Jane, asked on the other end of the line. "That you?"

"Yes, Jane, this is Cowney," I confirmed.

"Oh, good. Glad I got you. You sure are hard to get ahold of. Wasn't sure if you were even in Cherokee these days. Heard tell you might be there. Lishie's place make it through the fires alright?"

"Don't know yet about Lishie's."

"Well, okay. You keep us posted. I'm putting through a call, sweetheart."

"Yes, ma'am."

"Ello?" I heard on the other end. "This is Jon. I've got good news!"

"Well, that's a relief."

"They found the bone."

"Oh, really? Where? You sure it's the right one?"

"Yeah, pretty sure. Essie Stamper brought it to them."

"Why—" I couldn't finish the question.

"Well, I got to thinking about things. I called up Colonel Griggs after a couple of days, gave him some time to settle down. He gave me a few more details. Then I thought, if anybody knew where the bone got to, it had to be Essie. You know, we talked about that."

"Yeah. I mean, that makes good sense. Only she and I had been in that room, far as I know."

"Right. And Cowney, I understand why you didn't want to ask her. I get it. I made sure she knew that when I went to talk to her."

"You talked to her?"

"Of course. I had to. I mean, if we were going to get this sorted out."

"You didn't need to—"

"Cowney, you need to understand that as much as I like you, kid, it's also my job to get things like this sorted out, whether it turns out good for you or not."

"I see. Well, I'm just glad it did turn out good. That's what you said, right?"

"Yes, sure did."

"So?"

I could hear Craig laugh through the crackling line. "So . . . Essie had been hiding the bone. She was afraid that it would make things worse for you."

"How?"

"Who knows?"

"You think that means she thought I was some kind of murderer?"

197

"Like I said, I was just doing my job. It doesn't matter to me what she thinks about you. No offense. Listen, if it makes you feel better, she wanted to help after I told her what had happened to you."

"I guess it does a little."

"Well, good." He laughed again. "Anyway, after I told her, she brought me the bone and agreed to go with me to speak to Griggs."

"I bet he was livid."

"Yep. Threatened to put her in the brig for concealing evidence. Ridiculous, that inn doesn't even have a brig. I got him calmed down eventually, and told him to have his experts look at the bone."

"And have they?"

"Yeah, couple of local guys. Took them long enough, but he just called me a few minutes ago."

"What'd they say?" Craig was not talking fast enough for me.

"Said it was too old to belong to the girl. I felt like saying, 'Yeah, no shit, since the poor thing's only been missing a few days,' but I contained myself. And it wasn't the right size for a child, either."

"Is it even human?"

"Well, they're not entirely sure about that. They're going to have to send it off to Raleigh to determine that. Said it didn't look like any animal in our area, but couldn't be sure."

"Gosh, I really hope it's not a human bone. I mean, I knew there was a chance . . . but that just makes me sick."

"Yeah, you might still have some trouble if it is human, but at least we've bought some time."

"And that lieutenant's story? Is Franks still raising Cain?"

"I think he's quieted down, but he's already in Grigg's head. Even without the bone, Griggs still talks like you have something to do with this. Good news is that he doesn't have evidence. Can't even get Franks to sign a statement saying anything other than he *thinks* he remembers seeing you with the girl."

"That's all good to hear. And I think good timing, too. I got a letter from Lee. Said our job's finishing sooner than expected."

"That so? Well, we need to get you back to Asheville soon so you can make your tuition money."

"Who said I need tuition money? Right now I'm just trying to stay out of jail."

"Essie told me that, too. Said she's worried you won't have enough to leave in the fall."

"Essie needs to worry about herself."

"Well, either way, I told Griggs that I'd like to bring you back if he promised to let you work and not keep harassing you. Told him if they had questions for you, I had to be present."

"Why are you doing this for me, Mr. Craig?"

"I knew your father and your uncle when they were the men I wanted to become. I'll pick you up at the trading post at 8 a.m. sharp."

"Well, good morning, Cowney," Jones called to me as he arrived at the trading post to open for the day. His wide grin and disheveled hair made him look a little crazy, but in an endearing way. "Looks like you're headed somewhere." He nodded to my bag. "Glad to see you safe. Heard the fire got awfully close to your homeplace."

"Sure am. Headed back to work in Asheville. I didn't stay at home last night. Not sure just how close the fire got to us, but Bud will check on it."

"Well, that's good news, I guess. Waiting on your ride?"

"Yes. Should be here soon. Not exactly sure what time."

"Not your uncle?"

"No. Shoot, he's probably still sleeping one off." I sat down on the bench and leaned back.

"Last few times I've seen him in here, he looked pretty sober. Wouldn't say the picture of perfect health, but definitely sober."

"Well, you don't serve whiskey either."

"No, that's true, but once you've worked here a while, you start seeing patterns in folks. Drunks shop different from our sober customers. Locals shop different than tourists. And some of the craziest regulars even bring in squirrels to trade for photos." He laughed.

"People don't just change habits like that. Anyway, he's a grown man. He can do what he wants to. I found another ride to Asheville so I don't have to worry about Bud."

"Well, that's good." Jones opened the door to the shop.

"He might even be a good reference for me," I called to Jones.

"Bud?"

"Hell, no. Jon Craig. The man picking me up. He's a veteran and works for the FBI."

"Sounds like a real good reference. Good luck, Cowney. You be sure and get those applications in the mail. Send me what you have if you want. I'll have my father take a look, too."

"Thanks, Jones. I really do appreciate your help."

"Anytime." Jones let the door close behind him.

Not too long after, Craig pulled up in a whirl of dust. The car door creaked as he stepped out. "Morning, Cowney. You ready to get back to work?" He grinned.

"Think so," I called back.

"Okay. You need anything from here? I'm going to grab a snack and some cigs."

"Nope. I'm good."

"No Cheerwine today?"

"No, sir. Jones doesn't carry it, anyway."

"Well, what kind of establishment is this?" he asked in mock disbelief.

I waited in the car for Craig, cranking the window down and leaning out. He returned shortly with a Coca-Cola and a pack of Nabs crackers.

"Breakfast of champions," he announced as he climbed in behind the wheel and cranked the car. "Even better than Wheaties!" He went on, "So, how were things at home?"

"Fine, I guess. Same old, same old, you know. Had a bit of a scare with the fires last night."

"How's Bud?"

"Same old, same old." I shook my head. I looked at the charred pines on the mountainside. The grass, too, was black, almost clear down to the road.

"You get a chance to ask him the questions you had?"

"Nah. Didn't see the point in it."

"Hmm." Craig nodded. "It's just . . . last time we spoke, it sounded like you wanted some answers."

"You told me all I care to know."

"Really?"

"Yeah. Two guns. Both army-issued. No bullets in them. You told me they took the Indian soldiers' bullets, right?"

"Right."

"But there was at least one shot heard and the sleepwalker didn't have a gun," I continued. "You know, you're the first to actually verify that piece for me. The way I figure, it's like Lishie kind of thought, though she didn't know all the things you told me. I just figure my father heard the man struggling in the barbed wire, knew his own gun had been unloaded, found a bullet, and went out to help. Then Dad spotted the enemy and fired. Everybody else had probably been drinking, definitely Bud had, so when he got to Dad and the sleepwalker, he didn't have bullets. He probably just dropped his gun and ran."

"Oh, that makes sense to you?"

"Makes sense if I imagine what Bud would do."

"Son, you don't give your uncle any credit at all, do you?"

"No offense, sir, but if you grew up with him over your shoulder, you wouldn't either."

Craig shook his head. He wiped the sweat from his forehead with the back of his arm. "Cowney, I don't want to tell you what I am about to tell you. But I also don't want you to go your whole life thinking your uncle is a coward. He doesn't deserve that and neither do you."

I turned to Craig with my full body. I could feel my heart beating faster. The car was growing warmer by the second. I restrained the urge to tell Craig about my theory about Bud and the recent fires, remembering that he was a federal agent.

Craig sighed. "Your father did not know the sleepwalker was in the fence. Not at first. That is not why he went out there."

"Then why? Why would he be out there in the middle of the night?"

Craig turned and looked at me and then returned his gaze to the road ahead.

"And why would he have a gun? He had a gun, right?" I confirmed.

"Yes, Cowney. Your father went out with a gun and one bullet. He went out alone and intended to be alone."

"But Bud showed up?"

"Yes, he came looking for your father. And yes, he had a gun. But it's not like it sounds."

"Then who shot—?" I stopped before the words escaped.

Craig sighed again. "Your father. Cowney, your father shot himself. He had planned it well enough to get a bullet first." Craig attempted to look at me, but I turned toward the window.

It would have been so much easier if I had thought this man was lying, but I knew that he wasn't. There was a gentleness, an ease, in the way he was speaking that assured me he was telling the truth, and that this was something he had relived dozens of times for himself. I believed him because I could see how damaged he still was by this truth, and how badly he didn't want it to damage me. But sometimes not knowing your own story is the most damaging thing of all.

"Bud would have stopped him. You need to know that. He was protective of your father."

"It makes no sense." I shook my head. I couldn't understand why he would do that. I knew war is terrible, but they hadn't seen that much action. He had a family. He had us. The curves of the road exaggerated my hunger to the point of nausea.

"I know, Cowney. You remember I told you that you were on his mind when he died? I know it is true because—"

"How? How the hell do you know?"

"That night, Bud and your father got into an argument. Now, I don't know everything that was said, but I do know that Bud said something about your mother." Craig pulled a handkerchief from his back pocket, swerving the car a bit in the process. He wiped his forehead. "I sure as hell don't want to have to tell you this, but I want you to understand."

I needed him to tell me quickly. I couldn't breathe.

"I think your mother and Bud must have had an affair."

I wanted him to pull over. I wanted to hit him—hell, maybe even kill him—for saying something like that. But he looked as defeated as I felt. "Cowney. Just stop and think for a minute. Why would I tell you this if it weren't true?"

"Tell me how all of this is supposed to make me feel better?"

"It's not, but Bud has been shouldering a lot. He blames himself for your father's death. And up until that night, he probably saved your father's life a half dozen times, between fistfights at basic and tripwires on our marches. And you also need to understand that your father loved your mother so much he couldn't bear to remember anything imperfect about her. He was holding two pictures when they recovered him. One of her and one of you just after your birth."

"Why did Bud tell him? He'd never've known. Bud could have just kept his fat mouth shut and I'd still have a father."

"Maybe he did know. Maybe Bud just needed him to know to clear his own conscience. I'm not sure. Like I said, I only caught pieces of their argument."

My body began to cool a bit, or numb; I can't be sure which. "So, you think it was a better idea for me to go my whole life thinking my father was a coward instead of Bud?"

"Neither were cowards. Both served their country. Both loved you. Probably both loved your mother."

I was too mad to cry, so the tears pooled inside me until I almost drowned from the inside out.

Craig, still sweating, cracked his window. "I understand if you never forgive me for telling you. I do. But don't go another day without forgiving Bud. Neither of you deserve that. He's not well, Cowney. You can see that."

I let my face rest in the palms of my hands and inhaled the smell of my own sweat, earthy pine from resting on the trading post bench, and leather from clutching my suitcase handle. I lifted my head and exhaled. "Okay." I nodded, not that I intended to do as he suggested. "Is there anything else?"

"No. No. That's everything I know in the world."

"Good. I guess I'm my father's son because I just don't think I can take anything else."

"Cowney, you are your father's son and because of that, you can take a hell of a lot. He'd be proud of you."

"Well, I'll be damned!" Lee greeted me, standing hands on hips in the main corridor as I entered. "Sure didn't expect to see you walk through the door."

"Hello to you, too." I smiled, grateful to have something to smile about. I set my bags down and reached out to shake his hand.

"Would have thought you'd call first."

"I know, but I got your letter and also got word that the colonel had settled down a bit. Thought I best come on before you gave away my job."

"Well, glad to have you back. Go drop off yer things. Best check in with the colonel, too. Just so he doesn't get all riled up. Then it's back to work, straightaway. We're working in here today. I'll meet you back at the front desk."

"Yes, sir," I agreed. "Glad to be back." I picked up my bags and turned to seek out the colonel first. I figured it would be best to get that out of the way. Unfortunately, I turned directly into Sol, who had apparently arrived in the building shortly after I had. "Sol." I nodded.

"Mmm. You're back." It was a statement rather than a question.

"Yes." I almost asked him if he missed me, but thought I best not push my luck so early into my return. "'Scuse me." I ducked my head and headed toward the colonel's secretary's office. Sol stepped aside and stared as I passed.

Colonel Grigg's secretary wasn't very friendly, though I couldn't blame her. If I worked for that man, I'd be grumpy, too. "Can I help you?" she asked as I entered.

"Yes. My name is Cowney Sequoyah. I'm here to see Colonel Griggs."

She was accommodating enough to point to a worn couch and a pot of coffee. I poured myself a thick, black cup and positioned myself on the couch so that I could see who passed by the office's glass wall and who entered.

The inn seemed more hurried than I remembered. Soldiers and workers alike scurried across the wooden floors. Even guests were out in unusual numbers. Some carried suitcases, some waved papers as they entered and exited the officers' offices.

"What's going on today?" I asked the colonel's secretary.

"Nothing special," she responded without looking up from her desk. "Why do you ask?"

"Just seems busier than usual."

"When was the last time you were here?" She looked up at me, peering over her small square-framed glasses.

"Been a couple of weeks."

"Several of the guests are leaving in the next couple of days. All should be gone within a few weeks."

"Really? Where are they going?"

"Now, Mr. Sequoyah. You know I can't say." She raised her eyebrows and returned to her paperwork.

"Of course," I conceded, turning to watch the hurry again. Brooms and bags and files. The inn's grand entrance had turned into a railway station without a train. There was worry on some faces and anger on others. And navigating between the two were reassuring smiles on the faces of still others. None of them were directed at me. I felt invisible behind the glass, though I was far from it. Because I'd spent so little time in the main building, the sharpness of the men's suits and the vivid colors of the women's dresses and hats drew my gaze. They were beautiful. All of them. The fathers and mothers and children. They danced across a backdrop of khaki and green military uniforms and baby-blue maid's dresses.

And then a small piece of the backdrop moved forward, and the dancing stopped. She stepped forward, feather duster in hand, and made her way down the balcony staircase, sliding the feathers in rapid motion with each step downward. *Essie.* I watched her as she reached the final step and started toward the front desk. She leaned across it and spoke with the receptionist. They smiled and laughed. Then the receptionist pulled a folded piece of paper from her uniform pocket and slid it across the desk to Essie. I could see Essie's mouth form the words "Thank you" and she turned away. She was walking right toward me. I sank down in the couch as far as I could and grabbed a newspaper from the coffee table, holding it over my face.

"Cowney." I dropped the newspaper, relieved to hear my name from a male voice.

"Follow me," Colonel Griggs ordered.

"Yes, sir," I agreed.

As we entered his office, he nodded to a club chair, indicating for me to sit while he lit a cigarette. "I see General Craig got ahold of you."

"Yes, sir. Drove me in this morning."

"Well, wasn't that just sweet of him," the colonel drawled. "Too bad he didn't stick around to say hello. I guess he's told you that we have the bone."

"Yes, sir."

"You best be glad your friend Essie had a change of heart about what she did and didn't remember."

"Sir, with all due respect, I imagine she was scared. She didn't want to get anyone in trouble."

"Well, she managed to get herself in some deep trouble. And if they weren't scheduled to ship out in a few days anyway, she would have gotten her boyfriend and his whole family in deep trouble, too. And don't you think for a second that we're done with you. We'll have a report from Raleigh soon."

"Yes, sir. I'm just here to work as long as Lee needs me."

"Luckily for us both, that won't be long. Go on now. Just remember, I don't want to have reason to talk to you again."

I wasn't sure why he had wasted my time. I guess he wanted the final say. "Yes, sir. Thank you." As I walked out of the door, I laughed to myself. *Perhaps I should ask the colonel for a reference letter. I bet it would be a doozy.*

My smile did not last long. Standing at the end of the hallway, the only exit I had the option to take, was Peter. His face was so stern that I had to reassure myself that I was not the one who should feel guilty.

"I don't have anything to say to you." I tried to push past him, but he grabbed my arm. "Let me go," I demanded.

He released his grip. "Please. Just give me a chance to talk to you."

I could not see any way around this confrontation without drawing attention that I did not need. "I'm listening."

"I guess you know by now that I said some things that may have caused you some extra grief."

"You almost cost me my job and definitely cost me two weeks' worth of pay."

"I know. I promise I'll make it up to you."

"I don't know why you'd say those things in the first place, but why do you care all of a sudden what I think?"

"I didn't mean for them to accuse you." Peter's face was pale and his breathlessness made me nervous.

I craned my neck toward Peter. I could not hold back my anger any longer. "And what did you think would happen?"

"I wasn't thinking." He lowered his eyes. "I mean, it is all just one big mistake, all of it. It happened so fast."

I rubbed my forehead hard enough to leave noticeable reddened indentions. "It's more than a mistake," I almost whispered. Then my voice grew stronger. "And it certainly wasn't *my* mistake!"

"I would have lost my job, been court-martialed. I have a baby on the way. This is international. Goddammit. They'd string me up if it affects what's going on in Europe."

"What are you saying? What did you do?" But I did not need him to answer. Nausea crept into my gut for the second time in one day. It was his work the photograph showed. As much as I had tried to expand or contract the background of that picture, it had always been a soldier I had blamed for the crudeness of the fence. I knew as soon as I realized the wires had been cut and pulled back from the inside of the property. "How does it make it better to be my fault?" I shook my head.

"I didn't frame you. I didn't accuse you. I just had to get them off my tail. Oh, God, Cowney. What am I going to do?" Peter paced the floor.

"You didn't *have* to. Don't you get it? You didn't have to gather evidence. You didn't have to plant my fingerprints or pretend to be an eyewitness. All you had to do was give them a reason. Make it okay to restart their hatred for me and of anybody who dares to share their space and not be one of them." I was the brown boy they needed.

Peter clenched his jaw. "I just told them to question you again."

"You say it like they ever stopped questioning me." I glared back at him.

"They let you go. You could have just told them the truth about the bone. Shown it to them. They would have left you alone." Peter bared his palms, pleading to be understood.

"Why should . . . how *could* I tell them the truth if you refuse to?" It was obvious that the colonel had not shared Essie's confession and submission of the bone with the other men. He probably thought it better if suspicion remained firmly intact for the remainder of their duty.

"They don't need my truth," Peter reasoned.

"And they don't want mine," I sighed. "My God! That little girl. Who speaks for her?"

Peter paced, eyeing the exits. "Tell me what to do, Cowney. Tell me what to do." His body lurched forward as if he were about to vomit, but he recovered, hands grasping his knees, bending over in search of his next breath.

I walked over to him, placing my hand on his back. I didn't want to touch him, but I needed him to gain some sort of composure to tell me what happened. "First I need to know what you did?"

"I was out by the property line, shooting at targets during my break, when I noticed that the girl was standing at the fence crying." Peter went to a window and looked out without actually looking at anything. "The back of her dress was hung on a piece of barbed wire. It must have been hanging down and she backed into it. I told her to stay still but she must not have understood. I don't know if she even spoke English. She was scared. Her hand was bleeding. She kept pulling no matter how much I told her to stand still. I yanked hard on the wire and she screamed and flung her arms out. She knocked my sidearm from the holster and fell to the ground." His hands cupped his mouth as he drew in a deep breath. "Oh, God. What have I done?"

"And it went off." I finished his sentence.

"Yes. One shot. There was nothing I could do." Peter grabbed my arms, pulling me toward him. I pushed him back hard. His desperation disgusted me. I have never felt such a desire to hit another person. I wanted to lay him out—to make him feel pain over and over again until it dulled, drowning him in the numbness of violence. I wanted him to know what it is like to be a thrown-away person. I wanted to make him unrecognizable so he, too, would be forgettable.

"Help me, Cowney."

"Why didn't you just tell the colonel what really happened?"

"She was a goddam diplomat's daughter. It was bigger than me. The bullet went right through her heart. She was gone before I even realized what happened." He looked at me, angry but still composed. "Her face, Cowney. I can't shake that."

"So where is she? What did you do with the girl?" I didn't want to hear what I knew was coming—another white man taking the life of a brown girl, then moving her like a slain animal.

"I knew that I had to get her off the property, so I pretended that I wasn't feeling well and asked to drive into town for medicine. I took her body to Riverside Cemetery, waited until dark—"

"You buried her? Jesus Christ!"

"I know. I didn't know what to do. I thought if I could make it look like . . . Cowney, I even rigged the fence so they would think that she just ran off through a gap, but—" Peter was shaking, trying to steady himself with one arm on a high-backed chair.

"But you found a better story." I shook my head. *Wire cutters—one of the tools he had taken from the shed.* I had almost forgotten he was the one who had borrowed them.

"I'm sorry, Cowney. I'm so sorry. I'll be judged by God Almighty. I know that. I didn't mean to. Just tell me what you want me to do. They'll find more evidence. It's only a matter of time."

"Why do I have to make any decision? This is not mine to own. And you didn't mean to? You may not have meant to murder her, but you sure as hell thought you had a right to take her body from her family—make her disappear to make your life easier. You tried to erase her like her life meant nothing."

"You're right. I . . . I just don't know what to do. My family. They'll go through hell. If I go to jail, they'll have no one."

I saw the terror spreading through Peter's body. "Your family? Goddammit, she had a family, too!" I wanted to grab hold of him and shake him. For the way he had betrayed me. But also for how stupid and callous he had been. He might not be a murderer, but to have taken that little girl's body and buried her in some secret spot that way was unforgivable. He had been the only soldier to speak to me as friend, but he had betrayed me just as easily. He deserved whatever was coming to him.

"I killed her, Cowney. I didn't mean to. I'd change it if I could." He had gathered some sort of resolve, as if he were already beginning to convince himself of his complete innocence in the midst of his confession.

"I know." I nodded.

Peter turned from the window and faced me. "You don't get it." His voice slowly rose. "I buried a child in an unmarked grave. I destroyed a family not unlike my own. I was so eaten up with evil, trying to protect myself, I almost got you killed. I can't forgive myself for that. I can't keep going like this. I can't run anymore."

My eyes welled with tears. My body was suddenly too heavy to raise and steady Peter. I felt pity for the man. Pity. These thoughts are the shame of my youth. How could I feel pity for Peter—because he might go to prison after killing an innocent child, stealing her body, denying her the sanctity of burial, lying to the people who loved her, throwing me to the wolves to save his "good name"? Had I been trained to react this way? It came so easily to me to want to help him. No one would help that little girl. No one would help her family. I once had to be quiet to survive. I didn't have to be anymore.

So it came as a great relief to me when Peter nodded, acknowledging that he, too, would not choose silence.

When all was said and done, the government—like it has done many times before—shaped history the way it wanted. There was a war to tend to, so the story of a little girl was easy to bury. After his confession, Peter was born again. Free to continue his life on his terms. The incident was deemed an accident; his only censure for covering up the death was to be named a civilian. The little girl was erased. All I know is her first name, Sakura. That's all I ever heard. Her first name. But it is important for me to speak it, to you, in this moment. So that she is not completely forgotten. They tried to erase her. Though it meant one less body lying in these mountains in some unknown grave, her story was buried—was buried until now. I don't talk much of ceremony, a term so misunderstood and strip-mined, but that is all I know to call this. I offer her this rite.

I walked Peter back across the wide expanse of the entrance hall, bypassed the colonel's secretary, and stood with him in front of the colonel's door. I knocked, knowing Peter's hands were too shaky to do so.

"Sequoyah," Griggs blustered. "I thought I told you that I didn't want to see you again."

I looked to Peter and nodded, without offering a reply to Griggs. Assured by the fear and the clarity in Lieutenant Peter Franks's eyes, I turned and left, to finally deposit my bags in the dormitory. I would likely never see Peter again. His daughter might not either. War shouldn't be important enough to take another father from another child. It had already taken far too many fathers from far too many children. But when men in power continually make that choice for the rest of us, I am more than willing to sacrifice one of them for a semblance of justice.

It was barely noon, and I felt I had just lived ten years' worth of pain. I added another five years when I found that Essie had left a note on my cot. The note was simple, excruciatingly simple. Its coldness, like everything else she had done, was unforgivable.

Cowney,

Andrea has asked me to come with him and his family when they are released. I will not need a ride back to Cherokee. I have written my family, so they will not be expecting me. We will leave by the end of the week.

Essie

I crumpled the letter into a tight ball in my sweaty fist and let it fall to the ground.

CHAPTER TWENTY-THREE

I slept through lunch on my first day back at the inn. That's not wholly the truth. I lay on my cot, crying through most of the lunch hour my first day back at the inn. All of the workers were in the dining hall, so no one was there to witness my body overcome by the day, the summer—I was undone by sorrow. I was crying for Lishie, but also for my father. For Essie. But most of all, I have to admit, I was crying for myself. Because I didn't know what was supposed to come next for me. I tortured myself with thoughts of my father doing the same just before he searched out a bullet to load his gun.

I didn't want the men to find me in this condition when they returned, so I forced myself to stand, collect myself, steady my pulse, and seek refuge in the privacy of room 447. I knew there was no chance Essie would be there. Since catching a brief glimpse of her earlier in the main building, I knew she had returned to her normal schedule and had several more hours before she could choose where she wanted to be. I doubted that even then she would return to the room. Most likely, she was packing to leave with Andrea and his family. In truth, there was no assurance that 447 would be the 447 I remembered. It had been discovered. I had led it to be discovered, and nothing could ever be the same after its existence had become another's discovery.

I entered the main building with no concern for being stopped. It wasn't that I did not believe someone might stop me; it was just that I no longer cared if they did. I'd get back on the merry-go-round of questioning, play their game, and find my way off when the music stopped again. However, the lobby was still so busy no one even noticed me anyway. I climbed the stairs and found that the fourth floor was deserted; not a single guest remained. All the guestroom doors were wide open, as if they had been completely cleaned out. I did not know which rooms belonged to Andrea and his family, but wondered if they had been fourth-floor occupants. Had they already been released and Essie with them?

Room 447 was also unlocked and the door was partially open. 447 had surely been abandoned along with the other rooms on the floor.

Nevertheless, I pushed the door open slowly, fearful of allowing a memory to escape. Though the light switch no longer worked, the windows allowed just enough sunlight into the room for me to see clearly the wreck it had become. Every piece of its delicate architectural detail had been stripped, torn, or busted. Even the wallpaper had been skinned halfway down, ripped off in a jagged pattern and thrown into a trash heap in the corner of the room. It appeared that at some point in the two weeks I was gone, the army had considered using the room as an office space because two half-constructed wall dividers cut the room into haphazard sections. The carpet was filthy with mud and cigarette ashes. Even the couch had multiple cigarette burns. Every book had been cleared from the shelves. A few lay on the floor, open and torn, but so many had just vanished. I feared that there were words that I might not ever see or hear again. The mirror above the fireplace was cracked, and as unappealing as I had thought my image was the first time I looked into it, it was even more wretched and deformed by the broken glass. I was broken. Though the windows allowed some light in, the room was far darker than I had ever seen it, even in the latest of evenings. Not only had the soldiers pulled heavy curtains closed as far as they would reach (though they were falling from their rods now), the windows were soiled with smoke and what looked like ashy fingerprints, likely from someone tending the fireplace and then adjusting the window latches.

I turned to leave, but my left knee buckled when I attempted to steady my foot as it skidded across two errant dominos. I bent down and picked them up. I held the two alabaster pieces, the first with four small dots, the second with seven, in the palm of my hand. I scanned the room for more, but could not find even one. *Worthless*, I thought. There was absolutely nothing one could do with two dominos; not one game could be played. I placed the pieces on the coffee table, took one more look around the room, and closed the door behind me. I made my way back down the stairway as 447 hid in the corner of the fourth floor of the Grove Park Inn, the only door closed on the entire wing.

CHAPTER TWENTY-FOUR

I felt more at home at the Grove Park than I did waiting in Cherokee, especially since there was a good chance my Cherokee home was burned to the ground. There was always a part of me that hoped Essie would be there, that I would see her and she would see me, that she'd ask for one last ride home to Cherokee. But she wasn't there in the way she had been before, not waiting in 447 for our next game, and the Grove Park wasn't my home. I was being peeled from the fabric of the inn as easily as the wallpaper of the room. Easily tossed to the side and forgotten.

Even knowing this and willfully choosing to return, now back on the property, it was a bit unsettling to spend even a few more days in a place that had the capacity to change so drastically in the two weeks I was away. I tried to busy myself by helping others with their duties and even caught a ride into town with Lee one evening for dinner and to watch a reshowing of *The Great Dictator*. Lee navigated the streets like the local he was, always knowing where to park. He didn't talk much. He answered questions when asked, commented on how good the cherry pie was at dinner and how long it had been since he had a slice. But he didn't waste words. He didn't ask me any questions he didn't care to know the answers to.

"You getting along okay since you've been back?" he asked after the waitress refilled his water glass for the third time and had yet to bring me one at all. I was lucky she sat us in the first place, I suppose.

"Yes, sir. I haven't had any trouble."

"You let me know if that colonel starts harassing you again, that

S.O.B." The loud gruffness of his voice moved the already anxious patrons to crane their necks and whisper. I wondered if he felt them staring at us, the men especially.

"Yes, sir. But I haven't even seen him since the first day and don't reckon I will."

"It's just odd how that whole mess about the missing girl just seemed to go away. I don't hear a peep about it anymore. Colonel probably fouled it up and hoped everyone would forget." Lee shook his head and continued to eat his pie.

"Probably so," I offered. I saw no reason to tell Lee about Peter. I could see he had already grasped the most important details of the situation. Someone in charge had fouled up. Someone else in charge made sure to cover it up.

"Sol treatin' you right?" Lee asked as he took a sip of his coffee.

"Can't complain. Doesn't treat me any worse than he treats anyone else."

"Guess that's all we can ask," Lee said.

Lee pulled his wallet from his back pocket. He took out a few dollars and stacked them on top of the ticket.

I followed suit, but realized that Lee was leaving far more than his share. "You need change?" I asked.

"Nope," he answered, standing. "Best get going. Show starts soon."

We were able to walk to the theater from the diner, and I enjoyed the opportunity to feel the hum of a city night. Cars splashed through the remaining rainwater, and brassy music poured from open restaurant windows and club entryways. Lee and I did not say a word to each other. He seemed as content as I was to let Asheville speak for itself. Until it got way too loud.

At the ticket counter a stout woman with bleached blond hair (poorly masking her true gray) curled her lip as Lee slid money across the counter. "You gave me too much."

"I'm getting them both."

"Not for him, you ain't."

"Oh, it's on the house, is it?" Lee clutched the booth's ledge and leaned in.

"Don't serve Indians here," she snarled, taking a drag of her cigarette.

"That so? Sister, tell me how many Indians ye seen come through here in your time."

215

"Just that one standing behind you." She smirked.

"Then how you supposed to know if y'all serve Indians or not? You've got a balcony in this place, right? I reckon we'll pay full price and go sit up there. That way you can say you were a proper racist cuss and still make your money."

The woman snatched Lee's money from the counter, threw back two tickets and, clearly in a huff, waved us in with her chin.

We each ordered a small popcorn and Coca-Cola from the concession stand and found two worn leather seats in the balcony of the theater.

Charlie Chaplin's final speech of the film, the one in which he stands before thousands of people, the very image of Hitler, and pleads with the world to unite in the name of democracy, well, I have never heard a finer speech in my entire life. He quotes a verse from the book of Luke, one I can't say that I recall from any of Preacherman's services, though that is likely more my fault for not paying close enough attention than his for lack of thoroughness. Chaplin recites, "The Kingdom of God is within man, not one man, nor a group of men, but in all men." He continues by arguing that the power is within the people. I looked at Lee sitting next to me. I looked around at the dozen or so other moviegoers, those mindlessly stuffing popcorn into their mouths and those wiping tears from their eyes, so moved by the actor's words. I thought about how utterly different everyone seemed. How each of us were motivated by so many different things, and yet here we were all sitting together being reminded of our commonality by a comedian, a man whose voice we'd only just now heard for the first time, even though he had been a staple in our lives for years. I wondered if someone might try to take away his voice after they had heard what he had to say. That seemed to happen a lot.

When we returned to the estate after the picture show, Lee pulled to the front of the main building. "Gotta check on a job 'fore I turn in. Mind if I drop you here?" he asked.

"No. This is fine. Thanks for the ride." I offered him a couple of dollars for gas, but he waved it off. "Keep yer money. I know how hard you work for it." Lee smiled.

I started toward the dormitories, still able to make my way by moonlight. But something made me stop, made me face the entrance to that beacon of wealth and internment as if I were seeing it for the first time.

The massive, ornate entrance beckoned my immediate attention. Other than its staircase, I had spent all summer avoiding this building, especially the expansive guest reception lounge, but somehow knowing I only had a few days of access left tempted me inside the doors. I walked in, absorbing the grandness of the space.

Most of the military-issued furniture had been removed, presumably to make way for the inn's lavish, paying-guest-friendly fixtures that had been waiting in storage since the US Army took jurisdiction. In its absence, the inn appeared even grander, but cavernous and hollow. The massive fireplaces on each end of the lounge appeared to be shouting at each other with their enormous gaping mouths.

When I entered the barracks, I found a folded note on my bed addressed to me.

The Grove Park Inn
Date: 8/17
Time: 7:03 p.m.
To: Cowney Sequoyah (Maintenance)
From: Myrtle Hornbuckle (1 or 2 words?)

Message:
Uncle very sick. Come home as soon as possible. Bring bread and washing powders.

The news fell on me numbly. I played the note, its message, through my head a couple of times but could not bring myself to develop any kind of feeling toward it. It was as if I were still at the movie house, watching someone else's life play out. Regardless, I reasoned that I would leave at daylight. The shopping list eased any sense of urgency I might otherwise have had. I pulled my suitcase from beneath my bunk and laid my clothes out on the bed. There was something sad about knowing it took me only minutes to fold all of my possessions into my bag and forever be erased from that place.

In the morning, I found Lee and Sol at breakfast. I handed Lee his camera.

"Well, where are the pictures?" interrupted Sol.

"Already packed, sorry. Maybe some other time I can show you." I looked to Lee as I spoke.

"Packed?" Lee asked.

"Yes, sir. That's what I came to tell you. That and to give you back your camera. My uncle's not doing so well. Got a message last night that he's going downhill quickly."

"I'm sorry to hear that, Cowney. You sure can't catch a break, can you?" Lee shook his head. "Let me walk you out," he offered, standing up from the table. "Keep your fork off my plate," he instructed Sol.

Sol rolled his eyes.

"I guess I'll be seeing you, Sol."

Sol sighed. "Yeah, kid. See you around." He held out his hand to shake mine and managed a half-hearted smile before he continued eating.

Lee and I walked out of the hall and to the dorms to retrieve my bags. "You sure you don't want to just keep this old thing?" Lee held the camera up to his eye.

"It's yours. You've done enough for me," I answered.

Lee handed me the camera. "Take pictures of some of those pretty co-eds at college and send 'em to Sol to make him jealous. Consider it a graduation present. Just not sure if it is a late high school graduation present or an early college graduation present . . . either way."

"Lee, I appreciate it, but I don't even know if I can go to school now."

Inside the dorm, Lee picked up my suitcase and handed me my duffle bag. "I was afraid you'd say something like that."

"It's okay. I mean, that's life, right? Just couldn't save enough this summer. I'm not even sure what kind of shape my house is in. Maybe in a couple of years—"

Lee set down my suitcase, pulled a wallet from his back pocket, and handed me three $100 bills.

"Lee! I mean, I appreciate it, but—"

"I know. I know it's not enough for tuition, but it's a start. And don't worry about it. The army can't have us here for our full original contract, but they have to pay out. That's the way government budgets work. If you're a line item, you're going to get paid one way or the other. They have to clear the books. Please, Cowney. I've got no one to do things like this for. I surely don't need it. If ye don't take it, I'm just going to give it to Sol."

Lee picked up my suitcase again, and I folded the bills into my shirt pocket. We walked out of the inn together and loaded the bags and camera into the Model T.

"Now, I'm not one for good-byes, son." Lee shook my hand.

"Me neither," I said. "Come visit me, will you?"

Lee nodded. "If'n I can find my way over the mountain, I'll be sure to do that. Ye let me know if you need anything. Hope the homeplace is still standin'."

I turned to open the driver's side door but remembered one last thing. "Hey, Lee," I called to him as he was walking away.

"Yeah?" He turned back.

"Would you write me a letter of reference for school?" I asked.

"Oh, hell. You really do ask a lot of an old man, don't you? Ahh . . . whatever . . ." Lee mumbled, most of which I couldn't make out. But his wave said it all. I knew I'd have a letter in the mail within the week.

When I arrived in Cherokee at Bud's house, heaviness greeted me. Bud's health had deteriorated far more rapidly than I had expected. Bud's truck was the only vehicle parked in front of the house and, though I knew Myrtle was likely inside, I wondered how long Bud had suffered alone. He was not one to let on about his health, a characteristic that only supported his apathetic demeanor. So from the moment I received the message, I knew the summer cough and work-worn muscles he hinted at before I left were far more serious. He had always been quite capable of concealing the slow progressive effects of his gangrene and diabetes, and I never knew how to ask. I took a deep breath before I entered the cabin and righted myself with the resolve I knew it would take to face both my uncle and his condition.

Inside his bedroom, Bud twisted the white bedsheet in his blackening fists, contorting his torso with the influx of pain. According to Myrtle, he had already soiled one sheet earlier in the morning, and I was grateful to her for replacing it, both for Bud's sake and for my own selfish queasiness. Myrtle was clearly done now, and she exited the tiny bedroom, leaving me alone with Bud, a pitcher of water, and a table of useless Indian Health Service prescriptions. I sat down in a worn wicker chair beside his bed.

The stench of rotting flesh was much stronger that I had remembered from a week ago, probably because I had been away from its constant suffocation. I inhaled fresh air into my desperate lungs. Bud's face was the shade of piss.

The last time I had seen Bud I had chosen to not really see him. We exchanged a list of words, meaningless in their essentiality. Eggs, milk, here, there, time, go, come. Words that meant absolutely nothing except to ensure our bodies' subsistence for the week. By the end of that week, I knew deep down that his body had deteriorated further even in that short time. And he was just as reluctant as I was to talk about it. I guess we both figured that if we kept our words brief and our actions separate, neither of us would notice the pain of the other. I hadn't pushed him on the fires and he hadn't offered. What difference did it even make now?

Sitting by his bed, I couldn't remember ever spending this much time in the same room with Bud. I imagine I did when I was a young boy, out of a lack of options. Now it felt very different. I was now the one with the responsibility. I could see he understood that as well.

"Cowney, it's lookin' like you won't have to put up with me much longer." Bud turned his face away from me as he spoke and appeared to stare out the sooty bedroom window.

"Ah. Don't be talkin' like that. We both know you're too mean to let something like this get you down too long."

"You're probably half right." He turned to face me again. "Even so, there's something I think you ought to know. I ain't got the energy to explain why things are the way they are, but you need to know the hard line."

I sat back in my chair. I was not prepared for Bud to share any secrets with me. He was the bluntest man I knew, so I had never imagined he even had any secrets left to give after what I'd heard from Craig. Our conversations had always been built around what he needed and what I was not doing. "I don't want to know about the fires, Bud. I don't think I can take it."

"The fires? Ah. Yeah. Well. There's that. Lishie's place is okay."

"I'm awful glad to hear it." And most of me was. But there was also a part of me that wanted a reason not to return—to never have to face the reminders of her absence again.

"Her headstone's ready, too. You need to pick it up. Just promise me one thing."

"What?"

"Don't ask me how I paid for it. I know that's what you're gettin' at. If I thought it'd be of any use to you, I'd tell you. But it won't be. That's not what I wanted to talk to you about anyhow."

All I could manage was a nod.

"I know you're real proud of your daddy. You should be." Bud took a coughing fit, an interruption that nearly drove me mad. "He was a real good man and no matter what, it's true you take after him."

This was the first time I remember Bud favorably comparing me to my father. Even more than the physical state of his body, this was evidence of his failing health.

"No matter what I tell you, you need to know my brother loved you. He wanted to raise you. Ah, hell . . ." Bud paused again and gathered himself.

"Bud, you know Mr. Craig told me—"

"There's more, Cowney. Craig doesn't know the whole story."

I stood abruptly from my chair and stared hard at Bud. "What the hell are you saying?"

"There's fathers and there are *fathers*, and you need to know—"

"Don't tell me what you think I need to know. If you think for one second I am going to believe anything you say about my mother or my father, you've got another thing coming."

"Cowney, I just want you to know that they weren't the only ones proud of you. I may not have acted like it much, but—" He looked at me with fading eyes and nodded softly. "Do me one more favor and call for Preacherman. It's about that time."

I shook my head and left the room. I guess he wanted sympathy or thought telling me all this right now, right when he knew he wouldn't have to fill in the years of blanks, was fair enough. All I deserved. I was glad he hadn't finished his original statement. I could not have handled hearing the words my heart already knew. Yes, he was right. There are fathers and there are *fathers*, but there was no place in the world for him to be either to me. And there certainly was no place in my heart for my birth to be the reason both my parents had to die either.

I could hear him coughing behind the door as I made the call from the kitchen and waited for the preacher to arrive. I paced for a minute, thoughts eating themselves inside my head. Then I ran to the front porch and vomited onto the newly fallen leaves, parched from a summer of smoke and heat. I lowered myself onto the porch step, waiting for the world to stop spinning. I pictured him lying there alone, and I finally knew that so much of this summer had been about me and my fears. He had done his best. I had to make room for him. He had made room for me.

I sat on the porch steps for over an hour until I heard the crunch of gravel signaling Preacherman's arrival. Looking back, I probably ought to have stayed with Bud, but I couldn't force myself back into the room. Nobody deserves to die alone, and so I was grateful that he had held on until others could join me.

Preacherman Davis stepped out of his truck with the King James tucked under his arm and a cup of coffee in his hand.

Then the passenger side door swung open.

Out stepped Essie. Even from a distance, I could tell her face was flushed. She wore a muted blue dress so threadbare I am sure she had never intended to wear it in public. For a moment, I thought I might be sick again.

Preacherman began his slow approach toward the porch, a practiced walk of solemnity. Essie stood by the truck and stared at me. She wiped the corners of her eyes with her index finger. I no longer had the energy to turn her away. I craned my neck toward the front door, motioning her to come in the house. I waited there, only stepping aside so the preacher could enter first.

Essie practically ran up the steps, tears burgeoning into sobs. When she reached where I stood, her head down, long strands of hair shading her face, I grasped her shoulder, causing her to stop and turn toward me. She looked up with only her eyes, and I lifted her chin with my timorous fingers.

I felt as if I were seeing a ghost. "I thought you left," I forced out.

"No, no—" She couldn't continue through her tears.

"Where's Andrea?"

"Gone." Essie's chin fell onto my shoulder.

"Gone? You mean—?"

Essie pulled her head up and wiped her eyes with the palm of her hands. "The whole family. They just left. He left some ridiculous note at the front desk. Lord, Cowney. I was so stupid!"

I shook my head, stepping back to invite space between us.

"Said that we'd always known that it had to end. I've never been so naive. And I can promise you, I never will be again."

I wanted to push a fallen strand of hair from her eyes. Seeing her cry made my chest tighten.

"Why would he have done that?" she asked.

"Maybe he didn't have a choice." It pained me to take up for Andrea. And I hated to see her hurting, but in all honesty, some small part of me was glad she had finally seen the truth about him. She was my friend, but she had been wrong, done wrong, in so many ways.

"Oh, Cowney. Look at me. I'm a mess. I was supposed to come to comfort you." She patted the sides of her hair and smoothed the skirt of her dress. In a moment, she had transformed herself. It was as if she was abruptly ending a tragic scene onstage and was now ready to take her bow.

Her instant resolve for composure shook me. I took another step back.

Essie dropped her hands and stared at me, wide-eyed.

"Whether you admit it or not—hell, whether you know it or not— you use me." I dropped the accusation so hard and heavy I barely had the strength to pick it back up. "You know I love you," I continued in a whisper. "You know I love you beyond what makes any kind of good sense, and I will do just about anything for you. But if we are even going to be friends, you have to stop." I shook my head and wanted to walk away, but my feet remained planted. "I can forgive you because I know you were scared. I can forgive you because that is all I know to do with this. But what are we? What do you want from me? When will you realize you've used me up?"

"Oh, Cowney. I don't *want* anything." She looked surprised that I would say such things. Her face had fallen as if I was now the one hurting her. "I'm not using you. We're victims of circumstance." She said it with such ease I knew she believed it. My mouth grew as dry as the dirt road stretching out in front of us.

"Seems to me you're the one creating the circumstances, and getting dumped sure as hell doesn't make you a victim. You got everything you ever wanted out of these *circumstances*, except a husband." I paused a moment to scan her reaction, to confirm in some tiny change to her face that she knew she had been discovered. "And that is what you're saying also, isn't it? I'm nothing more to you than a ride home and an alibi."

223

Her gaze fixed on me. She clenched her lips before emitting a long, deep sigh and then spoke. "Cowney, why do you think I wanted to leave with Andrea?"

I wouldn't answer her. I had said all I needed to.

"Do you think I love him—love him more than I love you?"

I couldn't bear to hear her say it and certainly couldn't affirm it myself.

"I don't. He's handsome and fun and I did think we cared for each other, and what else can I ask for in this life? I would have taken the burden from my family. I could have settled into a perfectly fine life for myself. I could have taken care of him."

"Listen to yourself, Essie. You used me—sacrificed me to save him. Or at least you thought you'd save him. From what, I have no idea."

"You still don't understand, Cowney. I might dream about dancing in New York, but I'm not a fool. You have purpose. I don't. You know what you want to do. You don't have anybody telling you what to do or who to be."

"You're right about one thing: I don't have anybody."

"Don't talk like that. You will always have me. I do love you, Cowney. I always will, but we have to accept the hand we're dealt. Or maybe in our case, the dominos we're dealt." She offered a small, careful smile. "I have to get out of here and there is only one way for me to do it."

"Not with a Cherokee man."

She shook her head and her eyes fell. No trace of a smile remained. "I wish I felt differently."

My throat tightened. There was nothing left to fight for or about. It wouldn't change anything. "Me, too."

Essie reached for my hand, cautiously working her fingers into mine. At the first sensation of her skin, I flinched, but gave into the embrace all the same. "Cowney, I couldn't see past the moment, past the threat of everything—every chance of getting out of here being taken away. I thought I was protecting Andrea and by doing that I could protect myself. I thought you threw me away just like Peter did that little girl—outed me and Andrea because you were jealous and you wanted to preserve what you and I have."

"Have? Do we still have us, Essie?"

"It may be all we have. Everything else is temporary. The soldiers and the prisoners will go home. This summer will pass. Even that bone will eventually disappear. So when I say we are victims of circumstances, I mean we are victims of temporary things. No matter how hard people may try to do it, what we have can never be erased."

"What do we have, though?" I asked her. "Because you are confusing as hell."

"We have a true friendship, a kind of love that can't really be named," she said. "I think that's the best thing two people can have. But we have to try to be Essie and Cowney separate for now. It'll be hard, but it's what has to happen if we are ever to know who we are really meant to be."

We held each other and for a moment there was nothing but our breathing. This summer, the fires, everything fell away, and we just breathed together.

Though he was in another room, we breathed into Bud as well. The damp, warm air washed over everyone and everything. I didn't know then that no matter how much we want to believe papers make laws and bodies move the world, we are ultimately awash in the spirit of our lives, not their physicality.

Essie and I collected ourselves and moved to the front door before I could muster the courage to return to Bud's room.

"You know, I just realized. I don't even know what Bud's real name is," Essie said as she readjusted a bobby pin in her hair.

"It's Cecil." I laughed, appreciating that I had never called Bud by his real name. It seemed ridiculous that a man such as him could be attached to such a benign name.

"Cecil? I did not expect that." She laughed with me. "And what were your parents' names?" she continued.

"I figured you knew."

"No, I don't think so. Just grew up hearing people calling them Cowney's mother or Lishie's son, things like that."

"My mother's name was Ga-lo-ni." I nodded. Saying her name made me smile.

"That's a lovely name. Ga-lo-ni. August." Essie let the name curve off her lips. "And your father's?"

My smile grew. "It was Cowney. I'm a junior."

"I bet your father is proud of you."

I wanted to tell her that she could go inside and ask him for herself, but figured she did not need any more shocks that day.

A nearby tree branch bent in front of us, shaking both Essie and me from far-off contemplations. "Oh, did you see that?" I asked.

"Yes, I think it was a flying squirrel," Essie suggested.

"Oh, yeah. I think you're right." *Sa-nv-gi. It is soaring.* The animal leapt again and confirmed Essie's guess. "I was hoping it was Edgar. I don't think Tsa Tsi has found him yet. Last time I talked to Tsa Tsi he said that he hadn't seen Edgar for a few months. People think they've heard him, though."

"I sure hope nothing bad has happened to him." Essie frowned. "Stupid monkey," she muttered.

"He's survived this long, surely he just got curious and took off somewhere further away."

"How far does he go usually?"

"Tsa Tsi said he's been known to go clear into Buncombe County. Even asked me if I had seen him while we were at the inn."

Once Essie left, I eased into Bud's room. Myrtle was spooning some sort of clear broth into his mouth. It was obvious that just swallowing caused him significant pain. Bud periodically looked at me while he ate, but did not try to speak. When he refused to take another sip from Myrtle, she shook her head and left to wash the bowl in the kitchen. Preacherman stood as well, patted my shoulder, and followed her out with his coffee cup in hand.

"You need anything?" I forced myself to ask Bud.

"No, no. Thank you." Bud looked up at me with weak, yellowing eyes. He could barely keep them open and failed to when rushes of pain surged through his body.

"Is there anyone you want to see?" I offered. I wanted someone else to be there, someone who might find cause to stay the night, unlike Myrtle and Preacherman, who I was sure would be leaving for the evening soon.

Bud managed a breathy laugh. "No. Not like I have a lot of friends."

I shrugged. It was sad to think a man might not have a single friend to call in his greatest time of need.

Bud groaned.

"What is it?" I stood and leaned over him.

"Sit down, Cowney. I'm fine," he reassured me.

"You don't sound fine."

"It's just— Ah . . ." he groaned again. "Go ahead and call him."

"Who? Preacherman? I think he's still in the—"

"No," Bud interjected. "Call Jon."

"Jon Craig?"

Bud moved his head, attempting to nod. Even that slight motion sent him into a fit of coughing. "He doesn't need to come," Bud continued when he regained his breath. "Just let him know. He'll help you if you need it."

"I don't need any help. If you don't want him around, I won't call him."

"No. He should know. No sense in being mad now. You already know everything and that war was a long time ago."

"I'll call him in the morning," I promised.

Bud nodded and let his eyes close. Preacherman came back in with a full cup of coffee and I stepped out again, searching for my own cup to fill.

Bud struggled to hold on for two more days. I was able to reach Craig before Bud passed, but encouraged him not to come. I think it would have been good for the former soldiers to see each other once again, but I also considered Bud's vanity. He would not have wanted Craig to see him weak, unable to defend himself.

"Will you give him a message for me then?" Craig asked before we hung up.

"Of course," I agreed.

"Tell him that he's a hero," Craig said.

I promised Craig I would, but when I went into his room to tell Bud, it all came out much differently. He was sleeping, but I could not hold the words in. I leaned over his bed, put my hand on his arm, and spoke. "I talked to Craig." Bud did not stir. "I'm sorry," I said. I hadn't meant to say that. I had meant to tell him how sorry Craig was. "You're a hero, Bud. Craig says you're a hero. He's sorry." I'll never know for sure if Bud heard those words. There was never an opportunity to tell him again with his eyes open.

When Preacherman spoke the final words over Bud and everyone who had filled our home for the past twenty-four hours accompanied his body to its final resting place, I closed the door behind me and made the journey up the hill alone.

Before the cabin was completely out of sight, I turned and watched as the smoke, a sign I had always taken to indicate civilization, ascended from the chimney of the now empty home, and I realized how wrong I had been about that. All around me the mountains exhaled fine, white morning mist. By Western standards, this was far from civilization. Then again, it was probably the most civilized society I could imagine—a society of essentials. The sun edged its way over the mountaintops just as it had done every morning since the beginning of time. It struck me that years from then, even years from now, the fog and the sun would be two of the very few constants in this landscape, just as our spirit, not our flesh, our blood, or even our bones, will be the only remains of our existence.

I am an old man now and I still look at those mountains every morning. When I was a boy I wanted nothing more than to be as far away from here as I could get. Now I want nothing more than to stay in these hills for the rest of my life, and even beyond it. I want my bones to stay here, unbothered. Essie was not altogether different; she just stayed away longer—first in New York and later settling in Connecticut to raise a family. She wrote me letters the whole time. Even came to visit periodically. Oh, the stories I could tell about those visits! But those are for another time. This is the most important story.

That's why your grandmother sent you, after all. Essie wanted you to hear her story. That's why the note she left for you to share with me is so specific. She wanted you to hear this story. Her story. Our story.

Ageyutsa,

I have said this to you many times so that you memorize it. I've taught you to mistrust papers, especially those with lawyers' signatures, so this paper exists only so that you can show Cowney my words in my own hand and prove to anyone else who might question you. I am asking you to break with one tradition to honor a truer one.

When I pass, you are to take my body home to Cherokee—to the Qualla Boundary. I want to be laid to rest in the ground where my friend, my love, my Cowney will one day join me. If he should pass before me, please find his resting place and bury me there so